Ros Demir
is not
the One

RosDemir is not the One

LEYLA BRITTAN

HOLIDAY HOUSE NEW YORK

Library of Congress Cataloging-in-Publication Data

Names: Brittan, Leyla, author.
Title: Ros Demir is not the one / Leyla Brittan.
Description: First edition. | New York : Holiday House, 2024. | Audience:
    Ages 12 and up | Summary: "Sixteen-year-old drama-magnet Ros Demir is
    determined to score a hot homecoming date as part of her big comeback,
    but when she hurts her only friend in the process, Ros questions whether
    her plan is worth it after all."— Provided by publisher.
Identifiers: LCCN 2023046285 | ISBN 9780823457137 (hardcover)
Subjects: LCSH: Teenage girls—Juvenile fiction. | Interpersonal
    relations—Juvenile fiction. | Dating (Social customs)—Juvenile
    fiction. | CYAC: Teenage girls—Fiction. | Interpersonal
    relations—Fiction. | Dating—Fiction. | LCGFT: Bildungsromans.
Classification: LCC PZ7.1.B757427 Ro 2024 | DDC 813.6—dc23/eng/20240215
LC record available at https://lccn.loc.gov/2023046285

ISBN: 978-0-8234-5713-7 (hardcover)

To my family, and to all the girls
who are still figuring themselves out

Prologue

You should know before you get started that this is not my love story.

I mean, it is, but not in the way you'd expect. Definitely not in the way that I expected.

The other thing is that this story isn't just mine. This is my version of a shared story. Because people who play supporting roles in the movie of someone else's life have their own movies, ones in which they're the protagonist. Have you ever thought about that? It's kinda wild.

Chapter One

The thing about Pine Bay is that it's the kind of place I *wish* my parents were cool enough to stay at every summer.

The first time I remember hearing the name was back in sixth grade, when Lydia's family started going. She came back from summer vacation with a face almost as tan as mine, a miniature braid in her straight blonde hair, and something new in her attitude, something she never talked about explicitly, but that was more than evident to me in every confident step, every cold-eyed look at someone in our grade who had said or done something that revealed their immaturity, every twirl of her tiny blonde braid around her finger. I *knew*, watching Lydia, that Pine Bay held some sort of magic.

I, meanwhile, had spent the first half of summer visiting both sets of my grandparents, and the second half at sailing camp, which could have been cool if any of the other kids were cool, but we weren't the *cool* type of kids who sailed—the ones whose parents owned yachts, who were taught how to sail by their parents' friends to pass the time while anchored in the turquoise-blue water in the bay of some Greek island. No, we were the *nerds* who sailed—the ones whose parents wanted them out of the house in the summer, doing something active, but who weren't quite athletic enough for soccer camp.

I begged my parents to go to Pine Bay instead the next summer: I had dreams of beachside bonfires with cute boys, of wearing a bikini for the first time, of getting my own tiny braid. Of course, my parents said no. And when my parents say no to something, they're usually saying no for good.

"We can have a fun summer without spending a fortune. Didn't you like sailing camp?" my dad asked.

My mom tried another tactic. "It's a resort for wealthy families to hang out with other wealthy families and pretend they enjoy nature. Wouldn't you rather *actually* be in nature than stay in a manufactured summer camp for adults?"

So I let it go. At least on the outside.

But four years later, when Eleanor told me her family was going to Pine Bay for the summer, I *had* to ask her to bring me along.

The drive got things off to a disappointing start. Eleanor's mom drove, her dad was in the passenger seat, and I was crammed into the back row with Eleanor and her little brother, Mason. Between the five of us, we had too many suitcases and backpacks to fit in the trunk, so the floor of the back seat was lined with bags, and I had to sit cross-legged. Eleanor had volunteered to take the middle seat, though, so at least I didn't have to suffer through that. Mason spent the whole drive from Connecticut to Maine playing games on his phone, and Eleanor, predictably, spent it with her nose in a book—a massive tome about female workers during the industrial revolution that I couldn't *imagine* reading outside of a class assignment.

Luckily, I had plans to make. I spent the drive distracting myself by manifesting my perfect Pine Bay experience. We were going to find the coolest people to hang out with, I would get a hot boyfriend, and we'd have tons of stories to tell when we got back to school.

That was maybe the hardest part about my parents refusing to go to Pine Bay. Everyone worth hanging out with always came back to school in the fall blabbering on about the awesome stuff they'd done that summer, and who'd hooked up with who in the boat house and whatever. And every year it was a social setback for me. Who wanted to hear about the month I'd spent going on walks with my gran and grandpa in their bland Ohio neighborhood, or the month I'd spent helping my babaanne cook köfte in her stuffy Istanbul apartment? Eventually, of course, as homecoming and Halloween parties approached, people stopped talking about summer, and I stopped feeling so out of place, but the month of September generally sucked.

Even this year, the year things were supposed to change, my plans for the perfect Pine Bay summer were hampered by the fact that we'd only have eight full days there—not including arrival and departure days. The original plan had been to spend the last three weeks of summer at the resort, but then Eleanor got into some kind of camp for history geeks, and apparently getting in was such a big deal that she just *had* to go.

Whatever. I was trying not to focus on that, and instead focus on the fact that I was *finally* going to Pine Bay. I was going to spend my time making friends, sneaking out at night, and flirting with cute guys, with the ultimate goal of securing a boyfriend. This last point was deeply important, because it was part of a long-term plan I'd made as a freshman. Now that we were going into junior year, it was time to set that plan into action.

We pulled into the Pine Bay parking lot, and before Eleanor's mom had even shifted the car into park, I'd opened my door and jumped out.

Pine Bay smelled exactly how I'd imagined it would: like pine trees, sunscreen, and campfire smoke. At the far end of the parking lot stood a long building that looked like it was made out of giant, shiny Lincoln Logs, with a sloping blue roof and a sign that said RECEPTION next to a propped-open door.

Eleanor got out of the car and sniffed. "It smells weird." It was her first time at Pine Bay too. She had always been too busy with camps and summer classes, but even with that aside, I had the sense she had never picked up on the social significance of vacationing here.

"That's the scent of summer," her dad said. He opened the trunk and began lifting out suitcases.

From inside the car, Eleanor's mom said, "Mason, get off your phone. We're here."

There was a disgruntled sigh and then Mason, a quintessential seventh-grade boy in baggy jeans and a backward baseball cap, emerged from the depths of the back seat. Like his sister, he looked around and made a face. "I thought this was supposed to be a resort."

Eleanor's mom climbed out of the car looking faintly like a movie star in white capris, a white button-down, and huge tortoiseshell sunglasses. She was the type of mom who told everyone to call her Sherry and always wore a full face of makeup. She regularly took me and Eleanor to get mani-pedis at the expensive salon two towns over, instead of at the cheaper but perfectly good one nearby—something my mom would never do. Privately, my mother called Sherry "high maintenance"; I tried to explain to her the difference between that and "glamorous." Sherry was definitely the latter.

Eleanor's dad, Harry, was a little goofy and *way* less put-together than Sherry, but he could be pretty funny, and I liked him.

Eleanor's parents checked in at reception, then led us down a neat dirt path to a fork in the road, labeled with a cluster of polished wooden signs. On one side: REC CENTER. DINING HALL. GUEST SERVICES. LAKE CERULEAN. On the other: COTTAGES 1–30. "Looks like we're this way," said Eleanor's dad. "Come on, folks."

Our "cottage" was made of gray stone, with a sloping brown roof and a rocky path leading through a small garden bursting with purple flowers. A sign beside the front door proclaimed that its name was ORCHARD ORIOLE.

Harry hoisted up a suitcase and crossed the stone path to the front door in a few lunging steps, while the rest of us struggled behind. He swung the door open and said, "Welcome to our humble abode!" Exactly the sort of thing that American dads said in movies, but I could never imagine my own dad saying.

The interior of the Orchard Oriole was tastefully rustic. Inside the small living room were two white couches, facing each other across a rug that appeared to be made of rope, beside a stone fireplace with wood stacked inside and a glass jar of matches on the mantelpiece. It was smaller than I'd expected, but cozy and beachy.

"This is where the girls will sleep," said Sherry.

"Where are our beds?" asked Eleanor.

"One of the sofas is a foldout," Sherry replied. There were three open doors leading off the living room, and she peered into each one. "You'll just have to make sure you fold it up in the mornings."

Eleanor looked around. "Where are we supposed to put our stuff?"

Sherry had disappeared through one of the doors, into the primary bedroom. "Mason's room has closets. You all can share, I'm sure."

Eleanor and I peeked into the other bedroom. Mason had a bunk bed, a dresser, and a desk. I waited for Eleanor to say something—that bunk bed was clearly meant for us—but she didn't. Instead, she dragged her suitcase from the living room into Mason's room, where she started hanging up her dresses in one of the closets.

"You should ask your parents to let us switch with Mason," I whispered, following her.

Eleanor shook her head. "It's fine," she said.

I wanted to press further, but then Mason trudged in, dragging a duffel bag and wearing his backpack on one shoulder. He dropped the bags on the floor, looked around, then flopped on the bottom bunk, still wearing his sneakers, and started watching a video on his phone.

I leaned against the wall and crossed my arms. "Fine, then," I said. "Let's go look around!"

"I want to get settled first." A wraparound dress with little purple roses came out of the suitcase and into the closet.

"Come on! You can 'get settled' later," I pointed out. Eleanor just frowned and kept unpacking.

I went back out into the living room, where a pair of gauzy white curtains covered a glass door. I opened them and found myself on a small porch with two rocking chairs. The house sat on the side of a hill that sloped down into dense forest by the edge of the lake. The lake itself was enormous, bordered all the way around by dark green foliage.

"Gorgeous, isn't it?" Sherry asked, coming out onto the porch. "I can't believe we've never been here before."

"Me neither."

"The PTA moms never shut up about this place, and I've been so curious about it. I've offered to bring Eleanor a few times over the years, but she's never had much interest. I'm so glad it finally worked out this summer." She gave me a warm smile. "What do you think?"

"It's pretty great. Thanks again for letting me tag along."

She smiled. "Of course, Rosaline. We love having you around. You're good for Eleanor, you know. You bring her out of her shell. She needs that."

"She's a really good friend," I said.

Sherry nodded and stepped back inside, and I returned to contemplating the view, thinking again about how different Eleanor's parents were from mine. Sherry *cared* what the PTA moms said. My mom tended to assume anything that was popular among Bardet parents was overpriced and pretentious.

In the middle of the lake, someone was sailing a dinghy with a rainbow sail. I closed my eyes and let myself slip into a daydream, in which I sailed beside a tanned boy in sunglasses. His lean muscles rippled as he tugged on the mainsheet, tightening the sail against the wind, urging us faster over the water, faster, faster, as he turned to smile at me....

———

That night Eleanor and I lay side by side on the foldout couch, nestled under a large blue comforter.

"This is comfier than I thought," said Eleanor.

"The bed?"

"Yeah."

"Why didn't you ask your parents to let us switch with Mason? He doesn't need that room to himself."

"He's the younger sibling. We can handle sleeping out here."

"Since he's younger, doesn't that mean *he* should get the couch?"

"That's not how it works." She paused. "And besides, I got to bring my best friend on this trip, and he didn't. It's fairer this way."

Eleanor and I had only really become friends in ninth grade. Our school was one of those awkwardly medium-sized schools: not tiny enough that everyone knew everyone, but not big enough that there were people in your grade you'd never heard of. Everyone knew *of* everyone, if that makes sense.

At the beginning of freshman year, I mostly just had sort-of friends. The type of people you said hi to in the hallway or could ask for notes if you missed class one day. After everything that had happened in eighth grade, I wasn't exactly close to anyone. Most of my sort-of friends were guys—I didn't think I could trust other girls anymore.

That year, though, I sat next to Eleanor in AP Bio. I didn't know much about her except that she was quiet and really smart, and those types of people typically annoyed me. I got good grades, but I didn't make it my whole personality. So I wasn't all that interested in being friends with her at first. But our teacher kept pitting the assigned-seat "pods" against each other in quiz competitions, and my competitive side came out. Eleanor and I won—every single time. Soon we started hanging out to study for tests, and then we started hanging out just to hang out.

If I'm being honest, part of why I liked Eleanor was that she was so different from Lydia. If Eleanor had been anything like my last best friend, I would've run in the other direction. Instead, Eleanor was sweet and earnest. Her timidness got on my nerves, but in those moments I'd just take a breath and remind myself that I was trying to be more forgiving…and that Eleanor wasn't Lydia. She had believed and supported me when it mattered.

"You're too nice," I said, flipping my pillow over to the cool side. "I still want to switch rooms."

"Of course you do." Eleanor rolled over. Before I could ask why her voice had an edge in it, she was sound asleep.

Chapter Two

I leaned against the bathroom sink, getting as close to the mirror as I could, stretching my left eyebrow with my left hand and wielding a pair of tweezers with my right. I'd plucked my eyebrows yesterday morning, but new hairs had sprouted overnight. It was like they *knew* it was my first real day at Pine Bay, and they wanted to sabotage me.

There was a knock on the bathroom door. "Ros?" Eleanor asked.

"Just a second!" I plucked another thick hair, then moved to the right brow.

My mother made a point of calling them my "Turkish eyebrows." My dad made a guilty face whenever he heard that, and would say, "Yep, those are definitely from my side of the family." His mom—my babaanne—had the same dark, thick brows. When she went too long without waxing them, they crept up onto her forehead and toward each other, just like mine.

My mom, on the other hand, had thin eyebrows. Too thin, she said, because when she was a kid she saw her mom—my gran—plucking hers, and my mom decided to do her own eyebrows too. "Gran had to draw them on me with brow pencil for months," she said. "Promise me you'll never do that, Rosaline. You've got beautiful eyebrows, okay? A lot of girls would kill for them."

I appreciated that she was trying to make me feel better, of course, but what I really wanted was a mom with eyebrows like mine, who knew how to wax and pluck, so I didn't have to learn from YouTube videos and slowly suffer my way through trying to shape the caterpillars on my forehead.

There was another knock. "You okay?"

"I said just a second!"

"You've been in there for like half an hour. Breakfast is gonna close."

I plucked out one last thick hair before sighing and dropping the tweezers into my toiletries case. Standing outside the bathroom, Eleanor wore a cute floral sundress, but her brown hair was still in the braid she wore to sleep. "You ready?" I asked.

"No, because *someone's* been hogging the bathroom." She went in and shut the door. I fell onto the couch and pulled out my phone, swiping through Instagram stories, trying to find out who was around. I swiped quickly through the influencer stories that I'd usually linger on—aesthetic morning routines, gorgeous tropical getaways, glittering nightlife shots—in search of classmates. After about twenty, I hit gold.

"Did you know Ben's here?" I shouted.

"Ben Whittington?" Eleanor shouted back.

"Yeah!"

She opened the door, brushing her hair. "I didn't know that."

"His story says 'Home sweet Pine Bay.'"

Eleanor shrugged. "Cool." She disappeared back into the bathroom, and I kept swiping. I didn't know Ben well, but we'd had a few

11

classes together. He seemed nice, and I'd heard his family was old money. Not a bad person to have around, I figured.

The door to Mason's bedroom opened and he appeared, still wearing pajama pants and a T-shirt. "You guys are being loud." He yawned.

"Sorry, dude."

He frowned at me. "Where are you going?"

"Breakfast."

Eleanor called from the bathroom, "Mason, do you want to come with us?"

"No thanks." He disappeared back into his room.

Eleanor emerged a few seconds later. "Let's get a move on. My parents are probably wondering what happened to us."

The dining hall looked like the type of place you'd rent out for a wedding or a fancy sweet sixteen. Long tables with white tablecloths, dark wood chairs, light blue carpeting with a subtle white fleur-de-lis pattern, a parquet wood dance floor in the middle of the room, and an immense floor-to-ceiling window looking out onto a green lawn where little kids chased inflatable beach balls.

Eleanor spotted her parents, who were lingering over cups of coffee. She started walking toward them, but I pulled her aside. "We can't sit with your parents," I said.

"Why not?"

I sighed. Sometimes, she really was clueless. As cool as Eleanor's parents were—especially compared to my parents—hanging out with them was *not* going to help the chill, independent, down-for-anything image I wanted to project. "Eleanor. We're not here for a family vacation."

She crossed her arms. "Um. It *is* a family vacation, though."

I crossed my arms too. "Do you trust me?" She glanced toward her parents. "We agreed that we were going to use this summer to set ourselves up for the best junior year ever, right?"

"Fine," she said. "Whatever. Where do you think we should sit, then?"

I found an empty stretch of table, far away from Eleanor's parents, and we set down our phones to save seats. Then we made our way to the breakfast buffet, where a short line had formed in front of the pancake station.

"I see Ben," Eleanor whispered as we stood in line, jerking her head toward the corner of the room. I glanced over, trying not to make it obvious. There was Ben, with his curly, dirty-blond hair, one arm draped over the back of his chair and the other arm gesticulating wildly as he talked, like he was telling an unbelievable story. Beside him, listening, was another guy whose face was turned away from us. He had thick, dark hair and wore a dark blue button-down with the sleeves rolled up to his elbows. I jumped when Eleanor whispered again, close to my ear, "Don't look behind you."

"What?" I asked.

"Franklin Doss."

I wrinkled my nose and instinctively reached to tug down the edges of my shorts, just to make sure I was well covered. "Ew."

"Yeah." Eleanor looked toward the corner again. "Who's Ben with?"

"Can't tell." We'd reached the front of the line, where a man in a white chef's hat served me three chocolate chip pancakes. Eleanor asked for blueberry.

I waited with my stack while Eleanor helped herself to scrambled eggs and fruit salad, and then we walked back to our table. I glanced over at Ben Whittington again, wondering if we should try to sit with him, but his table was full. A well-dressed middle-aged couple, who I assumed were his parents, sat next to him. As I watched, Ben's mother, whose hair was the exact same shade as his, reached over and adjusted the collar of his shirt. He gently swatted her away. She brushed invisible dust off his shoulder instead.

I dug into my pancakes. They were unbelievably good. Fluffy and sweet.

"There you two are!" Sherry said. She and Harry had appeared next to our table. "How did you sleep?"

"Very well, thank you," I said.

"We might go on a bike ride around the lake," Harry said. "You girls want to join?"

Eleanor glanced at me.

"Haven't you heard?" Sherry joked. "It's not *cool* to go biking with your parents." She looked at both of us. "Do you two already have plans?"

"Nothing really," I said.

Harry nudged his wife. "That just means they're up to no good and they can't tell us."

"Well, that sounds like fun," said Sherry. "See you later, gals!"

As her parents walked away, Eleanor said, "OMG." Her phone was on the table next to her plate, open to Instagram.

"What?"

"Did you know Chloe is coming?"

Of course not. Chloe Choi and I had pretty much never spoken. "How do you know?"

Eleanor flipped her phone around to show me the selfie that Chloe had posted, her soft smile illuminated by golden light. Her skin was makeup-free and flawless, as usual, with a smattering of the daintiest freckles across her nose and high cheekbones. It looked like she was in the back seat of a car; her long dark hair was tied up in a messy bun. The caption: *See u soon, pine bay.*

"Why is she so perfect?" Eleanor asked.

"Oh, come on," I scoffed. "She's not."

"Have you *seen* her? How does someone take a selfie that actually looks that good?"

"She's full of herself."

"I would be too, if I looked like that."

"Eh." I shrugged and took another bite of pancake, pretending not to care.

The truth was that I was unbelievably jealous of Chloe. When we were younger, Chloe had been a sort of ugly duckling. She had braces and glasses by sixth grade, and her mom dressed her in those terrible shirts that were a long-sleeved shirt and a T-shirt all in one, sewed together so it looked like you were wearing layers. It definitely didn't help that she was half Korean. I remember kids doing that horrible, stupid eye thing at her and making fun of her dad's accent.

Even back then, I had always paid attention to Chloe because she was like me: one "American" parent, one immigrant parent. In our super-white town, where most kids' parents had also grown up in Connecticut, we stood out. When someone made a joke that I didn't get, or talked about some TV show that I wasn't allowed to watch, it was okay, because Chloe didn't get the joke or watch the show either. And while I got good at hiding those things, it was always obvious with her. It was like she never even tried to hide it. At the time, I saw this as a sign of naivete. If you had the ability to change the things about yourself that made you different from your peers, why wouldn't you?

Though we never spoke about it, I imagined that she had the same feeling of not-belonging that I did: I wasn't as American as the kids at our school, but I definitely wasn't Turkish. I was a weird blend—two halves that didn't quite make a whole. And so was Chloe, in an even gawkier, more obvious way. While I worked my way up the social ladder, putting in tons of effort, piecing together social codes and figuring out how to hide parts of my identity, Chloe stayed awkward. We weren't friends, but I was watching her out of the corner of my eye. It was comforting to know that as out of place as I felt, as *half*, as unfinished, someone else was even more so.

And then, a couple of years ago or so, Chloe got hot. Like certifiably hot. She had the absolute definition of a glo-up. Long, shiny, perfectly straight hair, gorgeous dark eyes, and…*freckles?* Like, how unfair is that? Overnight, she became the type of girl my babaanne would give a nazar boncuğu to, for protection, because with all the gifts the universe had given her, she was sure to be a target of people's envy.

And, of course, she became popular. She didn't even have to work for it. It was like she showed up to school one day and suddenly everyone was in love with her. It wasn't just that she was gorgeous—somehow her mixed identity, the thing that I had always thought tied us together, became *cool.* Kids began listening to K-pop and hanging out at the local Korean BBQ restaurant. After years of asking my dad to stop packing Turkish food in my lunch and avoiding wearing anything that looked vaguely Middle Eastern, I watched as Chloe wore clothes from Korean brands to school and got compliments, as she shared her skincare routine on Instagram and inspired half the school to order Korean serums and face masks.

So yeah, I had complicated feelings toward Chloe.

Eleanor was still staring at her phone. "She said in a comment that she won't be here for a couple of days. She's been visiting her grandparents in California and her family is driving back across the country."

"That's a long drive."

Eleanor was glued to the photo.

"Well," I said, sighing, "I guess this is a good chance to get to know her better. Once she gets here."

"I wonder who she'll hang out with. She's so cool."

I rolled my eyes. "If you just faced the world with a little more confidence—"

"I'm actually not in the mood for a lecture right now," Eleanor interrupted.

I shrugged.

"I assume you have plans for us today," she said, changing the subject and setting her phone facedown.

"Of course."

She propped her head in her hands. "Do I want to know?"

"We've got to get a running start," I said. "Get the lay of the land. Including today, we've only got eight days here; we have to be efficient."

"And what does that mean specifically?" Eleanor asked suspiciously.

"We should go say hi to Ben and see what he's doing."

"No need," she said, straightening up and looking over my shoulder. "He's heading this way right now."

"Really?"

Before Eleanor could answer, I heard Ben's voice behind me. "Hey, Eleanor! Didn't know you were coming this summer."

"Me neither! I mean, I didn't know you were coming." I could tell that one of her panic blushes was coming on. Eleanor had a tendency to turn tomato red whenever she was embarrassed, which was often, and I'd been trying to coach it out of her for months.

I swiveled to take over the conversation and give her time to collect herself.

And that was how I found myself staring straight into the most beautiful pair of green eyes I'd ever seen.

Chapter Three

"Do you guys have plans tonight?" Ben asked.

I was still staring at Ben's friend, I realized. *And he was still staring at me.* With his hands stuck in the pockets of his dark jeans and something like a smirk on his well-tanned face.

"Oh shoot," said Ben. "I totally forgot you guys haven't met."

Before he could introduce us, I gave the new guy a small wave. "I'm Ros."

He nodded and said something that sounded like "eye-din." He must have noticed the baffled look on my face, because he spelled it out: "A, Y, D, I without the dot, N." Then, with a shrug, he added, "You can just call me Aiden."

"Cool," I said.

Ben looked at Aydın, then at me, then said, "*Anyway,* what I was gonna say was, if you don't have plans tonight, you should join us."

"What are you doing?" Eleanor asked. She sounded unsure.

"We were talking about hanging out down by the lake."

"Who else is going?" I asked.

"No one, yet." Ben paused and scanned the room. "Have you seen anyone else from Bardet around?"

Eleanor shook her head. "We just got here yesterday."

"We haven't had the chance to do much," I explained. "We were *exhausted* last night."

Aydın was still looking at me. I could feel it. I refused to return his gaze, keeping my eyes firmly fixed on Ben.

Eleanor perked up and said, "Chloe Choi is coming, though!"

All three of us turned to look at her. "What?" asked Aydın. His voice sounded tight. And was I imagining tension in his shoulders?

"Um, our classmate," said Eleanor. "I remembered—"

"*Anyway,*" I cut in. "Getting back to the real question. We're down for whatever."

"Depending on what it is," Eleanor added. I resisted the urge to kick her leg under the table.

"Sick," said Ben.

Aydın pushed the rolled-up sleeves of his button-down past his elbows. "Dude, let's go. The boats are all gonna be taken."

Hearing this, I perked up. "Are you guys going sailing?"

Aydın laughed. "You think we know how to sail?"

"I do."

He considered this, running a hand through his thick, dark hair. "You'll have to give me a lesson sometime," he said, then winked an impossibly bright green eye and turned away.

Ben gave a little *see you later* wave and followed his friend.

Eleanor leaned in, her eyes wide. "Okay. That guy was *totally* flirting with you."

I shrugged and took a big bite of pancake.

Eleanor glanced back at the boys. "You two would be *so* cute together," she whispered.

"Ew."

She giggled. "You *like* him, don't you?"

I shoveled more food into my mouth so I wouldn't have to answer.

———

After breakfast we decided to explore Pine Bay. It was impossible to tell how large it was since so many buildings were hidden in the dense forest around the lake. Pine Bay was car free, so the resort provided bicycles for every guest. It gave the place a sort of old-timey feel, seeing families whiz by, picnic lunches packed in their bike baskets, with the little kids struggling along behind on their training wheels. I, for one, loved the aesthetic of the whole thing.

We walked down various paths, taking them as far as they led before turning around and trying a different route. In the process, we passed dozens of other cottages, a few buildings deep in the woods with signs that read STAFF, an adorable soft-serve ice cream shop, a fitness center, a kids club with a mini golf course, a smoothie stand, a coffee shop, a gift shop with swimsuits and silky blouses and fancy jewelry, and a spa.

At some point Eleanor had to pee. I waited outside the bathroom, leaning against the building's smooth, dark green wall, and closed my eyes, feeling the warmth of the sun on my eyelids. I took a deep breath, smelling the pine trees, and wondered for a moment if this was what meditating felt like. If it was, I was sold. I was going to start meditating. Maybe in the mornings. On the deck?

"Rosaline?"

My eyes snapped open. Standing in front of me was the one, the only...Franklin Doss. He looked like himself, only somehow *more so*: salmon shorts and a light blue button-down, unbuttoned just a little too far down his chest. He was wearing dark aviator sunglasses, which he took off. Instinctively, I crossed my arms over my chest, and sure enough, a moment later I could see his eyes traveling up and down my body. Deliberately, I realized. He wanted me to see him doing it.

"Rosaline Demir. I'm surprised to see *you* here," he said.

I wanted to punch him right in his pale stubby nose. "Same to you."

He raised a thick blond eyebrow. "Yeah?" he said. "Why's that?"

I had made my signature mistake: letting my words get ahead of me. And now I was stranded with no comeback prepared. "I...didn't think you came here."

"Of course I do. My parents have been coming here their whole lives," he said. "Which is why I'm so surprised to see you. I know this isn't the sort of place *your* parents hang out."

"What's that supposed to mean?"

He shrugged—slowly, casually. "It's sort of a Bardet High tradition. And traditions like that are hard to...join in later?"

"Franklin, what do you want?"

He put up his hands. "Nothing. Just came over to say hi."

"Great. Hi. See ya later." I gave him a sarcastic wave. Then I heard the bathroom door open behind me. Franklin's eyes shifted there with a look of real distaste.

"What are you doing here?" Eleanor asked.

"Nothing. Didn't realize you'd brought your boring friend," he said to me.

"Come on, Ros," she muttered, grabbing my arm and pulling me down the path.

"See ya later, Rosie Posie!" Franklin called after us.

When we were a safe distance away, Eleanor asked, "'Rosie Posie'?"

"He came up with it in like third grade."

"That sounds about right. His sense of humor hasn't matured since then." Eleanor spotted a picnic table tucked into a stand of pines and took a seat on one side. I sat across from her. "What did he want?"

"Nothing," I said. "Just to throw some microaggressions my way. You know, all in a day's work."

"That's so fucked up!"

I shrugged. "Honestly? I'm used to it."

"Franklin's a creep." She paused. "And still kind of obsessed with you."

At that moment, I wanted nothing more than to forget that Franklin Doss existed. "It's fine," I muttered.

"It's not." Eleanor's face was lined with concern. "What he did was really shitty."

A memory was playing over and over in my brain, unbidden, and bile rose in the back of my throat. "Yeah, I know," I managed to say.

"And it's been more than two years at this point. You'd think he'd have gotten the message already."

I picked at my nails.

Eleanor bit her lip. "I'm here for you, Ros," she said. "I know you don't like to talk about it, but—"

"Thanks," I said, standing up. "But can we please just go *do* something? I just want to cleanse myself of the Franklin vibes and pretend that interaction never happened."

As we stood in line for the bike rental shop, Eleanor was telling me a story about the time her extended family had a big reunion in the countryside in France, and they'd rented a villa and bicycled everywhere. I, meanwhile, was scanning the crowd. No one interesting, unfortunately. A lot of older folks and couples with little kids.

When we got to the front of the line, however, I saw that the guy behind the counter was about our age. He was a little on the lanky side for me, but he could reasonably be described as cute, with red hair, a scattering of freckles across his cheeks and nose, and big blue eyes. "Finally!" he said. "I was starting to worry it was all grandparents around here."

Eleanor laughed, slightly too loud and too long. I stepped in, worried she wouldn't stop. "Is this place a retirement home or what?"

The boy smiled and said, "So what can I get for you two?"

"Uh, bikes?" said Eleanor. It wasn't sass. When Eleanor talks to a guy she thinks is cute, she always gets this uncertain tone in her voice, like everything is a question.

"Oh, bikes?" the boy asked. "Sorry, we don't have that here."

"Oh," said Eleanor.

The boy grinned. "I meant, what color?" he said. "Also, room key?"

Eleanor, now blushing hard, pulled our room key, with its thick wooden tag, out of her pocket. The boy took it.

"Orchard Oriole, huh? That's a good one. Right on the lake, right?"

Eleanor nodded.

"Yeah, it's great," I said.

While he typed some stuff into a computer, he said, "I haven't seen you guys around. Did you get here today?"

"Yesterday," I said.

"Good stuff. What have you gotten up to so far?"

"Not much. Getting the lay of the land. It's our first time here."

"Gotcha," he said. "Well, for what it's worth, there are themed dances in the rec center, and they're actually kinda fun. The next one's on Sunday."

"That sounds great!" Eleanor blurted.

The boy smiled again. "You guys should definitely come."

Eleanor's face, which had almost returned to its natural color, immediately flushed again.

"Any other tips?" I asked.

He handed the key back and made a thoughtful face. "The boats are cool," he said. "And how do you two like bingo?"

I raised an eyebrow—a move I've been told is intimidating and far more effective than I ever expect it to be.

"Kidding!" he said, raising his hands in surrender. "But," he whispered, leaning toward me over the counter and looking left and right secretively, "you *can* win some cash from the old folks. Just saying." He straightened up and glanced at the line behind us. "Bike colors?"

"Oh right! I don't know. Blue?" asked Eleanor.

"I don't care," I said.

He raised an eyebrow at me. "I've got just the thing for you."

"Hit me."

He slipped into the back of the bike shop and came back skillfully wheeling two bikes, which he pushed through a swinging door at the side of the counter. Eleanor's was a glossy pastel blue, with a basket attached to the handlebars.

Mine was mint green and sleeker, and somehow more...aggressive? Maybe more of a mountain bike than a road bike. "This one seems just right for you," the guy said, holding out the handlebars. "I'm Cameron, by the way."

"Nice to meet you," I replied. "I'm Ros, and this is Eleanor."

"Good to meet you guys," he said. He paused. "I should probably..." He jerked his head back toward the counter.

"Oh," said Eleanor. "Right, of course."

"Get back to work, slacker," I said, and took Eleanor's arm, turning her away.

"See you guys later," he called after us. I felt Eleanor trying to turn to say something back, but I held her arm steady. Always better to leave with a little mystery.

Eleanor's parents found us at dinner, so we had to eat with them and a grumpy Mason.

"We were thinking after dinner we could go to that family board game night they're putting on," Sherry said. "Wouldn't that be fun?"

"God no," Eleanor and Mason said simultaneously.

Sherry didn't miss a beat. "The brochure says there's Scrabble!" she sang.

"Mom, we're not going to family board game night," Eleanor said.

"Why not? You love board games."

"Not tonight, okay?"

Eleanor's parents exchanged a look. Sherry turned back to us. "What if we bring one of the board games back to the cottage? Would you play then, if none of your friends could see us?"

I couldn't help but think, *Sherry, I thought you were better than this.* This was the sort of thing *my* parents would do.

"No, Mom," said Eleanor. "You guys go to family board game night. But Ros and I have other plans. Don't worry about us; just do your own thing."

"What are these 'other plans'?"

"Some friends from school are here," I said. "We're going to hang out with them down by the lake."

"Be careful down there," Harry warned. "I don't want anyone drinking and trying to swim."

"We won't be drinking," said Eleanor.

"*Sure* you won't," said Mason, not looking up from his phone.

Chapter Four

"What are the chances that guy from the bike place is here?"
Eleanor whispered, holding my arm as we made our way down to the lake that night.

"Probably not very high, right? I mean, he works here."

"And?"

So earnest. "I find it hard to imagine he got invited."

"What about Franklin Doss?"

"Ugh. Don't even say that."

We got close enough to see a roaring fire in the fire pit, and several people sitting in Adirondack chairs. The lake was dark and still: a glossy black mirror reflecting the stars. We reached the end of the path and took off our sandals to walk barefoot through the cold, soft sand.

A figure with curly hair—Ben, for sure—twisted in his chair to look back at us. "Eleanor and Ros?" he asked.

"Hi!" Eleanor said.

"Welcome!"

We found our way to a pair of unoccupied chairs, across the circle from Ben. Aydın was beside him. When he saw me looking, he winked. My heart started beating faster, but I kept it together and played my usual card: I rolled my eyes. Always safer to feign disinterest.

There were a few other people, none of whom I recognized. I leaned toward the boy to my left. "I'm Ros," I said.

"Pleasure. I'm Garrett."

Garrett, who had longish dark hair, was wearing a polo shirt and shorts—an absolute Vineyard Vines type. He had already turned away, but I couldn't help myself. "Do you play golf?" I blurted out.

He turned back with a momentary look of surprise. "Nah," he said. "Tennis. Although I can hold my own in golf—been out with my dad a lot. Why?"

I searched for a quick lie. "I, uh, I'm on my school's golf team and thought we might have played against you. You looked familiar." Did we even have a golf team? How did golf teams work?

He raised his eyebrows and I thought, *Shit, he's caught me,* but then he just said, "We should play sometime."

"Oh," I said. "Yeah, maybe."

He smiled, then turned to listen to his friend beside him, who was wearing a backward baseball cap and had leaned over to show Garrett something on his phone screen. I glanced involuntarily across the circle, at Aydın. He was still watching me, and now he lifted both his eyebrows and blinked. I smiled back innocently.

Breaking the moment, Eleanor nudged her chair closer to mine and whispered, "You don't actually play golf, do you?"

"Course not."

"Then why—"

"Just observing the animal in its natural habitat."

"What?"

"I had an urge to find out how accurate my stereotyping impulse was."

"You're terrible."

I batted my eyelashes. "I know."

"Anyone want to play a game?" Ben asked, standing up.

"Spin the bottle!" someone shouted.

"Do we have a bottle?" Ben asked.

"Spin the bottle is gross," someone else said.

"We could play Truth or Dare," I suggested.

Ben pointed at me. "I like it." A murmur of general agreement went around the circle. "Rosaline, you're first," Ben said. "Truth or dare?"

"Dare," I replied.

"Alright," he said. "Ros, I dare you to…" He paused, rubbing his chin like a beardless old man. "I've got it. I dare you to jump in the lake."

Everyone turned to look at the water. There was no wind, and the surface was still, reflecting a moon almost fully intact. On the far shore, the pines were looming, inscrutable sentinels. What kind of creatures could be hiding in that water, waiting out the sunlight and the crowds and the boats, only coming out at night to prey on unsuspecting solitary swimmers?

Before anyone could say another word, I ran straight down to the edge of the water, and when my feet got wet, I kept running, until I was deep enough to dunk my head. I resurfaced, smoothed my wet hair back, and stayed there for a second, just to destroy any suspicion that I might've been afraid.

"How's the water?" Ben called.

"Kinda nice! I might stay here," I called back. It was, in fact, quite chilly, but I wasn't going to let them know that. Then I felt something brush my foot. Holding back a squeal, I made a quick return to dry land and squeezed out my hair.

When I got back to the campfire, a girl said, "Just for the record, there's no way I'm doing that."

Aydın smiled sweetly and said, "But that's the point of Truth or Dare. Right, Rosaline?" he said.

"Oh, totally," I replied, walking back to my chair. "That's the fun of it." Eleanor was curled up in her seat, arms around her knees, looking nervous. I wanted to pick her to go next, but she turned her pleading brown eyes on me. I sighed. "Garrett, truth or dare?"

"Truth," he said.

"When was the last time you took a shower?"

"Really?" he asked. "That's so boring."

"The lady asked a question!" said Ben.

"This morning, I guess? Are you trying to tell me something?"

I shrugged and grinned. He looked taken aback, so I rolled my eyes and said, "It's a standard question, dude. Don't get all worked up."

As the game made its way around the circle, I found that the adrenaline of my lake adventure was wearing off and I became aware of the chill in the night air. I wrapped my arms around my knees, just like Eleanor, and sat there shivering. Suddenly, someone was laying a thick towel over my shoulders. I turned and found Aydın. His eyes met mine. "You looked cold," he said.

"I was." I took the towel and pulled it tight around myself. "Thank you."

"At your service," he joked, and then he went back to his side of the circle. Eleanor was staring at me, but I didn't have time to say anything because my name was being called.

"Again?" I said.

"Everyone else has gone," said Garrett. "I've gone twice."

"Fine. Dare. Hit me with it."

"Alright," said Garrett. "I dare you to call your dad but pretend you think he's your dealer, and when he asks what you're talking about, say, 'Sorry, wrong number,' and hang up."

Some of the girls giggled. Hunter, the guy with the backward baseball cap, said, "That's an old one."

"But a good one."

"Get more creative, bro."

"I think it's funny. Oh, and," Garrett said to me, "it has to be on speakerphone." Then he saw the look on my face. "What?"

"I can't do that."

"Of course you can. Dude, it's a dare. It's supposed to be embarrassing."

I swallowed and shook my head. "Yeah, but there's a difference between embarrassing and..."

"Just do it!" someone yelled.

"Can you give me something else?"

Ben must've seen the terror in my eyes, because he leaned toward me. "It'll be fine."

I was running through scenarios in my head, trying to figure out how I should handle this. I didn't know how to explain.

Scanning the circle as though I might find an answer there, I noticed that Aydın was sitting forward in his seat, looking as anxious as I felt. He made a face like a question. I nodded, although I wasn't sure what exactly he was asking.

"Drop it, Garrett," said Aydın. "Give her a different one."

Garrett turned on him. "Why? The *point* of this game is to make people uncomfortable."

"It's just different for me, okay?" I blurted.

Both Garrett and Aydın turned to look at me, and I realized that I had to keep going. "Um, you guys have parents who are used to stuff like that. Maybe. Like, they might be mad, but it wouldn't be the end of the world. Right?" I looked around for confirmation, and I got it. "Okay, well, for my dad, it would be a big deal."

"I didn't realize you were such a Goody Two-shoes," muttered Garrett.

"My dad's not from the US. You don't get it." I was getting heated. The circle went quiet.

"Where is he from, then?" Garrett pressed.

"Türkiye. He came here for grad school."

"So he's Muslim?"

"Sort of. Yes. Casually. But that's not the point. Weed is a *huge* deal to him. If he thought I was smoking, I—I don't know what would happen."

"So tell him afterward that it was a dare."

33

I shook my head. "I'll do any other dare, just please don't bring my parents into this."

"What about your mom?"

"Leave it," Aydın said.

Garrett held up his hands in mock surrender. "Whatever. I was just asking."

I didn't wait for him to come up with a dare. Instead, I stood and walked to the edge of the beach. I stepped into the shallow water, watching the reflection of the moon, and heard laughter as the game moved on behind me.

My parents had always been different from my classmates' families. My dad, born and raised in Istanbul, who came to the US for law school, was always cheerful and often a little cringey. And my mom, with her Midwestern roots, who was practical and honest and too nice for her own good. Eleanor's parents were friendly with them, but they didn't talk to most of the other parents at Bardet. Neither of them had the desire—or the know-how—to navigate our town's complicated social scene. My mom had made it clear that she didn't like playing games: she wanted nothing to do with the PTA feuds or the drama in the infamous Facebook group Moms of Bardet.

I was different. I wanted, desperately, to fit in. I'd learned from their mistakes and had crafted a savvy, confident image—and I knew that sometimes you had to be ruthless to get what you wanted.

I didn't hear Aydın approach, but suddenly he was standing beside me. "You okay?" he asked.

"Yeah," I said. "Just needed a minute to cool down."

He nodded. "Understandable." He sat down on the sand and I sat beside him. "That was pretty awkward," he said.

"No kidding."

"You handled it well."

I grimaced. "I usually don't have any trouble standing up for myself."

He frowned, watching the water. Then he asked, "Why didn't you tell me you were Turkish?"

"Why would I tell you that?"

"Because I am too?"

"How was I supposed to know that?"

"Um, from my name, maybe?"

"Aydın is a Turkish name?"

"Very much so."

"I thought it was just a weird spelling of Aiden! You know, like when people spell 'Ashley' with a thousand *i*'s and *g*'s and *h*'s just to be 'unique.'"

He laughed.

I was embarrassed, but I pretended not to be. "I'm not, like, *that* Turkish. My dad is. But I grew up here."

"So did I."

I shrugged and wrapped my arms around my legs. "I guess I don't have a list of all the Turkish names memorized."

"Fair enough."

A voice behind us asked, "What's happening over here?" Ben plopped down in the sand next to me. "Everything alright?"

"Yeah," I said.

"Sorry about all that," said Ben. "Garrett can be a jerk."

I shrugged. "He probably didn't mean anything by it."

"He's still a jerk," said Ben. Then he looked at Aydın. "You bonding with your future classmate?"

"What?" I asked.

"My family just moved. I'll be at Bardet this fall," Aydın explained.

"Oh," I said. "Wow."

He laughed. "You sound disappointed."

"Not at all!" I said.

Ben reached across me to lightly punch Aydın in the arm. "Well, I can't speak for Ros, but I know *I'm* excited to have you there."

"How do you two know each other again?" I asked.

"Long story," said Aydın.

"Not that long," said Ben. "We met at soccer camp three years ago, and then we came here together—"

"Ben let me tag along with his family," Aydın interjected.

"I was trying to force Aydın to hang out, and bribery with a Pine Bay trip seemed like the best strategy," said Ben, grinning. "He didn't make it the last two years, but this year I finally convinced him to come back."

"Cute," I said.

"Isn't it?" said Ben.

"Adorable, really."

"Alright," said Aydın, standing and brushing sand off his pants. "I'm ready to go back to the game if you two are."

As we reentered the circle, a girl named Courtney, whose massive tangle of light brown curls was tied back with a pink-and-orange scarf, was asking Eleanor who her biggest childhood crush was. It could've been juicy, but the answer was a guy who'd moved away in third grade.

Next, Eleanor asked a blonde girl named Mary, who was wearing a navy sweatshirt that hung past the edges of her jean shorts, what the biggest lie she'd ever told was. Then Mary asked Garrett how many people he'd had sex with, and he said three. *Bullshit,* I thought. Garrett dared Ben to lick the bottom of his own foot (gross).

"Aydın," Ben said. "Truth or dare?"

"Dare."

Ben stared thoughtfully into the fire. I watched as an evil grin spread slowly across his face. His eyes flicked up to meet mine for just a second before looking back at Aydın. "Okay," he said. "I have one. But only if Ros is cool with it."

"I'm scared," I said, only half joking.

Ben's grin only widened. "Aydın, I dare you to kiss Ros. For at least five seconds." Then he looked back at me. "You okay with that?"

I gaped at him for a moment. On the inside, I was jumping up and down. Of *course* I wanted to kiss Aydın. He was hot, and charming, and *transferring to our school.* I leaned back in my chair and said, "I'm down," in the calmest voice I could muster.

"I accept your dare," said Aydın. He sounded chill, like this was no big deal to him. It occurred to me that maybe it wasn't, but I didn't have time to finish that thought before Aydın stood, strode across the circle, leaned over my chair, and kissed me.

It was pure magic.

I was vaguely aware of Ben counting down from five, but it sounded muffled, like something happening in a dream. My whole world narrowed into the feeling of Aydın's lips against mine.

And then, suddenly, it was over.

Aydın leaned back, but his eyes lingered on mine for another moment or two before he turned and returned to his seat.

Someone whistled. I glanced at Ben, who was now wearing a self-satisfied smirk. I crossed my arms, sank deeper in my chair, and tried to look unimpressed.

"Eleanor," Aydın said. "Truth or dare?"

"Truth," said Eleanor, her voice a squeak. I realized she'd probably made up her mind then and there to never choose a dare.

"What's your least favorite thing about Bardet High?" Aydın asked.

"Hold on a sec," said Garrett. "Bardet? I swear I know someone else who goes there."

"A lot of Bardet kids come to Pine Bay," said Aydın.

Garrett frowned. Then he snapped his fingers, brightening. "That girl, the blonde! She's cute. Here every summer. She goes to Bardet, right?"

"Do you mean Lydia?" asked Ben.

"Yeah!" said Garrett. "That's it! Lydia!" He elbowed his friend beside him. "She's great, right?"

His friend nodded. "For sure."

Courtney chimed in: "Lydia is *so* sweet! Do you guys know if she's coming this year?"

"You alright, Ros?" Ben asked, and I realized that my expression had shifted to something between irritation and disgust. I tried to smile, but Eleanor had already looked over and noticed as well.

"You really don't like her, do you?" she asked.

"Forget it," I said quietly.

Aydın, noticing this, changed the subject. "Eleanor, I'm waiting for an answer!"

She rested her elbows on her knees, looking thoughtful. "My least favorite thing about Bardet is how self-centered everyone is."

"Wait, did something happen with you and Lydia?" Courtney asked me.

"I'm actually curious too," said Ben, raising his hand. "It seemed like you two used to be so close, and then you weren't."

"That's exactly what happened," I said.

"Okay," said Courtney. "But why?"

I looked up and realized the whole circle had their eyes on me. "I feel like this is just going to be a letdown. It's not that good of a story."

"Just tell us," said Garrett.

Screw it. "We went to summer camp together and I...kissed her crush."

Garrett raised an eyebrow. "That's it?"

"It was worse than It sounds," I said.

"Like, how though."

39

"She *really* liked this guy. And she thought he was flirting with her, leaving her little notes, but…they were actually for me. I knew, and I didn't tell her. I let her think that he was really into her, and something was going to happen between them." I paused.

"And then you kissed him," said Ben.

I nodded. "In front of her. At the camp dance."

"Oof."

"But there was more to it," I added quickly. "I mean, I didn't mean to—I wasn't going to kiss him, but then…" I squeezed my eyes shut. Talking about it was bringing up a memory that I really didn't want to resurface.

"Girls are so sensitive," declared Garrett.

Mary cut in. "No, that's pretty bad."

"Agreed," whispered Eleanor. She looked shell-shocked.

"It's complicated," I said. "She…deserved it." Everyone went quiet.

"Alright," said Ben, breaking the silence. "Whose turn is it?"

———

"Why didn't you tell me what happened with Lydia?" Eleanor asked. We were in our pajamas, lying side by side on the pullout couch in the dark.

"You never asked."

"I kinda think I did."

I rolled over to face away from her. "I don't like talking about it."

"Yeah, it sounds like you were pretty shitty."

"You don't know the whole story."

"Right," she said. "Because you won't tell me!"

"Why does it matter?"

Eleanor hesitated. "Because," she said slowly, "you're my best friend, and I feel like I deserve to know why you decided to hurt your last best friend so badly."

I stayed silent.

Then she asked, "How do I know you won't do the same thing to me?"

I sat up and turned to face her in the dark. "I won't."

She sat up too. "But how do I know that?"

"You're not Lydia."

"I just want to know what happened."

I sighed. "You're nicer than her. Nicer than most girls. That's why I get along with you."

Eleanor said nothing.

"Lydia isn't as nice as she seems, and yeah, I got upset tonight when everyone was talking about how *sweet* and *great* she is," I said. "But you're generous and thoughtful and kind—too kind for your own good, really—and I would never do something like that to you."

"What did she do that was so bad?"

I hugged a pillow to my chest. "Honestly, Eleanor, I don't want to talk about it."

Eleanor made a frustrated sound.

I continued, "You just have to trust me when I say that Lydia isn't as nice as everyone seems to think. She did something really shitty to me, and yeah, maybe I made a mistake, but it wasn't just on me, it was on both of us. And I would never do anything like that to you because you'd never do anything to deserve it."

There was a moment of silence. "I don't know, Ros. It kind of sounds like it still bothers you. Maybe talking—"

"It doesn't," I said, although this was a blatant lie. "And I don't want to talk about it anymore." I lay down facing away from Eleanor, closed my eyes, and let exhaustion wash over me.

Chapter Five

After breakfast the next morning, I decided I wanted to go sailing. The weather looked perfect: blue skies and a light breeze. Eleanor and I walked down to the boathouse, and I picked out a Sunfish for us.

"I don't know," Eleanor said, eyeing the boat. "I might just stay here and watch you."

"Chicken," I said. "Come on! It's fun!" I grabbed a life vest and started strapping it around my chest.

Eleanor sat down on the bench of a nearby picnic table. "What you think is fun isn't always what I think is fun."

"That's because you're scared." I took off my shoes and placed them in one of the wooden cubbies that lined the side of the pale blue boathouse. The boathouse attendant, a wiry, gray-haired lady, helped me rig the sail and push the small boat into the water. "Come on, Eleanor, please?" I asked.

She just wrapped her arms around her knees and watched as the Sunfish entered the water. I was knee-deep in the lake. I scrambled up and into the boat and called back, "Last chance!"

"I'm good," Eleanor replied.

"Suit yourself."

I grabbed the tiller and the mainsheet and slowly began pulling the sail in, bit by bit, until it caught the wind. The mainsheet went taut in my hand, and the boat began to move away from shore. I dropped the centerboard.

There's a dreamy, almost mystical quality to sailing alone on a good day. The way the sun sparkles off the water, the wind in your face, and the way you glide over the surface of the lake, quickly, perfectly, effortlessly. If you get it just right, it feels like flying.

I closed my eyes for a moment and let that feeling wash over me. It was early, and there was no one else out on the water. I had the whole lake to myself.

I sailed for a while, reveling in the physicality of it and the technical aspect of harnessing the wind. Figuring out which way the wind is coming from, and how to adjust your sail to play into it and use it to move you into the direction you want to go, trips up a lot of beginners. But once you've gotten past that stage and start to get the hang of it, it gets pretty intuitive pretty quickly.

By the time I made my way back to the boathouse, Eleanor was gone. Someone else was there, though, talking to the attendant. Someone who turned to watch as I brought the boat in to shore. Someone with inscrutable green eyes.

"Welcome back, sailor," he said as I hopped out of the dinghy, back into knee-deep water, and began to drag it back onto shore.

"Thanks, dude."

"You said you knew how, but I didn't realize you were an *expert.*"

"A couple years of sailing camp."

"Damn," he said. "I've always wanted to learn."

"Once you get the hang of it, it's amazing." I turned to the attendant and asked, "Should I leave it here?"

She nodded. "Just beach it if you can. I'll deal with the rest."

As I struggled to pull the boat all the way out of the water, Aydın appeared at my side. My heart started beating faster, and I was too aware of how close he was to me. I couldn't help but think about the kiss, how soft his lips had been, the smell of his soap mingling with the scent of campfire. I gritted my teeth, trying to focus on the task at hand, and together, we pulled the boat onto the sand. Aydın brushed his hands on his shorts. "Thanks," I said, trying to sound casual. "You going out on the water?"

He shook his head. "I came to ask if someone would take me out. But apparently, they don't do lessons." He paused, looking at me. "I'm pretty sure you said you might be willing, though."

"Oh," I said. "I mean—"

"Not right now," he said quickly. "But some other time?" His voice had lost its usual smoothness. For once, he sounded like any other teenage boy.

"Okay," I said. "Maybe."

Aydın grinned. "Great. Okay."

I slipped off my life jacket and handed it to the attendant. When I turned back to ask Aydın what he was up to today, he was gone.

"He went that way." The boathouse attendant pointed. "Let me just say, the two of you are *adorable*."

Eleanor wasn't at the cottage when I got back. **Where are you?** I texted her.

Rec center, she replied. Then: **Don't come. You won't like it.**

Eleanor knew better than to say something like that if she *really* didn't want me to come.

When I got to the rec center, I opened the door to find rows and rows of people with white and gray hair seated at long tables, facing a woman who stood alone at the front of the room. At first, I thought it was some sort of performance, but then the woman called out, "B-2. That's B as in boy, B-2." Her elderly audience all shifted forward, leaning over their bingo boards to search for the number.

I scanned the room and located the single head of long brown hair in the crowd. I slipped between the rows, whispering, "Excuse me!" and "I'm so sorry!" until I reached Eleanor.

The caller announced the next number and there was another shuffle over the boards. "Bingo!" someone shouted. The room froze and I turned to look at the little old woman who was holding her hand in the air triumphantly. Her friend tapped her on the shoulder and pointed at something on the board. She looked down. "Oh, darn it!" she said. "Sorry, everyone. Carry on."

Eleanor was leaning over her board, apparently totally absorbed. "Hey," I whispered. She looked up and gave me a tight smile. "Want to get out of here?"

"Go get a board. I think they'll let you join late."

"I don't want to get a board. I want to go do something fun."

Eleanor sighed. "This is why I told you not to come."

"So I couldn't rescue you from this hell?"

"It's actually fun."

A lady with short, curly gray hair and turquoise jewelry was sitting on Eleanor's other side, and now she leaned in and said in a half whisper, "Maria always does that, calling bingo when she doesn't have it. She *knows* she doesn't have it too. She's sharp as a tack. I suspect it's a distraction tactic."

Eleanor giggled. "How's your board looking, Sandy?"

"Not good, my dear, not good." The woman looked at me. "Does your friend want to play? She can have my board if she wants."

"I'm good, thanks," I said.

"At least sit down," said Eleanor.

I did. "Are you mad I went sailing without you?"

"Nope." The caller said another number, and Eleanor marked it on her board. "Just having fun my way."

"I saw Aydın this morning."

"Oh."

"He asked me to teach him how to sail."

"What did you say?"

"I said maybe."

"Classic."

"How's that classic?"

Eleanor shifted in her seat. "Just…classic Ros. Noncommittal, I guess? Always having to keep them guessing?"

I crossed my arms. "And?"

"There's no 'and.'"

I scanned the room, still trying to figure out why on earth Eleanor liked this. "Have you seen Cameron lately?"

"Hmm?" She was avoiding my gaze, I was sure of it, watching her board studiously.

"Bike shop guy. Remember? Love at first sight?"

"No, I haven't seen him."

"Want to walk by the bike shop after this, see if he's there, chat him up?"

Her mouth twisted thoughtfully. "Maybe…I don't want to come on too strong."

"Oh, come on. You're incapable of that."

"Fine."

"Yay! Right now?"

She silenced me with a glare. Sinking deep into my seat, I pulled out my phone and started scrolling.

When the game finally (finally!) ended, Eleanor packed up her board, said goodbye to her friend Sandy, and thanked the caller, who replied, "You're welcome, dear. Hope to see you here again!" Then we headed out the door.

When we got to the bike shop, Cameron was taking care of an unusually large family: six kids and two harried-looking parents. I nudged Eleanor. "You should talk to him."

"I can't. Do you see all these people?" she said.

"Not now, dumbass. Some other time."

She bit her lip, watching him laugh in response to one of the kids. "I feel stupid," Eleanor said, turning away from the booth. "This isn't me."

"You like him."

"I don't usually get worked up about guys. I just...why him?" she asked.

"Because he's cute and charming?"

"I have more important things to focus on. Like school."

"It's literally summer vacation."

"Vacation is almost over." She glanced back in Cameron's direction. "But I can't stop thinking about him."

"You have a crush!" I sang.

She rolled her eyes. "I'm not the only one."

"What does that mean?"

"I've seen the way you look at Aydın. The second he pays attention to you, you turn into a lost puppy. And that *kiss*—"

"Shut up." I pointed at the bike shop. "Are you going to talk to Cameron now or are we going to find something else to do? Something that doesn't involve old people, preferably."

Eleanor hugged her elbows. "I'll talk to him later."

"Good." My phone buzzed. I pulled it from my pocket at the same time as Eleanor reached for hers.

It was a group text from Ben: **Found something in the woods, super fun. You guys in?**

"Sketchy," I said.

"What do you think he means?" asked Eleanor.

"There's only one way to find out."

Chapter Six

It turned out that "something in the woods, super fun" was an obstacle course: a bunch of wooden platforms and ropes, and a row of tires sticking halfway out of the ground. Ben and Aydın were sitting on a low platform when we arrived.

"Pretty cool, right?" asked Ben.

I jumped up onto the row of the tires and walked along the line. They squished under my feet, shifting my center of balance so that I almost fell. I caught myself and quickly glanced back to see if Aydın had noticed. Luckily, he was looking in the other direction. "Why is this here?" I asked.

"Kids camp, maybe?" Eleanor suggested.

"Oh, good thought!" said Ben. "Aydın and I figured it was a corporate retreat thing."

"Team building," Aydın said.

"Maybe it's both," I said, hopping off the last tire and wandering over to a web of ropes that stretched to about ten feet off the ground, ending at a wooden platform. I put a foot into one of the holes in the web and started to haul myself up.

"It's kinda fun, right?" asked Ben.

I made it to the platform and looked down to see Ben

walking the balance beam and Aydın doing pull-ups on a metal bar. I snort-laughed, noticing this. Who did he think he was showing off for? Eleanor was standing off to the side. "Come try this one!" I called to her.

She walked to the base of the web. "It looks hard."

"It's not, I promise."

She grabbed the net with both hands and tried to step up into it, but her foot slipped through and she let out a squeal.

"It might be easier barefoot."

She kicked off her sandals and slipped one foot in. With my continuous encouragement, she made her way up the web and dragged herself onto the platform beside me. "Not that bad, right?" I asked.

Eleanor lay on her back. "I'm never getting back down."

I lay next to her. Above us was blue sky bordered by pine branches, waving slightly in the breeze. It was unbelievably peaceful.

Then Ben's excited voice cut through. "Ros! Eleanor! Get down here!"

We made it back down—slowly but surely—and found Ben and Aydın next to a pair of low platforms with a rope dangling between them from a thick tree branch above. "Remember this? I'm pretty sure we did it in elementary school gym class."

"Your gym class was way more fun than mine was," said Aydın.

Ben had a huge grin on his face. "Who wants to swing across?"

"Let's do it," I said, climbing onto one of the platforms. Aydın followed.

"Is it safe?" asked Eleanor.

"Come *on*," I said, holding out a hand. Eleanor grabbed it, letting me help her step up onto the platform.

Ben grabbed the end of the rope and followed Eleanor. "Alright, who's first?"

"I'll go," I said.

"Be my guest."

I took the rope and stood near the edge of the platform, looking across the gap. Somehow, the other platform looked much farther away now. I took a deep breath, pulled back on the rope, then pushed myself off the platform.

I swung faster than I expected, and as I reached the end of my arc, I realized I would have to release the rope and fall to the platform or else swing back in defeat. I let go, hoping I wouldn't overshoot and tumble into the dirt.

I landed on the platform in a crouch.

"Nice one!" said Aydın.

"That looked terrifying," said Eleanor.

"You'll be fine," I said.

Aydın grabbed the swinging rope and took a couple of steps back, then flung himself off the platform. He did it with graceful athleticism, and as he tightened his grip, I happened to notice his biceps under the sleeves of his white T-shirt. I stood there staring, which was why I forgot to step out of the way.

Right before the collision, he locked eyes with me, and there was a split second during which we both knew exactly what was going to happen and were powerless to stop it.

His body slammed into mine, and I stumbled backward, instinctively clutching his shirt to keep myself from falling. Our feet tangled, and then suddenly I was on my back on the wooden platform and Aydın was on top of me, his eyes wide, his chest heaving.

"Ros!" Eleanor shouted. "Are you guys okay?"

Aydın wasn't moving. Why wasn't he moving? I realized that I still had the front of his T-shirt bunched in my fist. I let go, embarrassed. "I'm so sorry! That was my fault," I said.

"Not at all. I should've warned you that I was going." His eyes were locked on mine.

"Are you two done with whatever you're doing over there?" Ben called.

Aydın scrambled off me, then grabbed my hands and helped me up. He turned over my right hand. I immediately cringed—there was an actual woodchip stuck halfway into my palm. How had I not felt that? "Oh my god."

"I can get it out if you want."

I nodded, squeezing my other fist tight.

"One sec!" Aydın shouted to Ben.

With concentration, he lifted my palm toward his face, grabbed the tip of the woodchip between his pointer finger and thumb, and slipped it out. It was clean: no blood, no dirt, barely even a sign that it was there. "You'll want to put some antiseptic on that when we get back, just in case," he said. He didn't let go of my hand, and I caught his gaze shifting to the bracelet around my wrist: a simple black thread with a small blue nazar bead.

"I guess it didn't do its job of protecting me, huh?" I joked.

Aydın's eyes crinkled with amusement. "I don't think that's quite how the evil eye is supposed to work." He brushed a finger over the tiny nazar, sending a shivery feeling through my forearm. "My mom used to pin these on the inside of my clothes," he said. "She refused to send me to kindergarten without one."

I nodded. "I know it's just superstition, but it helps me feel... safe?"

"Everything alright?" called Ben. He stood at the edge of the other platform, holding the rope.

"Yep," Aydın said, dropping my hand and stepping out of the way. With a whoop, Ben leaped from the platform and came swinging in hot.

We had to coach Eleanor through the process, but once she took the leap, she was fine, and she landed gracefully with the rest of us.

"I feel like I remember that being more difficult when we were kids," said Ben.

"Ros and I managed to fuck it up," said Aydın.

I could feel Eleanor wanting to say something more, but I elbowed her before she got the chance.

"Should we do it again?" Ben asked.

That night, after Eleanor and I had brushed our teeth and put on our pajamas, after we'd said good night to her parents and brother, after she'd turned out the light, I lay on my back, staring straight up into the darkness.

The sofa bed creaked as Eleanor rolled over beside me. "It's obvious, you know," she said.

"What?"

She snorted. "Aydın. You guys are *so* into each other."

My first instinct was to deny it. Then I reminded myself that this was Eleanor, and that she meant well, and that I was trying to be a better, more honest friend. "I never said I didn't like him."

"Come on," said Eleanor. "I want to hear you say it."

With a groan, I grabbed my pillow and put it over my face, as though this would protect me from having to be vulnerable. "Yeah," I mumbled. "I kinda like him."

I didn't move the pillow from my face, but I could *hear* her gleeful grin when she said, "I knew it!"

"Don't be so proud of yourself."

"You should tell him!"

I took the pillow off my face. "Absolutely not."

"Why not? It seems like he likes you too. Why not just get it over with so you guys can date already?"

"Because," I said.

"Because what? Ros, this is perfect! You said you wanted a boyfriend, and here he is—like, the perfect guy for you. Now you're saying you don't actually want to date him?" She paused. "He's even transferring to Bardet this year! I mean, come on!"

"I do," I said. "I do want to date him. But..."

"But *what*?" Eleanor asked, sounding exasperated.

"I can't come on too strong. I have to let him come to me."

"Ah," said Eleanor. "Right. I forgot about your whole 'be the pursued, not the pursuer' complex."

I bristled. "It's not a complex. Look, not to be mean, but we both know that I know more than you do about guy stuff. And I'm telling you that this is the best course of action. I don't want to scare him off."

Eleanor was quiet for a moment. "I guess you're right," she said softly.

Maybe Eleanor had a point. Maybe I was hung up on this whole playing-hard-to-get thing. It's just, I had always wanted to be the type of girl that guys fell in love with, the girl who inevitably broke their hearts. And I liked that image of myself. I had never thought I would become the type of girl who fell in love.

I think anyone who knew the whole story would agree that I had fair reason to feel the way I did.

Eleanor stayed quiet, and I worried that I might've been too harsh. "I know you're looking out for me," I said. "I appreciate that."

"I guess I was thinking about how you said you wanted to run for homecoming court," she said. "And how you thought you needed a boyfriend to win."

"You *do* need a boyfriend to win," I pointed out.

"I'm pretty sure you can run individually."

"Okay, but if you look at the winners from the last few years, they've all run as couples. *Hot* couples."

"Why do you want to win anyway?" Eleanor asked. "The whole thing seems kind of…shallow."

I tried to find a way to explain it without going into the stuff that I didn't want to talk about. "I guess…it would prove that I belong. That people like me."

"So you're looking to the rest of the idiots in our school for validation of your self-worth," Eleanor said.

"Sort of, yeah."

"Is there more to it than that?"

"Can we stop talking about this now?"

I felt Eleanor tug the blanket toward her side of the bed as she rolled over to face away from me.

After a moment, I said, "Thanks for listening. I know how stupid it must sound."

"That's what friends are for," Eleanor whispered.

———

Here's the deal.

When I was a freshman, I went to our school's homecoming dance. Homecoming came at the end of Spirit Week, which I'd already decided was my favorite time of the year at Bardet. Getting to wear silly outfits to school every day for a week? The vibes were immaculate. *And* there was a trivia contest, in which Eleanor and I had competed as a team, which was an absolute blast.

But at the homecoming dance, I had a moment that changed my life.

Okay, that might sound dramatic, but that's what it felt like at the time.

The moment happened when they announced the winners for homecoming court. We always have two sets of royalty: a pair of seniors are crowned king and queen, and a pair of juniors are crowned prince and princess. I'd assumed that the junior race was sort of inconsequential—like, no one cares about the prince and princess, they just want to see the king and queen, right?

Wrong.

Hailee Benson was named homecoming princess, and the crowd absolutely lost their shit. I have never seen people my age get that excited. They were screaming and whistling and clapping—it must have gone on for ten minutes.

And here's the thing about Hailee Benson. The previous year, she'd dated this lacrosse guy named Josh. They were a picture-perfect couple, and everybody loved them…until Josh wrote something absolutely disgusting on the hot new Spanish teacher's whiteboard and ended up getting expelled. And because Hailee never made any sort of "public statement" denouncing Josh, people started spreading rumors that she was okay with his terrible behavior. It was the only thing that people talked about for, like, *weeks*. I'm sure there was some schadenfreude involved, because Hailee had always been so pretty and perfect, and when things are going that well for you, of course some people are going to want to see you fail. The fact that she'd been so popular made her downfall so much worse.

Hailee walked up on that stage in a sparkling silver minidress and matching silver heels, holding hands with her Ken-doll boyfriend, and they placed that tiara on her perfect, shiny, straight hair. She gave this gracious smile and a little wave, like she was actual royalty, and then she turned and kissed her new boyfriend, who had just been crowned homecoming prince.

I had gone to the homecoming dance alone—Eleanor didn't want to go, I didn't have any other close enough friends to go with, and I *definitely* didn't have a boyfriend. But I'd gotten dressed up and walked in with my head held high, ready to take high school by the reins and show everyone who I really was. And as Hailee walked up on that stage, I stood there, taking it all in, and I realized: the junior race wasn't a throwaway. It was the real race. To be crowned homecoming princess is to win the whole school's attention and admiration for the next *two* years. Not just senior year, when everyone's about to head off to college.

And more than that, it's a chance at redemption. Had poor Hailee not found a new guy and made it onto homecoming court, she might've lived in the shadow of that gossip, of her ex's mistake, for the rest of her high school career. Instead, all of that was erased and written over with her new story as the most popular girl in school.

I had just been through my own ordeal in eighth grade. I'd hoped the rumors wouldn't survive the jump from middle school to high school, but they did, and I was desperate for a way to erase them. Even now, going into junior year, I felt their aftereffects.

It was time to set in motion the plan I'd been working on ever since that coronation ceremony.

I needed to be Hailee Benson.

Chapter Seven

We woke up to texts from Ben that the campfire crew had gotten access to a speedboat—it belonged to someone or other's dad—and were going tubing on the lake.

"I wish I had a one-piece," I said, looking in the bathroom mirror as I tugged on my bikini straps.

"I have one if you want to borrow it," said Eleanor.

She was dressed in a turquoise bikini with a cute bandeau top. "Why aren't you wearing it?" I asked.

"Why should I?"

"Tubing? Wardrobe malfunctions?"

She leaned in close to the mirror, applying mascara. "I'm not going tubing."

"You're not?"

"Absolutely not."

I'd hoped that the obstacle course would have made Eleanor a little more adventurous, but it seemed to have had the opposite effect. Once she had decided that she wasn't getting on the tube, there was no changing her mind. While most of the group took turns, three at a time, holding on to the handles for dear life while Garrett whipped the boat around the lake in maniacal turns, Eleanor and a couple of the other girls sat at the prow, wearing sunglasses and trying to sunbathe, but having to grab the railing every other minute to keep themselves from getting flung overboard.

I had an absolute blast. Flying around the lake—going momentarily airborne, then crash-landing on the water with a jolt that shuddered through my whole body, holding on with every ounce of strength I had—cleared my head. I couldn't think about anything besides the cold water and the bright sun and staying on the tube.

Ben challenged Aydın to a faceoff, wherein the two of them would get on the tube and do everything in their power to knock each other off. "Winner gets to pick their next challenger," Ben declared.

The competition was fierce. We all gathered at the back of the boat to watch as Garrett sped around the lake, doing doughnuts and crossing back through our own wake, whipping the tube around as Aydın and Ben shoved at each other. At some point, Ben resorted to trying to pry Aydın's fingers from the tube handle, and Aydın used the opportunity to shift his weight leftward, toward Ben, just as the tube turned right, throwing the balance off and sending Ben hurtling into the water. Everyone cheered and clapped, and Garrett slowed the boat to a standstill.

As Ben swam back to the boat in defeat, Aydın knelt on the tube and looked straight at me.

"You and me, Demir," he said. "It's time."

"You're on," I said, grinning.

Once Aydın and I were settled on the tube, grasping our respective handles, Garrett said, "You guys ready for this?"

"Hell yeah, we are!" I said.

He glanced back at us with a wicked grin. "If you say so."

Immediately, the boat took off, and I could've sworn it was going twice as fast as before. I couldn't even think about trying to knock Aydın into the water—it was all I could do to stay on the tube myself.

But there he was, edging up against me. "Hey," he shouted, over the roar of the motor and the wind howling against our faces.

I couldn't help myself. I turned my head and looked straight into those bright eyes of his. *Damn it.* "What's up?" I shouted back.

He shouted something that I couldn't quite make out.

"What?" I asked.

"Are you competitive?" he repeated, shouting louder this time.

"Very."

"Well," he replied, with an exaggerated frown, "that's unfortunate for you."

"Why?"

He gave me a sideways smile, and I was all too aware of the heat of his body pressed up against my side. I couldn't help but think about how we'd locked eyes when we'd fallen together at the obstacle course, about how warm he was and how good he smelled....

"Because you're gonna lose!" Aydın shouted, breaking my train of thought as he hip-checked me straight into the water.

When I surfaced, sputtering for air, I heard the group laughing and cheering. I rubbed my eyes, trying to clear them, and swam back toward the tube, where Aydın was kneeling at the edge, clearly suppressing laughter. He reached out and helped me climb up, then held the tube steady so I could clamber back into the boat. "Sorry about that," he said.

"Don't be," I said, squeezing the water from my hair. "I'll get you back next time."

He climbed off the tube as well and took a seat next to me. "We'll see about that." His voice was low and soft, and it made me shiver. I glanced up and caught Eleanor watching us. She quickly pretended to shield her eyes.

Later, as we all lounged on the boat, Mary asked me and Eleanor what we were planning on wearing to the dance, which I vaguely remembered the guy from the bike shop telling us about.

"The theme this week is masquerade," Mary said helpfully.

"Oh," said Eleanor, looking skeptical. "Is it fun?"

"Totally," said Mary, taking off her sunglasses. "I thought it was going to be dumb the first time I went, but it's kind of a good time."

"Is it a parents thing?"

"Parents go too, but—"

"We bring vodka to spike the punch," said Garrett.

I grinned. "Sounds great."

Garrett punched me lightly on the arm. "That's the spirit!"

"Anyway," Mary said, "Courtney and I were trying to figure out how hard to go with the theme."

"How hard do people usually go?"

"Depends on the theme," said Courtney, who was attempting to tie back her curls with a hair tie. "The boys only put in effort if it's trop-ical themed."

"Hawaiian shirts look great on everyone!" said Hunter.

"We were thinking we'd go old-school for the masquerade," said Mary. "Cute dresses and those little masks that go over your eyes." She shot Garrett a look, like they'd discussed this earlier. "*Not* creepy Halloween masks."

"I'm down," I said. "Where are you planning to get them?"

"They've got a mask-decorating station set up in the rec center," said Courtney. "It's super cheesy, but like, what else are we gonna wear?"

Garrett had pulled the boat up to the dock, and we piled out, grabbing our towels and taking off our life jackets, throwing them into a wooden bin.

I slipped my flip-flops on, but before I could head for the Orchard Oriole, Aydın pulled me aside. "I'm sorry," he said.

"For what?"

"For going so hard on you back there." He looked almost nervous.

I laughed. "Honestly, I would've been offended if you *hadn't*," I said. "I meant it when I said I was competitive."

"Good," he said.

"Just watch your back when we have a rematch." I made an *I'm watching you* gesture and walked away without looking back.

Inside, I was bubbling over with happiness and another feeling, an excitement mixed with the hope that maybe, *maybe* he liked me just as much as I liked him.

Not that I was going to let him know that. I had to play it cool, I reminded myself.

In line for the mask table, Eleanor couldn't stop bouncing.

"What are you doing?" I asked.

"I don't know," she whispered. "I just have this, like, nervous energy all of a sudden."

"What do you have to be nervous about?"

She stopped moving and bit her lip. "Cameron," she said, like it was obvious.

"What about him?"

"He mentioned that he kind of liked these dances. So maybe I'll get to see him tonight."

I hadn't remembered that he'd said that. "That's fun."

We reached the front of the line and found a table piled high with stacks of white plastic masks in different shapes. I picked out an elegant mask that would cover just the top half of my face and flare out at my temples in little wings. Eleanor picked a simpler one and we moved over to the decorating station, which was covered in sequins, paint, and bottles of glitter glue.

I wanted my mask to match the one extra-nice dress I'd brought to Pine Bay. It was intricate forest-green lace over a slip, with thin straps that crossed in the back and a skirt that flared out just slightly. I would pair it with tan wedges and a set of dangling fake emerald earrings that I'd bought impulsively at one of those mall stands. So I decorated my mask with dark green and gold glitter glue, in swooping spirals and a set of dots down the bridge of the nose. Beside me, Eleanor was painting jewel-toned flowers onto hers.

"Anyway," she said, "I decided that if I do see him, I'm going to make a move tonight. I'm gonna let Cameron know that I like him, and we'll see what happens."

"Really?" I asked.

She frowned. "I'm just doing what you said I should do."

"I'm so proud of you!" I said. "That's great."

"Yeah," said Eleanor. "I guess." She paused, then added, "What about you and Aydın?"

I glanced around to make sure no one we knew was nearby. "What about us?"

"He'll be at the dance tonight too, right?"

I had this image in my head of me and Aydın twirling together under a crystal chandelier, of him leaning in to kiss me again, and it felt just like the first time, all warmth and joy and perfection. Of course, in this fantasy, we were both in full-on gala attire, and we were in some kind of grand ballroom that looked nothing like the Pine Bay rec center, but a girl could dream....

I didn't say any of this out loud to Eleanor. Instead, I shrugged. "Probably."

"And?" she said, her voice higher pitched. "Are you excited?"

I couldn't help myself. I smiled. "Yeah," I said. "I guess I am."

⸺

The dance wasn't until after dinner, so Eleanor and I spent the afternoon biking aimlessly around the lake and then trying on our outfits for each other at the cottage.

By six o' clock, though, it had begun to rain. Hard. Eleanor and I ran toward the dining hall crouched over, shielding our faces. I was grateful that we'd decided to wait until after dinner to get dressed and do our makeup. Thunder rumbled, and we squealed and ran faster, splashing muddy water everywhere. By the time we got to the dining hall, we were soaked.

We stood in the entrance, wiping our shoes on a black mat already caked with mud. Eleanor wrung water out of her hair onto the floor, giggling like a maniac. "I love rain."

We spotted Ben and Aydın nearby, seated with Ben's parents, who were somehow, miraculously, perfectly dry. Ben's mom was wearing a gorgeous off-white linen dress—she somehow managed to look almost *too* nice for this objectively very nice place.

"Is that Ben's mom?" whispered Eleanor. "She looks like a movie star."

"She totally does."

"I wish my mom dressed like that."

"Are you kidding?" I asked. "Your mom is so cool! And gorgeous."

She looked skeptical. "Ros, I know you're trying to be nice, but you don't have to lie."

"I'm not!" I said.

"My mom is so annoying."

"I don't think so."

Someone behind us called, "Eleanor! Rosaline!" We turned and spotted Eleanor's parents sitting at a table with another family, a younger couple with a pair of toddler twins in matching dresses. As we approached, Sherry said, "Girls! Hello!"

"You're a sorry lot," said Harry.

"It's raining," Eleanor pointed out.

"I know. We were lucky to get in before the worst of it," Sherry said. "Sit with us!"

"Where's Mason?" Eleanor asked.

"I think he found some kids to hang out with," said her mom. "Go grab food, you two."

The buffet continued to amaze me. There were so many options, so beautifully displayed, from so many cuisines. There was an Italian table, loaded with pasta in big silver trays—chafing dishes, as I'd recently learned they were called—and gourmet pizza topped with vegetables and fancy cheeses. There was a table where a guy stood behind a massive chunk of steak, and you'd tell him how much you wanted and he'd slice it right there for you. There was even a sushi station. Neither of my parents were into sushi, so I'd never actually eaten it. I figured I'd better try it for myself and find out what the rest of the world was so obsessed with.

I headed for the sushi station, and Eleanor followed. While we waited in line, I pulled out my phone and opened Instagram to keep us occupied.

Eleanor rested her chin on my shoulder, looking at my phone screen. "Wait, scroll back up," she said. I did. There was a picture of the Pine Bay check-in desk, posted by Chloe Choi, with the caption: *Finally here!*

"OMG, she's here!" said Eleanor.

"I guess so."

Eleanor looked around, as though Chloe might magically appear beside us. "Do you think we'll see her tonight?"

"Probably," I said, taking a step as the line for the sushi station moved forward.

Just then, Ben and Aydın walked past us, engaged in some kind of serious-looking discussion. Eleanor elbowed me in the side. "There's your man."

Aydın glanced toward us as though he'd heard her, meeting my gaze. He looked solemn. I gave him a small smile and a wave, and he waved back, but his expression didn't change.

When he and Ben were out of earshot, I asked, "Why the *hell* would you do that?"

"What's wrong?"

"I think he heard you!"

"So?"

"So?" I repeated. "*So* it's embarrassing!"

Eleanor looked hurt. "Weren't you going to tell him you liked him anyway?"

"Of course I wasn't!"

"You told me that I should let Cameron know how I felt. Why won't you take your own advice?"

"Because it's different for me!"

Eleanor frowned. "How?"

"It..." I could feel myself getting heated up, so I took a deep breath and tried to calm down. I heard my mom's voice reminding me not to let things get to me. "It just is, okay?"

We'd reached the front of the line, and each of us grabbed a plate. "Fine," said Eleanor. "But I wish you'd tell me why."

"Our situations are different," I said. "And we're different people. If you don't tell Cameron you like him, he'd never have a clue. Aydın and I already have something going. And I don't want to come on too strong."

"Fine," said Eleanor, loading her plate.

We walked back to the table in silence.

Eleanor's parents were chatting with the other couple, so we dug in. The second I tasted my first piece of sushi, I was in pure heaven.

The crispy, salty seaweed, the soft rice, the savory fish…I didn't even use the soy sauce that they'd given me in a little dish, because I wanted to taste the sushi in its full glory. *This* was what my parents had been hiding from me? What sort of monsters were they?

"Sushi is so good," I mumbled to Eleanor through a full mouth.

"Mhm."

I swallowed. "I can't believe I've never tried it before."

"OMG, what?"

Suddenly, there was a loud crackling sound, and then a man's voice came over the loudspeaker system. "Due to inclement weather, we are advising everyone to stay inside for the time being. Please do not go outside until we have further updates. Our chefs are working hard to make a special treat while you wait. We apologize for the inconvenience."

A wave of chatter rose up in the room. People shifted in their chairs. Kids got up and ran to the big windows to look out at the pouring rain. I spotted Ben and Aydın sitting with Ben's parents. Ben looked like he was up to something. He glanced toward us, saw me staring back, and quickly looked away, whispering something to Aydın.

"Well, this is exciting," said Sherry.

"Mom," said Eleanor. "Really?"

"How many times have you been in a storm lockdown?"

"A couple."

"When?"

Eleanor stood up. "I'm still hungry. Ros, you want seconds?"

I glanced down at my plate, which still held three pieces of sushi. "I'm good, thanks." Eleanor turned and headed toward the buffet.

"She didn't ask me if I wanted seconds," Harry said with a melo-dramatic sniffle.

"So tell us, Ros," Sherry said, leaning toward me. "What have you girls been up to?"

"Nothing much."

"Oh, come on. You can tell me."

Part of me actually did want to share our gossip with her. But I had a feeling Eleanor would hate that. "We've just been hanging out with some friends from school."

A huge rumble of thunder made the whole room jump. The tod-dler twins at our table started bawling, and their parents rushed to soothe them.

"We went canoeing this afternoon," Sherry told me. "It was so lovely. Have you gone yet?"

I shook my head. "I went sailing."

"By yourself?"

"Yeah."

Her eyebrows furrowed. "Are you sure that's safe?"

"I went to sailing camp for a couple of years," I said quickly. Her expression reminded me of my mom's when she thought I might've done something wrong. "I know what I'm doing. It's totally safe, I promise."

Sherry sat back in her chair, her concern appearing to evaporate. "Well, I didn't know you sailed! You should teach Eleanor!"

"I tried," I said. "She wouldn't get in the boat."

"That sounds like Eleanor," said Harry, chuckling.

I finished my sushi and glanced around to see where Eleanor had gone. She was standing in a corner with her arms crossed, listening to something Ben was telling her. They were close together. It looked private, and it looked intense.

The loudspeaker crackled again. "We would like to apologize once again for the inconvenience. Our chefs are now bringing out a special dessert. Please enjoy."

The room exploded in a cacophony of chair legs squeaking against the floor. Kitchen staff carried platters out to the dessert section of the buffet, and kids ran to meet them.

"Can you see what it is?" asked Harry.

"I can't. Let's go check it out," said Sherry. She stood. "Ros, do you want any dessert?"

I shook my head. "No thanks."

A moment later, Eleanor sat next to me, setting down a plate piled with more sushi.

"What was that about?" I asked.

"What?"

"You and Ben looked like you were having a serious conversation."

"Oh." She paused. "Yeah, it's actually kinda big news."

"Well? Tell me!"

Eleanor took a sip of ice water. "Ben said Aydın likes you."

I held back a squeal. "That makes sense."

Eleanor's mouth got tight in that way it does when she wants to say something, but she holds it back instead.

"So, what did you say to him?" I asked.

"I told him you're not interested."

"You did *what*?" I asked.

Eleanor bit her lip. "Wasn't that what I was supposed to do?"

"No!"

"I'm confused," she said, leaning back in her chair.

"Why would you do that?"

"Because you got mad at me when you thought Aydın might've heard me call him 'your man'! You said you had to play hard to get!"

"Yeah, but there's a difference between playing hard to get and… this!"

"What was I supposed to say?" Her voice was rising. "Tell me, Ros. Come on. You don't want him to know that you like him, but you don't want me to say that you don't?"

"Couldn't you have been more tactful?"

"*How?*" Eleanor was practically shouting now. "How am I supposed to know what you want me to do? Why don't you just give me the Ros Rulebook, so I can follow it without fucking up so much?"

"What are you talking about?"

"I'm sorry that I'm not you! I don't like boats, or the water, or climbing on top of tall things. I don't need to risk my personal safety to have a good time, and I'm tired of you making fun of me for it!" I tried to interject, but she continued, "And what the hell am I supposed to think after hearing about what you did to Lydia?"

I had never seen Eleanor angry before. Grumpy, sure. But angry? Never like this. "You don't know the whole story."

"No, I don't, because you won't tell me! I thought we were best friends, Ros."

"We are!"

"So *why* are you treating me like this?"

"Like *what*?" I felt tears of frustration welling up in my eyes, and I wiped them away. "I don't understand why you're so upset."

"I never know what you want me to say, Ros! Do you have any idea how hard it is to be your friend? To figure out what the hell you want at any given second of the day, and do exactly what's going to make you happy?"

At that, I was actually, truly speechless.

"You got mad at me for hinting that you might like Aydın in his vicinity, where he could *possibly* have heard. But then you got mad at me for *not* telling Ben that you liked Aydın? What on earth am I supposed to do?" Eleanor stood up. "I need a break," she said, and then she walked away, leaving her plate on the table and abandoning me with the other family, who were pretending not to have heard our conversation.

I folded my arms on the table and buried my face.

Chapter Eight

By the time I got back to the Orchard Oriole, Eleanor had already left. I got dressed and did my makeup alone, trying not to think too hard about our fight. I couldn't let it ruin what was supposed to be an amazing night. She would get over it. She had to. Right?

I approached the rec center with some trepidation, though. I hadn't anticipated showing up without Eleanor. Luckily, it wasn't my first time going to a dance alone, so I did what I always did: threw my hair back and stalked into the room projecting confidence and ease.

Whoever was in charge of decorating the rec center did a surprisingly good job. Fake candles flickered on every windowsill and unused surface, including the mantelpiece of the immense stone fireplace, illuminating the space with a soft yellow-orange glow. White fabric hung in arcs from the tops of the windows, and shimmering stars dangled from the ceiling on nearly invisible fishing line.

The room was about half full. Adults clustered in small groups, chatting with champagne glasses in hand. Someone nudged my elbow, and I found Ben standing beside me. "Fun party, huh?"

I nodded in the direction of the champagne glasses. "Where can I get one of those?"

Ben smirked. "No need." He held open his navy blazer to show me the small bottle of vodka tucked inside. "You want some?"

"Of course," I said.

He nodded toward the door and I followed him out, around the side of the rec center, where the rest of the group was perched on a couple of large white rocks. The rain had stopped and the clouds had cleared, and the needles on the pine trees glinted in the dim blue twilight.

The group was already passing around a bottle of something or other. As we approached, Aydın took a long sip, his head thrown back. The top half of his face was obscured by a plain black mask, but his thick tangle of dark hair was unmistakable. As always, he was the best-dressed among the guys—at least, I thought so. While the others went for traditional preppy, he had something a little more sophisticated going on, with black pants and a black dress shirt—as always, with the sleeves rolled to the elbows. He finally tilted forward again and removed the bottle from his lips, wiping his mouth with the back of his hand. A couple of the girls let out giggles, and Garrett clapped him on the back. Everyone was wearing a mask of some sort, except Garrett, whose mask—one of those cheap plastic Halloween things that looked like a politician—was hanging around the back of his neck.

Eleanor sat primly on top of a laid-out raincoat on one of the rocks, wearing a purple velvet dress. As Ben and I approached, she looked at us and then promptly turned her face away.

I turned to Ben. "Gimme the vodka." He passed it over with an old-fashioned bow. I unscrewed the top, tilted my head back as Aydın had done, and poured a stream into my mouth. I only lasted half a second before the alcohol started burning my throat and I leaned forward, coughing.

"Don't get in over your head, kid," said Garrett.

I glared at him, then coughed again. "That stuff is nasty."

"It's cheap," said Ben. "Sorry the quality isn't up to your standards."

I moved to sit on an open section of one of the smaller rocks.

Aydın passed his bottle to Eleanor, and she took a dainty sip. To her credit, she looked elegant: no coughing, no grimacing. She passed it along and gave him a sideways smile. As I sat, I noticed how she kept her eyes averted from me, her face always tilted in someone else's direction.

I told myself I didn't care.

Aydın also seemed to be ignoring me. He was laughing and flirting a bit with the other girls, but he hadn't so much as glanced at me.

Eleanor had screwed it all up. There was nothing I could do to fix things while we were with the group, but maybe at the dance I could find a way to get him alone, to tell him how I felt.

Right when things had started to get a little fuzzy from the booze, someone suggested that we should probably actually go to the dance. I agreed.

When we entered the rec center, the vibe had changed. The music was more upbeat, and people were dancing.

A few steps ahead of me, Eleanor looked at Ben. "Are you dancing?"

He was sort of shimmying to the music. "It's catchy," he said. Then he grabbed her hands and shimmied her farther into the middle of the room. "You're too sober!"

"I'm not sober!" she said, catching the ear of an older lady nearby who looked at her in surprise. "Sorry, Kris," Eleanor said, sounding embarrassed. The lady winked and kept dancing. Eleanor looked around the room as she danced halfheartedly with Ben. Searching for Cameron, probably.

Then I spotted Chloe.

She was on the other side of the rec center, dressed in white with a gold mask, talking to a group of little kids and smiling as they tugged at her hands, trying to bring her onto the dance floor. Her hair hung straight and glossy down her back. She looked like an angel.

A male voice behind me asked, "Ros?" I turned, hopeful, only to be deeply disappointed when I found Franklin Doss standing in front of me.

"Hi."

He looked approvingly at my dress. "You look great."

"Did I ask?"

He shoved his hands in his pockets with a frustrated sigh. "Look, Ros, I know you don't like me—"

"*No*," I said with exaggerated surprise. "*Really?*"

"I'm not sure what you said about me to everyone, but can you tell them you didn't mean it?"

This time, I was genuinely surprised. "What do you mean?"

The upbeat song that was playing ended, and a softer, slower one came on. Where the hell was Aydın?

"Everyone's been ignoring me," Franklin said. "I assume you told them to. You're the only one who hates me enough—"

"Who's been ignoring you?" I was half paying attention, but the other half of me was scanning the crowd, searching for Aydın.

"Everyone from school. And those other people you guys hang out with."

I turned around to scan the other side of the room, standing on tiptoe to peer over everyone's heads. That's when I finally spotted him. But he wasn't looking for me.

"Ros, please," whined Franklin. "It really sucks. I'm here with my family and I feel like such a dumbass. Even my little brother has people to hang out with."

It was like watching a movie in slow motion. As I stared at Aydın, the crowd in front of him parted, revealing Chloe, who was kneeling to help a little girl tie her mask on. Backlit by the flickering fake candles, Chloe looked like she was glowing. And Aydın? He was perfectly still, mesmerized.

"Are you even listening to me?" asked Franklin.

I had to tear my gaze away. "I didn't do anything."

"Look, I know I've said some things that have bothered you—"

"*Some things?*" Was he really this stupid? "Franklin, I haven't said anything to anyone. You occupy exactly zero percent of my brain space. People just hate you because you're an asshole."

He opened his mouth to reply, but I turned and weaved my way between the slow-dancing pairs, just to put some space between us. The song ended, and another even more romantic song began to play. Something about roses and the moon.

I found myself just a couple of yards away from Aydın, in a clear space on the dance floor. His back was turned to me, watching Chloe, and as I stepped forward to tap him on the shoulder, I saw her stand up, her eyes meeting his. He took a step toward her. I couldn't move. I could barely breathe. I watched, frozen, as Aydın offered Chloe his outstretched hand.

She took it, and they began to dance, joining the sea of swaying couples. It looked like neither of them said anything. It looked like they didn't have to. They swayed gently, tenderly to the music, Chloe's head resting on Aydın's shoulder, her eyes closed. An intertwined column—his black clothes, her white dress—under a night sky of sparkling, spinning stars. I remained stuck, my heart in my throat, as I watched the first boy I actually thought I might love dancing with another girl.

As they turned in place, Aydın noticed me watching, and he tilted his head up to look me in the eyes, his expression unreadable. Then Chloe lifted her head and he looked at her instead. She said something. He smiled, all white teeth, and tucked a strand of her hair behind her ear. It was so intimate, so gentle, that I felt guilty for watching. Turning away, I spotted Ben by a window, chatting with one of the other guys.

I made my way to him. "Is there any more to drink?"

He looked surprised, then grinned. "Yeah, dude."

The rec center had a loft, accessible by ladder from a back room. It was piled with decorations for celebrations of various sorts—autumnal wreaths made of red and orange plastic leaves, a couple of small plastic Christmas trees, a full-sized wooden sleigh, some red-white-and-blue tinsel. Ben led me to a box labeled UNDER THE SEA and pulled it open. Inside was a collection of bottles of various sizes and states of emptiness. "Welcome to the stash," he said.

"This place is nuts."

"I know." Then he looked at me closely. "Everything alright?"

"Mhm. Just too sober for this."

"Cheers to that," said Ben.

———

Let me just say that climbing up and down a ladder in a dress and wedges is not easy, and honestly, I was extremely proud of myself for managing it.

When I got back to the dance floor, Aydın and Chloe were perched together on a window seat, engaged in what seemed to be a deep and intent conversation.

I couldn't stop thinking about the look that Aydın had given me, before he did that thing with Chloe's hair. It was so intentional. He *wanted* me to see it, I thought. He was trying to send me a message. *This is what you're missing.*

I decided the only thing to do was to give him a dose of his own medicine. I couldn't just go talk to him and explain things like I'd planned; instead, I was going to have to show him that two could play this game.

I want to make it clear: it seemed like such a good idea at the time. Clouded by alcohol, my judgment was not at its finest, and of course, I had no inkling of how messy and complicated the consequences would be.

How could I have?

My first idea for a target was Garrett. He *had* been flirting with me, right? I wasn't sure, but it seemed likely. And he seemed douchey enough to go along with my scheme.

I wound my way through the crowd—which was now bopping around to a song that was very early 2000s—in search of him. Finally, I spotted his cheap plastic mask. It wasn't a politician after all...it was Nicolas Cage. I grimaced to myself but pushed forward and tapped him on the shoulder. "Hey, Garrett?"

He turned. He was sucking on a lollipop. "'Sup?" he asked, one cheek bulging with the candy. Mary appeared beside him, and he put an arm around her.

"Oh," I said, looking at Mary, who was watching me curiously, playing with a strand of her hair. "I was just wondering if you'd seen Eleanor."

Garrett shook his head. "Nope."

"I think I saw her over by the bathroom, but that was a while ago," said Mary.

"Oh, okay. No worries. Thanks."

"No prob," said Garrett.

I glanced back over my shoulder as I hurried away, and saw Garrett take the lollipop out of his mouth and lean down to kiss Mary.

I wondered, momentarily, what flavor it was, then shook myself out of it. *Dodged a bullet with that one.*

Distracted, I bumped straight into someone. "Sorry!"

"No harm done." The guy was tallish, on the skinny side, with bright red hair. He squinted at me from behind a blue mask that covered his whole face. I was still trying to figure out where I'd seen hair that color before when he said, "Hey! Ros, right?"

Then I remembered. "You got it. Cameron?"

He nodded enthusiastically. "What's up? How have you been?"

"I've been good!" The beat dropped and the dancers around us started jumping up and down. Someone bumped into me, and I fell against Cameron. He caught me with ease.

"This place is a minefield," he said, raising his voice over the music. "Want to get out of the line of fire?"

"Sure," I shouted.

He led me off the dance floor to one of the window seats. He took off his mask. He *was* sort of cute, I decided. I could see what Eleanor saw in him. Especially now, flushed from the heat and dancing, and his hair standing up wildly....

"So, what have you been up to?" he asked. "You and your friend—I feel terrible, I can't remember her name...."

"Eleanor," I said.

"Eleanor!" He snapped his fingers. "I remember now. Blue bike."

I nodded. "We've been good. It's fun here." The room was spinning a little, the second round of alcohol finally hitting me. "We went sailing. And made a campfire. And we found a—I can't remember the name—a thing, in the woods."

He nodded solemnly. "A thing in the woods. Sounds like fun."

I rolled my eyes, unable to suppress a smile. "I can't remember what it's called. With ropes and stuff?"

He laughed. "The obstacle course?"

"Oh. Yeah. Duh."

"I mean, it's not really an obstacle course. It's a 'team-building arena.' But everyone just calls it the obstacle course." He looked at me sideways, with an amused smile. "You've been into the loft stash, haven't you?"

"You know about it?!"

He laughed again. He had a cute laugh. "I work here. Of course I know about it." He leaned in and dropped his voice. "The younger staff always has a predance 'meeting' up there."

"Who buys the alcohol?"

"Sometimes us, sometimes you guys. It's our little shared secret."

"Huh." I thought about this. "I like that."

"Me too."

"It's not that obvious that I'm drunk, is it?"

"Lucky guess."

I squinted at him, trying to figure out if he was lying. I was pretty sure I was good at hiding mild levels of intoxication, but I didn't exactly have proof of that. "What have you been up to?" I asked.

"Oh, the usual. Work, more work, a bit of fun."

"Are you just the bicycle guy?"

Cameron shook his head. "I'm also the games-for-little-kids guy. And a lifeguard. And sometimes I stand in for the waitstaff."

"A man of many talents."

He winked. "That's what they call me."

It was then that I thought of Eleanor. A good friend, in this situation, would check out the situation for her, gauge Cameron's level of interest and report back. And I was trying to be a good friend.

But then I remembered that we were fighting. That Eleanor had ruined my thing with Aydın. That she'd tried to use my history with Lydia against me. And that she'd been ignoring me since.

An idea sparked in my brain, about Cameron, and I immediately squashed it.

Even if Eleanor wasn't speaking to me, it would be absolutely terrible of me to use her crush to make my crush jealous.

Then again, a small voice in my brain was saying, *doesn't she deserve it?*

I'd convinced myself that Eleanor was different from Lydia, that she would never do the things that Lydia did. But maybe she wasn't so different. She'd overreacted in exactly the way Lydia would have. I'd been burned before, and I'd taken a chance on trusting Eleanor, and look what I got in return.

But still. I couldn't hurt Eleanor in that way. I was trying to be a better friend, and good friends forgive each other.

Cameron nodded toward the dance floor. "You go to school with those guys?" I followed his gaze and saw Ben talking to Garrett, Mary, and Garrett's friend Aaron, who had a buzzcut and a standoffish attitude.

"Some of them. How'd you know?"

"The staff sees everything around here."

I lifted an eyebrow. "Creepy."

"Okay, not everything. But I've seen you guys all together, and since I know you're not a Pine Bay repeat, I figured you knew them from before."

"Have you ever considered a career as a detective?"

He smiled. "That's my other career, actually. When I'm not the bike guy or the games guy." Then he looked back out at the dance floor, rubbing the back of his head. "So, uh. This is kind of an awkward question."

"Ask away."

He looked at me, and his eyes were sea-glass blue. I felt my heartbeat speeding up. I knew what was coming, and I was powerless to stop it. And, more frighteningly, I didn't yet know what I would do in response.

"Your friend over there," he said, nodding his head toward the dance floor. "I think his name is Ben?"

This was not what I had anticipated. "Um. Yeah. What about him?"

"Is he...with anyone? Like, dating?"

I was stunned. "Um. No. I mean, not that I know of."

Cameron nodded. He was blushing now, bright red. "Sorry," he said. "I didn't mean to make that weird."

"No, no worries," I said. Then I prodded, "Do you *like* him?"

"I mean," he said, and he paused, glancing over at Ben again. "We haven't talked much. But. Sorta." Then he jumped up and offered me his hand. "But I work here, so I'm not really supposed to say that. Want to go dance?"

I stood up, taking his hand. "Absolutely."

As we danced, I tried to muster up the clarity of mind to figure out what I had to do. The alcohol had made my brain even fuzzier. And Cameron was standing so close to me, and his scent was distracting—he smelled faintly of herbs, like chamomile and mint, maybe. He smiled down at me, and a tiny dimple appeared in one cheek. *Goddamnit, that's cute.*

Eleanor. I was supposed to ask about Eleanor. I decided right then that I was going to set aside my frustration and be a good friend. Maybe it'd even get her to forgive me. "So, I don't know about Ben," I said to Cameron as we danced. "But I maybe kinda sorta have a different friend who might like you."

"Oh, really?" He raised an eyebrow.

I didn't want to tell him her name just yet. I needed to sell it first, see if there was any chance he was interested. *Then* I'd tell him. Because if I knew Eleanor, I knew there was no chance she was actually going to make a move on her own tonight. She needed my help. "She's super sweet and kind and thoughtful and like, *unbelievably* smart—"

He scrunched his nose. "I'm sorry, Ros. Your friend sounds really great, but I'm only into guys."

"Oh," I said. "I'm sorry, I wasn't sure."

"It's fine," he said. There was an uncomfortable pause. "She does sound great, though. Anyone would be lucky to date her."

I nodded emphatically. "They really would."

The music switched to another angsty early-2000s pop hit, and the awkwardness of our conversation dissolved as Cameron grabbed my hands and started jumping around, our dancing getting sillier and sillier. As he twirled me, I saw a flash of white out of the corner of my eye.

There they were, Aydın and Chloe, dancing close together, their eyes closed, swaying to a rhythm in their own heads, in an entirely separate world from ours. Aydın opened his eyes. He noticed me looking at him, and he glanced at Cameron. His eyebrows furrowed.

This was it. The perfect moment. The perfect opportunity to jab back at Aydın, to show him what he was missing.

Eleanor doesn't even have a shot with Cameron, said that tiny voice in my head. *He's not interested, so what could be the harm?*

And she'd been so pointedly avoiding me all evening, she probably wasn't anywhere near us. She wouldn't even know.

I glanced over to make sure Aydın could still see us.

Then I stood on my tiptoes and tilted my head up to plant a gentle kiss on Cameron's lips.

When I pulled back, Cameron raised an eyebrow at me and started to say something, but I didn't hear it, because over his right shoulder, I found myself making direct eye contact with Eleanor. It took one look for me to know: she had seen everything.

Chapter Nine

Eleanor spun on her heel and disappeared into the crowd.

"Ros?" Cameron was saying.

"Sorry," I said, blinking, wondering if I should run after her. *I can explain later. I'll explain later, and it'll be fine.* "What is it?"

"I said, I'm flattered, but I just told you that I wasn't into girls."

"I'm not into you either," I said.

He frowned. "Then what was that?"

"Cameron, I'm so sorry, but I'll explain later." I scanned the crowd again. Aydın and Chloe were nowhere to be seen. "Right now I need to go do some damage control."

"Damage control for what?" he called after me, but I was already on my way out of the rec center.

When I got back to the Orchard Oriole, I found Eleanor in her pajamas, wrapped in a blanket, lying on the couch facing the backrest so I couldn't see her face. She hadn't unfolded and made our pullout bed.

"Eleanor?" I asked. She stayed silent and still. I could tell from her breathing that she wasn't asleep. "Eleanor, don't be mad at me. Please."

"Don't talk to me." Her voice was a low growl.

I hesitated. I had to explain. I had to tell her that I wasn't planning to do it, that actually I was trying to be a good friend and check out the situation for her, and when I found out that he wasn't into girls anyway, and everything aligned so perfectly, well, I couldn't pass up the opportunity.

But I was suddenly utterly exhausted. I changed into my pajamas and curled up on the other couch, figuring she'd be more likely to listen in the morning. And then she would forgive me. She had to.

Except in the morning, she was gone. I woke up to Eleanor's parents tiptoeing through the living room to the front door. A grumpy Mason dragged his feet behind them. I sat up, yawning. "Good morning!" Sherry said brightly.

"Good morning," I mumbled. My head hurt.

"Did you have fun last night?"

I nodded, rubbing my eyes. *Maybe a little too much fun.*

"Sweetheart, leave poor Ros alone," Harry said. "Let her wake up in peace."

Sherry mouthed *sorry*, and the three made their way out the door, leaving me alone in the bright white living room.

I brushed my teeth, got dressed, and chugged a bottle of water, hoping to kick my throbbing headache. When that didn't help, I took two Advil and headed outside.

As I reached the dining hall, I was surprised to see Cameron leaning against the wall. He looked up and spotted me. "Hey."

"Good morning."

"How's it going?"

I made a *so-so* face. "Little tired. Little hungover."

Cameron gave a small smile. "Been there."

There was a moment of silence, and then he said, "Look, I just want to talk about what happened last night."

"I'm so sorry," I said. "That was deeply not okay of me."

He shrugged. "Why'd you do it?"

My head was still pounding. "I was trying to make someone jealous."

"Who?"

"Ben's friend."

"Green eyes?"

"That's the one."

Cameron nodded.

"He was dancing with someone else last night," I continued. "I thought...for some reason, I thought it would be a good idea for him to see me kissing someone else."

Cameron snorted. "That's a terrible idea."

"I know," I said. "And now Eleanor wants to kill me."

He looked confused. "What does she have to do with this?"

"Never mind," I said. "It doesn't matter. I just want you to know how sorry I am, and that I totally get it if you're mad at me. I wasn't thinking straight." My stomach let out a long, slow, incredibly loud growl.

Cameron laughed incredulously. "Was that *you*?"

"I think so."

"Need some breakfast?"

"Seems like it. Any chance you'd accompany me and let me continue apologizing over pancakes?"

"Sure thing," Cameron said. "I've got the morning off, and I'd never say no to a little more apology."

As we entered the dining hall side by side, I glanced around. It was late morning, and the place was packed with lingering families chatting over mostly empty plates. Eleanor's family was with a couple and a kid who looked about Mason's age. The two boys were studiously ignoring each other, as middle schoolers do. No sign of Eleanor, and no sign of Aydın and Ben.

I headed for the bacon, which at that moment looked to me like it was the only thing that could cure my burgeoning hangover. There was a line, of course, and I stood in it impatiently, tapping one foot and rubbing my temple, hoping this would somehow help.

Then someone behind me said, "Rosaline." I recognized Doss's voice.

At exactly the same moment, I saw Aydın approaching the line. Our eyes met. "What do you want?" I asked Franklin without turning around.

Aydın paused. "What?"

"Not you." I jerked my head backward at the jerk behind me.

"No need to be so aggressive," said Franklin.

"Why won't you leave me alone?" I asked.

"I'm just trying to have a conversation—"

I turned and faced him. "Franklin Doss, I hate you and I want nothing to do with you."

For a moment, it seemed like I'd stunned him silent. Then he crossed his arms and faced Aydın. "Aydın, great to see you, buddy. Been a couple of years, yeah?"

Aydın ignored him.

"Go away, Franklin," I said.

Franklin continued talking to Aydın. "I assume you've met my classmate Ros. Did you know that she's been fraternizing with the waitstaff?"

I felt my face heating up.

"That ginger is probably going to get fired," Franklin went on, turning back to me. "And tell me: Do you actually like him, or is he just the only guy who'll look at you?"

"Franklin," said Aydın in a low voice.

"I knew you were desperate, but not *that* desperate," Franklin told me.

"Knock it off."

I finally burst. "It was just a kiss! I don't even like him!"

"Oh, good," said Franklin. "I was starting to worry you had really lowered your standards. Dating the staff is basically dumpster diving."

I felt a shift in the air, and I knew that someone had walked up behind me.

"What's your problem?" said Cameron. His voice had the edge of someone just barely holding back deep anger.

"The man of the hour!" said Doss.

Aydın grabbed Franklin's arm and marched him away.

"I'm so sorry. If it helps, he's an asshole to everyone," I told Cameron.

He was rubbing the back of his neck. "I think I'm gonna go."

"What about breakfast?"

He shook his head. "I usually eat in the staff room anyway. We're allowed to eat here, but no one ever does. I guess now I see why."

"Cameron, I'm so sorry," I repeated.

"Don't worry about it. I just…I don't want to be here anymore." He stuck his hands in his pockets and walked away before I could say anything else. My head was spinning and my stomach hurt. I had no idea what to do. Should I go after him? Would that make it worse?

In a daze, I collected a plate of bacon and wandered to an empty table in the corner. I ate a few pieces of bacon, scrolling through my phone, but I felt more nauseous than before, and now I wasn't sure whether it was from the hangover or something else.

A few minutes later, as I neared the Orchard Oriole, I was relieved to hear Eleanor's voice coming through an open window. I started to plan out what I would say, how I would explain things to her and get her to understand. But as I reached for the doorknob, I heard another familiar voice. "It was stupid," Chloe Choi said, sniffling like she'd been crying. "I know it was stupid. I shouldn't have done that."

"It wasn't stupid," said Eleanor, her voice gentle. "You did nothing wrong."

"It just brought all the emotions back…." There was a sound like a small sob. I removed my hand from the doorknob.

"I know," said Eleanor. "I'm sorry."

"You're a good person," said Chloe. "Like, a really good person. I'm basically a stranger crying on your couch."

"You're not a stranger," said Eleanor. "We've gone to school together for forever."

"That's true."

"I'm here for you."

"Well then," said Chloe between sniffles, "you're a really good friend."

I was shocked. Eleanor and Chloe weren't friends. As far as I knew, they'd never spoken. What was this?

"So, what did you say to him?" Eleanor asked softly.

"That I didn't want to go through this again. That I wasn't interested. We both already know that he can't be with me. I don't know why he let it happen, why I let it happen...."

"It's hard to let go of old feelings. I get it."

Did she get it? Eleanor had never had a boyfriend, had never been on a date. *I'd* been the one who dispensed boy advice to *her.*

Then I heard Chloe sniffle like she was going to start crying again, and I turned and left.

I wandered aimlessly along the resort paths for a while, trying not to think about all the things that were making me feel guilty, and trying not to think about what this meant about Chloe and Aydın, or about Aydın and me.

I came across a trailhead labeled OVERLOOK HIKE, 5 MILES. With nothing better to do, I started down the path. If I couldn't have friends or a boyfriend, I figured, at least I could have killer legs.

———

By dinnertime I had cooled off and was ready to face society again. I was nearing the dining hall when I heard familiar voices around the corner. On the side porch of the building, I found Garrett and his squad. And…Doss. Weirder still, the asshole was wearing a towel on his head, clutching it under his chin. I was about to step forward and tell him to kindly fuck off when the group burst into laughter. In a high, sing-songy voice, Franklin called, "Aydın! Dinner time!"

Aydın wasn't there, I noticed. Neither was Ben.

"Allahu Akbar!" Franklin said then, and in his voice it sounded garbled, harsh, like a curse instead of a prayer.

Garrett leaned back in his Adirondack chair, smiling. "Aydın definitely has a hot mom."

"One hundred percent," said Franklin, switching back to his normal voice. "She's probably the hottest terrorist you've ever seen."

I burst out, "What the fuck?" The look on all of their faces told me that no one had noticed me standing there.

Franklin's grin was vicious. "Rosie Posie," he said. "What's up?"

"What the fuck are you doing?" I asked.

"What does it look like?" asked Franklin. "Hanging out." I saw something malicious flicker in his eyes. He looked *way* too pleased with himself, and it scared me a little.

I tried to collect myself, to convey pure disdain in my voice as I said, "That racist performance was low, even for you, Doss."

Garrett's gaze was flicking back and forth between Franklin and me. "You two know each other?"

"From school," I said, just as the Douchebag King said, "Oh, we *know* each other, alright."

I froze.

Chapter Ten

Aaron let out a laugh, then covered his mouth with his hand.

"What did you say?" I asked.

Doss shrugged. "I'm just saying we had a good time way back when, isn't that right?"

Before I knew what I was doing, my hand flew up and slapped him across the face. Hard.

This elicited a chorus of claps and "dangs" from the boys.

"It was that bad, huh?" asked Garrett, laughing.

Franklin rubbed his cheek and looked at me sideways. "Didn't realize I broke your heart."

"I think she wants to go for round two!" someone shouted.

I had momentarily found myself speechless, but no longer. "All we did was kiss."

He was quiet for a moment. The other boys seemed to be waiting to hear how he would respond. "All I'll say," Doss finally replied, "is that that didn't seem like a kiss slap to me, right, guys?"

Some more snickering, a few "yeahs."

Garrett looked at me and twisted his mouth in mock consideration. "Yeah, I don't know. Seems like the secret is out, Ros."

"What secret?" I spat.

Garrett held up his hands as though in surrender. "All I'm saying is that slap seems a bit overkill for 'just a kiss.'"

"What are you trying to hide?" Franklin asked.

I looked around at them, self-satisfied smiles on each face. "You're disgusting," I said to Franklin. "And don't you dare talk about Aydın's family like that."

"It was a joke," said Garrett.

"It wasn't funny."

Franklin looked like he was winding up to say something else, and I decided it was probably best that I didn't stick around to hear it. Rage was close to boiling over inside me, but I heard my mother's voice in my head repeating what I'd heard a thousand times as a kid: "You've already caused enough of a scene. Let it go."

I turned to leave, squeezing my hands into fists. Then the Prince of the Assholes called after me, "You don't like me joking about Aydın because you're into him."

I froze, willing myself not to turn around.

"What would your pool-boy boyfriend think of that?" Franklin continued. "But then again, that's just classic Ros. She needs to keep all her options open."

Before I knew what was happening, I was running at him. I shouldered his chest and heard him let out an *oomph* as he fell to the wooden porch floor. I jumped on top of him and started punching him in the chest. It felt good. There was nothing but anger inside me, anger built up over years and years and years. Franklin shielded his face with his hands and shouted something I didn't understand.

"Oh my god," a voice said.

Then, suddenly, a pair of hands slid under my arms and hoisted me off Franklin Doss. "What the hell is going on?" Aydın asked.

I slid out of his grasp and turned to face him. He looked concerned—*really* concerned.

Up until that point, I had been flooded with adrenaline, but the sight of his face, of his worried green eyes, broke something inside of me. "I—" I started to say, and then my throat got tight. "I—"

"She had a temper tantrum," said Garrett.

My shoulders were moving up and down in shudders, and my vision was hazy, blurred with tears. I realized I was hyperventilating. I felt distanced from my own body. Aydın wrapped an arm around me and looked at the group of boys again, then down at Franklin, still curled up on the ground, before walking me away.

I barely remember the walk, just coming to a picnic table off the path and shaded by trees. I sat down on one of the benches, facing away from the table, and Aydın sat beside me. I was still angry, but I was more embarrassed. I didn't want Aydın to see me like this. I closed my eyes and counted five seconds in, five seconds out as I breathed, trying to slow the shuddering of my shoulders. It worked for a moment, but then Aydın put his hand on my back to comfort me and something about it made me break into tears again. I squeezed my eyes shut.

"What happened?" he asked quietly.

All I could do was shake my head.

Several moments of silence passed. "Do—do you want me to leave? I can leave you alone if—"

"No," I said.

A pause. "Okay." His hand on my back moved slowly up and down, up and down. After another long moment, Aydın asked, "Did Doss hurt you?"

I half laughed at that, with a sniffle. "No, but I might've hurt him."

Aydın laughed. "Damn, Ros."

"He deserved it."

"I believe that."

My breath was slowing, and the tears had stopped. I looked sideways at Aydın, his eyes soft and concerned, and I smiled weakly. He smiled back.

"How can I help?" he asked. "I'd offer to go beat Doss up for you, but you've taken care of that."

I snorted, then sniffled. "I appreciate the thought."

"Seriously, what can I do?"

A thought crossed my mind then, a half-formed idea. "Let's go sailing."

"Right now?" He glanced at the sun, hovering dangerously close to the top of the tree-covered hills. "It'll be dark soon."

"I thought you wanted to learn."

He gave me a funny look. I kept my face still, trying not to betray any emotion. "I mean, if you think it's safe—"

"It'll be fine," I said. "I know what I'm doing."

He gave me that same searching look. "You think this'll make you feel better?"

"I know it will."

"Alright, then," he said, standing up. "Lead on, Captain."

———

The shack where the attendant usually sat was closed up, but I grabbed two life jackets from hooks on the side, handing one to Aydın. Then I rigged one of the little sailboats, and Aydın helped me push it into the water.

The water was cold when I trailed my fingers in it. There was a fresh breeze skimming over the lake, which made me shiver but would be helpful for teaching.

I had Aydın sit by the tiller. "You want to push it in the opposite direction from where you want to go," I said.

"Well, that makes no sense."

"You'll get the hang of it."

I sat in the middle of the boat and worked the sail. The breeze quickly filled it, sending us out into the middle of the lake.

Aydın pushed the tiller all the way to the left, turning us right, then pulled it all the way to the right. We turned left, and farther left, and farther left, and then we were heading upwind, making the sail hang limp and useless. "Oh shit," he said, "what did I do?"

"Nothing," I said, grabbing the tiller from him and maneuvering us so that the wind was at our back. The sail billowed out again. "The mechanics of the wind are kind of tricky. I think that'll probably have to wait for session two. For now, we focus on the basics."

"Oh," said Aydın. "I didn't realize this was a whole course."

He began playing with the tiller, moving it back and forth more cautiously now. The wind blew his hair into his eyes, and he reached up and brushed it away, only to pause when he noticed me watching him. He dropped his gaze to the water again.

"Franklin was saying stupid things," I said. Aydın didn't say anything, so I continued. "That's why . . . that's what happened. I didn't just attack him out of nowhere."

"I figured there was a reason."

The breeze was getting colder and the sky darker as some clouds rolled in, but I knew that if we turned back now, this fragile moment would break. I liked this, sitting on a boat in the middle of a lake with Aydın, just the two of us, with no one and nothing else around to interfere. I wondered if he liked it too.

I wasn't sure what else to say, so I asked, "Did you see the stash last night?"

He laughed. "Did Ben show you? He's obsessed."

"It's pretty sick."

"That it is. Dude was psyched when he first found it."

"I can imagine."

"Last night was your first time breaking into the stash?"

"You couldn't tell from how hungover I looked this morning?"

He laughed at that. "Welcome to Pine Bay then, I guess." He paused. "This is your first time here, right?"

"Mhm," I said. "But, I mean, I've been hearing about it for years. I feel like everyone's family at Bardet has had a Pine Bay summer except me." I paused. "What about you?"

He trailed his fingers in the water again. "I've only been here because of Ben."

"Oh yeah. After you guys met at soccer camp, right?"

"Yep."

"You a big soccer guy?"

"Not really." He shrugged. "I mean, I used to be."

I leaned my chin on my fist. "Are you gonna join the team at Bardet?"

He shook his head. "My parents want me to focus more on school these days. With college admissions being so competitive."

"Soccer could be good for that."

"I'm not good enough to get recruited. So they think I shouldn't waste my energy, should focus on other extracurriculars instead."

"That's dumb."

Aydın looked at me, and I tried not to stare at his eyes, the color of freshly cut grass. "I don't know," he said. "They have a point. And if it's gonna help me get into a better college—"

"If you love it, you should do it!" I said.

He shrugged. "I love my parents more, and I don't want to disappoint them," he said. Then he looked embarrassed.

I felt a wave of guilt, remembering that I hadn't yet told him what

Doss had said about his mom, and how the other guys had laughed. But I wasn't even sure I should tell him. I knew how much these things hurt. If it were me, I'd never be able to look at Garrett and his friends the same way again.

But on the flip side, if it were me, I would want to know. "About Franklin," I said.

"You don't have to tell me about it if you don't want to," Aydın said.

I looked down at the mainsheet in my hands. "He was making Muslim jokes," I said. "Terrorist jokes. About your mom."

"Oh."

"I just felt like I needed to say something. To tell him it wasn't okay."

Aydın's mouth was tight. "Seems like that asshole says all sorts of shitty things and gets away with it."

"I know," I said softly. "It's even worse at school."

"Yeah?"

"Franklin Doss's assholery knows no bounds."

"Has he said that sort of stuff to you?"

"Sort of," I said. "I mean, he loves to mention how my family is different from his, from most of the families in our town. But…" I hesitated. "I guess he's never gone quite as far with me. At least, not that I've known about."

Aydın nodded, looking at the floor of the boat. "Why do you think that is?"

I was caught off guard by the question. "Um. I guess…I've worked really hard to distance myself from my dad's Turkishness."

Now Aydın looked at me, his thick eyebrows furrowed. "Why?"

I suddenly felt exposed, like I was under a magnifying glass. I had never articulated these feelings out loud to someone else. "Um, because it made me feel different. And what I wanted most as a kid was just to fit in. Our town is pretty homogenous. And…I guess I was… scared. Of how other kids might see me. What they might think."

Aydın nodded. "I get it," he said.

"And I know I have some privilege," I continued, now unable to stop. "Because my mom's family is Scottish, and my features are pretty mixed, so people can't usually tell what my background is if I don't tell them."

Aydın smiled at that. "Both of my parents are Turkish, but I get that too."

I nodded. "I know I should feel shitty about pushing my dad's heritage away, but…this is just how I've learned to cope."

"How does your dad feel about it?"

"I don't know," I said truthfully. "I mean, we visit his family in Istanbul, and I eat his Turkish cooking, and all that. It's not like I'm rejecting his culture. But when I'm around other people…I don't know, it gets weird. And I know that he doesn't feel super comfortable with the other Bardet parents. I think that's probably why he and my mom have never wanted to come here."

"I can understand that," said Aydın.

I noticed that we were drifting aimlessly, and the wind had left our sail, so I leaned over and nudged the tiller.

"Sorry," said Aydın, "I keep forgetting about this thing."

"You'll never make first mate at this rate," I said. Then I felt bad about joking after having such a heavy conversation.

But Aydın grinned up at me, eyes shining. "I think I'm probably more along the lines of the guy who mops the deck at this point."

"Are you?" I asked, with mock indignation. "I haven't seen any deck mopping yet. Get to it."

He smiled. We sailed on in peaceful silence for a minute or two, and then he said, "Ros?"

"Yeah?"

"So, I'm sorry to fixate on this, but I just want to make sure I have it right. You...punched Franklin because he was a racist?"

I rubbed my forehead. "I'm sorry you had to save me from that."

"Not a problem," he said. "Seeing you obliterate Doss was pretty satisfying. Dude's a creep."

"Yeah." I took a deep breath. "But honestly, I mean, yeah, that was part of it, but there was something else too."

"What did he do?" Aydın asked. "If you don't mind me asking."

"It's not—" I broke off, trying to figure out how to explain. "It won't sound that bad because you don't know the context."

"Then tell me," he said. "We're on a lake. We've got all the time in the world." He pulled the tiller expertly to set us back on course. We were nearing the other side, and we'd have to turn soon.

"Okay," I said. I was realizing that I'd have to tell him the whole story now. "Basically, he made some comments in front of that group about how well we 'knew' each other. And...I may have slapped him. And things sort of just escalated from there."

"Why would he say that?" Then he stopped, realizing the potential mistake he had just made. "You didn't...with Doss...did you?"

I laughed, a little bitterly. "Nope," I said. "But half of Bardet thinks we did."

Aydın frowned, waiting for me to continue. So I told him the whole story.

Back in middle school, Franklin and I were sort of friends. Shocking, I know. I guess he wasn't so gross at the time, or maybe I just didn't notice it as much.

In any case, we got along fine, and sometimes we hung out. And…

We kissed.

It was once, in eighth grade, and it was just because I wanted to get it over with. I was tired of playing Never Have I Ever and having to admit I'd never kissed anyone.

I know eighth grade isn't, like, *late* for a first kiss. But it felt urgent at the time.

So we kissed, and then he asked me out. I guess he thought the kiss was validation that I felt the same way he did. But I rejected him, and he got upset. To save face, he told everyone that we'd been hooking up for months, and that I didn't want to date him because I wanted to keep sleeping around.

I showed up to school the next day and felt the difference right away: girls who were usually friendly to me were staring and whispering, casting pointed glances my way as I passed them in the hallway. Soon enough, Lydia clued me in that everyone was calling me a slut. I was a total pariah.

To the girls, that is.

With the guys, it was more complicated. Despite my best efforts, the guys in my grade had never paid me much attention. All my crushes had heretofore been unrequited. (Hence why I had to turn to Franklin for that first kiss.)

But now guys who I'd thought didn't even know my name were saying hi to me in the hallways. They picked me early for gym class kickball, whereas before I'd always hovered somewhere toward the end of the lineup. They started to flirt, and I started to flirt back, and I realized that I could get them to like me if they thought I liked them too.

I had a lot of feelings about the whole thing. Obviously. On the one hand, I felt betrayed by Franklin and angry that this stupid situation had had such an impact on my social standing. On the other hand, I saw the silver lining in the attention that I was getting from guys, even though I understood that it was coming from kind of an icky place.

It was a lesson. I learned that everyone just has to look out for themselves, because no one else is gonna do it for them. Girls, especially, were never to be trusted. They were always looking for an excuse to take other girls down a notch. I was done with girls.

Except for Lydia. We never really talked about what had happened after that first day, but she didn't abandon me like everyone else. We stayed best friends. And that's why what she did that summer was so unforgivable.

But I didn't tell Aydın this last part. Instead, I finished the story with how I'd felt like an outcast at school and waited, internally cringing, for his reaction.

Aydın was quiet for a long moment. Then he said, "Wow."

"Yeah."

"I'm so sorry that happened to you."

I shrugged. "It's okay."

"You wanted to be able to say you'd had your first kiss, and you got more than you bargained for."

I let out a laugh. "I guess so."

Aydın ran a hand through his hair, looking up at the clouds. "Why did Doss bring that up now? Is he really pathetic enough that he feels the need to perpetuate a rumor he started in middle school?"

"He was trying to get back at me," I said. "For telling him not to be a racist shit."

"I still can't believe he did that."

"It's like he hasn't caught up to the world we live in yet."

"Unfortunately, I think there are a lot of people in this world who haven't caught up yet." He looked lost in thought, so I stayed quiet too, not wanting to interrupt whatever angry reverie he had entered. Then he said, "That guy from the bike stand seems nice."

I looked over at Aydın, but he was looking at the water again. A strong gust of wind pushed the sail out, and I fought to pull the mainsheet back in, keeping control. We were moving at a fast clip now, skimming quickly over the lake's surface, which had become bumpier, ridged with small waves from the wind. The boat started to heel, so I quickly switched to sit on the opposite side, weighting it to keep us from tipping all the way over. I motioned for Aydın to do the same.

"Cameron?" I asked. "Yeah, he's a nice guy."

Aydın nodded. "I'm sorry about earlier. Did you…I mean…I hope you managed to fix it."

"Oh. Oh my god, no," I said, maybe too quickly. "We—um…" Frantically, I ran through questions in my mind. Why was he asking? What was the deal with him and Chloe? *Was* he just with her to make me jealous, as I'd thought, or was there a chance—*any* chance—that it was…real? I thought back to the conversation that I'd overheard. "I mean, it wasn't anything serious. We're not…together."

"Gotcha."

"So," I said, against my better instincts. "Did you and Chloe used to date?"

Aydın gave me a funny look. Then he nodded, looking toward the trees on the opposite edge of the lake. "We did."

"Can I ask what happened?"

I saw the hesitation in his eyes as he looked at me. He was trying to figure out whether or not to say what he wanted to say. "We were really young. We met at Pine Bay the summer I came here with Ben. And then we sort of dated long-distance for a while. But I broke up with her. For…personal reasons. Not because of her or anything. She's…amazing."

I nodded, trying not to reveal my jealousy.

Aydın sighed. "Last night was the first time I'd seen her since then. And I thought…maybe…but it wouldn't have worked out between us. Seems like the timing is never right."

As much as it hurt, I wanted to know more. But just as I opened my mouth to ask what he meant, a clap of thunder sounded.

Chapter Eleven

Within seconds it had started to rain. "Shit," Aydın said. "What do we do?"

"It's okay," I said, trying my best to channel my inner levelheaded sea captain. "Let's head for shore."

Aydın switched the tiller to try to turn us in the direction of the Pine Bay dock, and I hauled in the mainsheet. The rain was picking up, and I was already shivering, my hair plastered to my shoulders. The wind was blowing much harder now than before, and I held the sail steady as it billowed outward and began to propel us across the water. The surface of the lake had gotten choppy, and the boat rocked as we made our way back toward shore, the spray from the waves dampening us even more than the rain.

I glanced back at Aydın, and when I saw his nervous expression—his eyes wide, focused on our landing spot—I said, "That's perfect. Just hold us steady."

"Bad luck on the weather, huh?"

"Yeah, seriously." I didn't say anything about the fact that I had seen this storm coming—the signs had been there. It was my own selfish fault that I had wanted this moment to last.

The rain was falling harder, the water getting choppier, until it felt like we were surrounded by gray sheets. The shore was barely visible. Aydın was a soaked-through mess, and the wind was roaring in my ears. But I had a singular goal and purpose: to get us safely back on land. Though every muscle in my body was tensed, I felt strong and confident. I knew what I was doing, and I could get us back just fine. I was—

A forceful gust blew into the sail, and we started to tilt. The port side, where I was sitting, lifted out of the water as the starboard side dipped dangerously low. I watched the waves lapping at the opposite edge of the boat, starting to make their way in. The wind was fighting to tear the mainsheet from my hands, to let the sail go free, and instinctively, I tightened my grip, pulling the sail even tighter against the wind. It was all I could do to maintain my hold. All of the sailing knowledge I had built up, all of the confidence I had in my abilities, had flown straight out the window. I was blank, a total beginner. In my panic, I had no idea what to do.

"Ros!" Aydın was shouting. He had let go of the tiller and was desperately holding on to the boat, trying not to fall out. The sail looked just inches away from touching the water. We were going to capsize. "Ros! What do we do?"

The sound of his voice brought something back to me in the split second before the mast went underwater. "Bail!" I shouted. "Jump away from the boat!"

The next thing I knew, I was underwater in the freezing dark, bumping up against something large and immovable above me. The boat. Desperate, panicked, I picked a direction and swam, trying to find the edge, to escape out from under it.

For a moment, the only thing I could think was *I'm going to drown.* Then it became: *Aydın is going to drown.* That kicked me into high gear, and I paddled through the water as hard as I could, pushing myself away from the boat above me, and then, suddenly, miraculously, I rocketed up to the surface, buoyed by my life jacket, and sprang out into the glacial air, taking massive, desperate gulps of breath.

"Ros!"

I caught my breath, bobbing in the waves. Everything was blurry and the cold stung. Aydın was beside me, also bobbing. He grabbed a strap on my life jacket to keep us from getting washed apart by the waves. "Are you okay?" he asked, almost shouting over the wind.

I nodded. "You?"

"I'm fine," he said, then looked at the boat beside us, which had turned turtle: all that was visible was the underside of the hull, sticking up out of the water like some massive crustacean's shell, with the centerboard protruding from the middle. "That was…insane."

"I've never had that happen before," I blurted. "I don't know what happened! I froze up, I—"

"It's fine," he said. "Let's focus on the important stuff. What do we do to fix it?"

"I don't know that we can." I could've made an excuse—about the rain, about the waves—but the truth was that I had no idea how to right the boat. At sailing camp, the counselors did that for us. "We should try to swim out. We don't want to be out here too long."

"Right," said Aydın. "It's really damn cold."

"Also lightning."

"That too."

It was going to be a rough swim, but I thought we could do it. At least we'd had the foresight to put on life jackets.

Then we heard a megaphone blare: "Remain where you are. A rescue team is coming to get you. I repeat, stay put."

I squinted toward shore through the sheets of rain. I managed to spot a cluster of people in what looked like black rain ponchos scurrying around a small motorboat.

"Well, that's good," said Aydın. His teeth were chattering.

"This is so fucking embarrassing," I said.

He shook his head. He was still holding on to the strap of my life jacket; we were twin buoys, bobbing up and down in the water. "We're Pine Bay celebrities now," he said.

I smiled, appreciating his readiness to make a joke, even in this situation. Even when I'd gotten him capsized in a lake in a rainstorm, when we shouldn't have been out sailing at all. And when he met my gaze with those brilliant green eyes, I was aware of how close we were, even though we were floating in a freezing lake.

"I have to ask you something," he said.

It was all I could do to nod.

"Did you really have to go to all this trouble just to get back at me for knocking you off an inner tube?"

I swatted gently at his head.

"It's not my fault I'm better than you at tubing," he said with a grin, holding up a hand to defend himself.

"Shut up," I said.

Aydın opened his mouth to say something else, but instead got a mouthful of lake water. As he sputtered, I giggled. "Don't laugh at my pain, Demir," he said.

"I'm so sorry."

He smiled, and the look in his eyes as he watched me took away the laughter and replaced it with something nervous and fluttering. "Alright, I'll forgive you. But only if you tell me what you're thinking about right now."

"Really?"

"I'm freezing and I need something to keep my mind off it until we're rescued."

"Alright, fair." I took a breath. I had to be honest. "I guess I'm thinking about what Eleanor told Ben at dinner last night."

Aydın narrowed his eyes, questioning.

"About me," I said. "And how I feel about you."

"Oh."

"Eleanor lied," I said.

"Why would Eleanor lie about that?" Aydın asked softly.

I heard the growl of a motor and looked up: the rescue boat had departed the shore. I had to make this quick. "I think I've made a lot of bad decisions the past couple of days," I said. "And things haven't really gone the way I wanted them to."

Aydın was quiet.

The waves were pushing me closer to him, and I didn't fight them. I looked him straight in the eyes. "I really like you, Aydın. That's a hard thing for me to say, but for some reason I feel comfortable with you and you make me want to be vulnerable, which is something that, trust me, I *never* want to be, and—"

Then he was kissing me. One of his hands pressed against the back of my life jacket, holding me to him as the water rocked us up and down, and his other hand tried to wind into my wet hair. I melted into it.

The next thing I knew, someone had grabbed my life jacket and hoisted me out of the water. They pulled me over the side of the boat, and I collapsed to the floor.

Now that I was out of the lake, the air felt even colder. My teeth started chattering violently. Someone wrapped a heavy blanket around my shoulders. I saw Aydın trying to clamber over the side of the boat, with the help of a large man in a jacket that said LIFE-GUARD. He looked shell-shocked; his wet hair was plastered wildly across his forehead. I could only imagine how I looked.

They sped us back to shore, where several more staff members—including Cameron—were waiting to escort us to the infirmary. As we walked, Cameron fell in step beside me and asked softly, "You alright?"

"I...think...so," I managed between chattering teeth.

I heard someone behind me say into a walkie-talkie, "They're walking to the infirmary now." There was a staticky response. "I don't know."

In the infirmary, we were met by a woman who introduced herself as Nurse Aditi. She looked like she was in her fifties, and wasn't dressed much like a nurse—at least not the way I thought of nurses. She was wearing a navy-blue quarter-zip sweatshirt and jeans. She ushered me into the bathroom, took the now-sopping-wet towel from me, and handed me a pile of clothes. "Do you think you can change into these?"

My body was convulsing with shivers, but I managed to say, "Can do."

She nodded and left, closing the door behind her.

I changed into a baggy sweatshirt and sweatpants, both two sizes too big, and left my clothes in a soggy pile on the bathroom floor. Aydın was already sitting on the couch when I got out, wrapped in a massive duvet. It was funny to see him in sweats too—he looked jarringly casual without one of his usual tastefully rumpled button-downs. Nurse Aditi had me sit beside him and wrapped me in a duvet as well. A younger man, also dressed in a navy quarter-zip, came into the room, and Nurse Aditi asked him to get us some tea.

Then she pulled a wooden chair up and sat down in front of us. "How are you two feeling?" she asked, making deliberate eye contact.

"Never been better," Aydın said.

She rolled her eyes. "Oh, so you're a smartass." She looked at me. "How about you?"

"Okay, I think," I said. I was still shivering, but the blanket helped.

Nurse Aditi took our pulses and listened to our breathing. She asked us to write out our full names on a slip of paper. The other nurse brought two steaming mugs of chamomile tea. I was too nauseous to drink, but I was grateful to hold the hot mug between my frozen fingers and let it thaw them out.

Nurse Aditi pulled a pair of reading glasses out of a backpack, put them on, and began filling out a packet of papers attached to a clipboard. After a few marks, she paused and peered at us over her glasses. She looked like a stern librarian observing a couple of troublemaking kids, and I found myself wondering if summer resort nurses are school librarians during the rest of the year. Was that even possible?

"What were you two doing out on the lake so late?" Nurse Aditi asked.

"I wanted sailing lessons," Aydın said. "Rosaline was nice enough to offer to teach me."

She looked skeptical. "I'm assuming you're both at fault here, so no use trying to throw yourself under the bus. You're not going to get your friend out of trouble."

"It's true, though."

"How did you get the boat?" she asked, ignoring this. "The sailing station was closed."

"We just took it," I said. "It wasn't locked up or anything. We didn't know it wasn't allowed."

She wrote something down in her packet, and I started to wonder exactly how much trouble we were in. "Did you know there was a storm coming?" she asked.

Aydın shook his head. "No idea." I was grateful that he answered so I didn't have to, but I wondered how true this was. I found it hard to believe he hadn't noticed the clouds.

She let out a short huff. "I hope you realize you both could have gotten seriously hurt. There was no lifeguard on duty."

It occurred to me for the first time to wonder how we *had* gotten rescued. "How did you guys find us?"

"A staff member happened to see the boat capsize, and he called it in. Let's just say you got lucky." She leaned in and looked us in the eyes, one at a time. "I don't want this to happen again. You can't rely on that sort of luck."

"We won't," I said.

"We promise," said Aydın. Then, with a slight grin, he made the Boy Scout salute and said, "Scout's honor."

Nurse Aditi remained unamused. "We're going to keep you here, just for tonight. In that rain and wind, when you fall in the water, there's a very real possibility of hypothermia."

"I'm feeling okay, ma'am," said Aydın. "I don't want to speak for Ros, but I don't think we need to stay here."

I wondered why Aydın was pushing back. Then Nurse Aditi picked up a landline phone and asked, "Where are your families staying?"

Aydın winced and tried again. "It's really alright, ma'am."

"Your parents are going to know about this incident one way or another, hun. So let's make this easy, alright?"

Aydın sighed. "I'm in the Ruby-Crowned Kinglet. Whittington family."

Nurse Aditi frowned and looked down at the clipboard in her lap. "I thought your last name was Muhtar."

"It is. I'm here with a friend's family."

A subtle look of understanding flickered across Nurse Aditi's face. "Ah." She turned to me. "And you?"

"Blake family. Orchard Oriole. Same thing."

Nurse Aditi nodded. "I'll still have to call your friends' parents."

"Understood," I said.

She dialed the Whittingtons first. "Hello? This is the Pine Bay infirmary. We have Aydın Muhtar here." A pause. "Yes, everything's fine. He just got a chill in the lake water. We're going to keep an eye on him overnight. But he's doing great." Another pause. "You can come see him if you'd like, anytime before eleven o'clock." She smiled at something the other person on the line said. "Perfect. We'll see you then." She hung up the phone and turned to Aydın. "Your friend will be over as soon as he can. He's very worried about you."

Aydın nodded. "Thank you. For not—making it sound—"

She waved a hand. "Don't mention it."

I had a feeling she really did understand how I was feeling about the whole thing—and how I assumed Aydın was feeling too. To do something stupid and get yourself in trouble when your family was around was bad enough. But to do it when you were with a friend's parents, when you were supposed to be on your best behavior? I could hear my dad saying, "Do you want them to think we raised you wrong?" I was sure I would never hear the end of it.

Nurse Aditi's call to the Orchard Oriole was similar. After she hung up, she informed me that the whole family was coming to check in on me, which was a surprise. I figured Eleanor was still mad, and rightfully so. Maybe this would provide the perfect opportunity to explain everything.

Nurse Aditi moved back into nurse mode, ordering the other nurse to get us some warm soup and saltine crackers. My mouth started watering at the thought. Nothing had ever sounded so good in my entire life.

The rest of the evening was kind of great. It was like being sick at summer camp, when the counselors just coddle you and give you whatever you want. Except without the bad parts, like being young and homesick and alone. And, you know, sick.

There was a stack of DVDs next to an ancient TV, so Aydın picked out *The Princess Bride* and we watched it with bowls of chicken noodle soup on our laps. I wanted to scoot closer, to wrap ourselves in the same blanket and get cozy, but when I glanced over at Aydın, he seemed wrapped up in the story of the beautiful Buttercup and the daring farmhand-turned-pirate Westley. I tried to ignore the swirling storm of thoughts that had started up in my brain.

Did he think the kiss had been a mistake? Was it an adrenaline-fueled act, the decision of someone caught up in a life-or-death moment, mistaking fear and camaraderie in the face of danger for something else?

Or, even worse, had he just been trying to comfort me?

I shook my head and focused on the movie. I'd loved it as a kid but hadn't seen it in years. This time around, I realized Buttercup was kind of the worst, but Westley was as hot as I remembered, so...I didn't mind too much.

After about ten minutes, Ben charged into the room. "Are you guys okay?"

Aydın paused the movie. "Yeah, we're doing alright."

"We're living the life," I said, gesturing to our setup.

Ben gave us a once-over. "Yeah, actually, looks pretty cushy to me." He took a seat on Nurse Aditi's wooden chair. "What happened?"

Aydın glanced at me. "We had a run-in with a storm."

"You've got to give me more than that."

"We went sailing," I said.

Ben frowned. "At night?"

"It wasn't night when we left."

"Ros was teaching me," Aydın said. "She's a pro."

"Clearly not, since I capsized us," I said.

"You *what?*" said Ben.

"The boat flipped over," said Aydın.

"Jesus. I'm glad you're okay."

Aydın shrugged. "It wasn't a big deal."

"I don't know, dude," said Ben. "Sounds like a big deal to me."

"Just because the water was cold," I said. "And it was storming. Otherwise, it would've been fine."

Ben glanced around the room. "Eleanor leave already?"

"She and her family are on their way," I said.

"Gotcha," said Ben. "Can I stick around? This movie looks wild."

"You've never seen *The Princess Bride?*" I asked, at the same time as Aydın exclaimed, "Dude! Tell me you've seen this movie before."

Ben stared at us. "I didn't realize this random movie was mandatory viewing. Did that cold water do something to your brains?" Then he furrowed his brow. "Actually, that reminds me of this thing I was reading about brain-eating lake amoebas—"

The infirmary door swung open again, and Eleanor's parents and brother hurried in. "Rosaline, sweetheart, how are you feeling?" asked Sherry, striding over to give me a hug.

"I'm alright, Mrs. Blake," I said.

She held me at arm's length and looked at me carefully. "Are you sure?"

"Absolutely sure."

She gave me another hug. "That must have been terrifying!"

Mason took a hesitant step toward me and held out a box of fudge-striped cookies, his eyes on the ground. I took the box and said, "Thank you so much, Mason."

"We thought they might help you feel better," he mumbled.

"They definitely will."

He finally lifted his gaze to look at me. His eyes were wide. "Did you almost drown?" he asked.

"Not really. Aydın and I just fell in the water and went for a very cold swim." I looked at Eleanor's mom and dad. "Is Eleanor here?"

They exchanged a look. "She's not feeling well," said Mr. Blake.

"We tried to bring her along, but she said she was under the weather," said Sherry. "Do you know what's going on?"

"I have no idea," I lied. "I'm sorry to hear that."

Sherry nodded. Then she turned to Aydın and Ben. "I'm Eleanor's mom, Sherry."

"Ben Whittington. Nice to meet you," said Ben, shaking Sherry's hand.

"Whittington," she repeated. "Is your mom on the committee for the Bardet holiday auction gala?"

"Every year." His smile was brilliant. I had a sudden vision of Ben twenty years from now, an accomplished young politician, greeting an adoring supporter.

Sherry's smile mirrored Ben's. "I've heard nothing but good things about you. Your mom is so sweet. And you," she said, turning to Aydın. "What's your name?"

"Aydın Muhtar," he said, also shaking her hand. "You can call me Aiden. Very nice to meet you, Mrs. Blake."

"What a lovely name," Sherry said.

"Thank you."

"Well," she said, straightening up, "it seems you're being well taken care of. I'll get on the phone with your parents, Ros, and let them know that you're okay."

I sat up straighter in my seat. "You don't have to do that."

"Of course I do. They'll want to know how you're doing."

"I can call them myself."

She waved her hand. "Don't worry about it, sweetheart."

I nodded, but my mind was racing, trying to figure out how to convince her not to call my parents.

"It's getting late," said Harry. "Let's leave the kids to their movie."

As the family turned to leave, I said quickly, "Will you ask Eleanor to come see me when she's feeling better? I need to talk to her about something."

"Of course, dear," said Sherry.

———

That night I got a small room in the infirmary to myself, with a nightstand and a twin bed and a massive stack of blankets and quilts. Nurse Aditi gave me a toothbrush, toothpaste, and a set of pajamas—again, a couple sizes too large. I brushed my teeth in the bathroom, changed, and got under the covers.

The curtains were open, and through the window, I could see an almost-full moon peeking over the tops of the pine trees. For the first time since I'd arrived in Pine Bay, I wondered what my parents were up to. It was weird to have a movie night without them.

My dad is a film buff, and when I was in middle school he decided that we needed a weekly family movie night. The person who chose the movie always had to give a presentation introducing their pick, and we took turns from week to week. Classics were welcome, but so were cult films, movies with historical significance…even epically bad movies were part of our repertoire.

The discussion afterward was the part that my dad lived for: talking about the decisions the director had made, analyzing the color palette, grading the screenplay and each actor's delivery. At first, I'd seen this as a chore. It was basically extra homework from my dad. But the more we did it, the more I got into it, and the more I began to understand what he was talking about. I guess it turned me into a kind-of film buff too. I was *really* into old high school movies—the Brat Pack and that whole bunch. There was just something about them. The aesthetic, the clothes, the touch of wild teenage recklessness.

Of course, a lot of them were seriously problematic. But I imagined that, if I ever made movies, they would look and feel just like those eighties high school films. Just *better.* All the good vibes and fun banter and pretty colors with none of the casual racism, homophobia, or misogyny.

I'd been so wrapped up in my excitement about Pine Bay that I hadn't been thinking about my parents much since Truth or Dare. But I had to admit, I missed them a little. A part of me wished they were there to dissect the movie we'd just watched. I pictured them at home, wrapped in cozy blankets on the couch as they watched some old movie without me.

The door to my infirmary bedroom creaked open and I propped myself up on one elbow. A silhouette appeared in the doorway, dressed in baggy infirmary-issued pajamas. "Hey, Ros," it whispered.

"Aydın?"

"Yeah. Can I come in?"

"Sure."

He tiptoed in and shut the door behind him. It was dark except for the faint, clouded-over moonlight coming in through the window. As my eyes adjusted, I saw him standing by the door, arms crossed. I sat up and patted the bed, and he sat down a couple feet away from me.

"Is everything okay?" I asked.

He nodded. "Yeah."

I wanted to ask what he was doing here, but instead I stayed quiet—maybe a first for me—and waited for him to speak.

"Today was kind of a lot, huh?" he said.

"You could say that."

"I read that people who experience life-threatening situations together get kind of bonded. Like, in plane crashes and things like that. The adrenaline makes them feel closer."

"Really?"

He was quiet for a moment. Then he said, "I feel like we've gotten a lot closer, just today."

Was he going to say that kissing was a mistake, that he just did it because of the adrenaline in the moment? "I'm not sure capsizing a boat is on par with a plane crash."

He shook his head. "You know, that all sounded much smoother in my head."

"Did it?" I was aware of how shallow and loud my breaths were. Could he hear the panic in my voice? I curled my legs up toward my chest and hugged them close.

He put his hand down on the bed between us. "I like you, Rosaline, capsize or no capsize."

"I—" I stumbled over my words. "Me too." My chest was tight, like a giant hand was squeezing all the air out of my lungs.

He was looking at me. "Are you sure?" he asked.

I nodded. "One hundred percent."

Still looking at me, but hesitant, he moved a little bit closer. I closed the gap between us, kissing him. His breathing hitched, and then his hand was on my cheek as we sank deeper into the kiss. I could *feel* the silence in the room, how loud my heartbeat sounded in the absence of all other noise. Then Aydın kissed me again and I couldn't think about anything else. I pulled away and his fingers wound into my hair as I climbed onto his lap, putting one knee on either side of his hips. I touched his face—strong eyebrows, high cheekbones, sharp jaw. He pulled me in and kissed me, harder this time. I kissed him harder in return, and then I remembered something.

I pulled away. "I have a confession," I whispered.

"What is it?"

"Cameron? The guy from the bike shop?"

Aydın looked worried. "What about him?"

"I only kissed him to make you jealous."

Aydın arched both his thick eyebrows. "Really?"

"Yeah. I just thought you should know."

"Well," Aydın said, pulling me close again, "it worked."

I fell back into his embrace, kissing him even more desperately than before. We had our hands in each other's hair, on each other's backs, as though we could become one person if we got close enough. I was lost under his spell.

His hands found my hips and he lifted me off his lap, then gently laid me on the bed. His mouth on my neck sent shivers through my whole body. I closed my eyes for a moment, and when I opened them, I saw him looking at me, green eyes bright even in the dark. "You're beautiful," he said.

I didn't know what to say to that, so I said, "So are you," reached up, and pulled him back down to me.

I have no idea how long we lay there, kissing in the dark. It could have been ten minutes; it could have been two hours. It felt like a blissful lifetime.

At some point, Chloe's face appeared in my head, along with the echo of the words I'd overheard her saying to Eleanor: *We both already know that he can't be with me.* I pushed it down as hard as I could. I was here, and I was getting exactly what I wanted. Why couldn't I just enjoy that?

Then I felt his hand moving downward, and I froze.

I could tell he felt it, because he immediately stopped and sat up. "Is everything okay?"

"Yeah, I just—" I was breathing hard. "I'm not—"

"We don't have to go any further if you don't want to," he said quickly.

"It's not that I don't *want* to," I said, "I mean, of course I want to, but I just haven't—I've never—"

"That's okay. We don't have to do anything."

"Are you sure? You're not…disappointed?"

He laughed. "Ros, you think there's any way I can be disappointed after *that*? I'm on top of the world." Then his expression turned serious. "Hey, it's okay."

"Okay," I said. "Thanks. I'm sorry."

He whacked me playfully on the shoulder. "Don't apologize." Then he lay down beside me, took my hand, and squeezed it.

We lay in silence for a long time. I sighed, content.

"I just wanted to say," Aydın said, but he paused.

"What?" I asked.

He shifted to face me before he said, "Thank you. For telling me that what Eleanor said wasn't true."

"Of course," I said. Then I added, "I figured you could probably tell anyway. I thought it was obvious that I liked you."

"I had my suspicions, for sure," he said. "And I'm fully aware that getting Ben to ask Eleanor was kind of a little-kid move. Sorry about that. But I'm someone who second-guesses himself about stuff like this."

"Really?"

"You sound shocked."

"I am."

"Why?"

"You're so charming," I said.

He laughed. "I am *not.*"

"You are," I insisted. "And funny, and slick sometimes."

"Slick?"

"Yeah," I said. "Smooth."

He groaned. "I hate that word."

"We'll stick with 'charming', then," I said.

"Agreed." He paused. "Do you ever feel like it's weird to hear other people describe you? Because it doesn't match up with how you see yourself?"

I thought about it. Half of my high school had based their

perception of me on a blatant lie, but somehow that felt different. "What do you mean? How do you see yourself?"

"I was a really anxious kid," he said slowly.

I didn't know how to respond to that, so I said, "Oh."

"I didn't talk at school until second grade."

"At all?"

"Yup. I spent preschool, kindergarten, and first grade absolutely silent. Social anxiety."

"Why?"

I felt him shrug beside me. "I remember being terrified I was going to say something wrong."

"You were a little perfectionist."

"Something like that. I put a lot of pressure on myself."

"Do you think," I began, and then broke off, unsure whether it was okay for me to ask what I wanted to ask.

"What were you going to say?"

"Do you think maybe it's because your parents put a lot of pressure on you?"

"That was part of it. But I don't blame them. They've given me everything. It's my job to take those opportunities." Then he asked, "Do you feel pressure from your parents?"

Of course I did. They wanted me to be good at everything. And most of the time, I succeeded. They didn't know about my social struggles, though. They didn't know what had happened with Franklin, or the full story of what had happened with Lydia. My mom had asked about it, multiple times, when she noticed that Lydia and I weren't hanging out anymore. I'd tried to brush it off, but finally I had to explain, giving her an extremely abridged version that omitted the worst parts.

I didn't feel quite the same sense of duty that Aydın seemed to feel toward his parents.

"A little bit, yeah," I said.

Aydın sat up. "I should get back to bed, or else I'll fall asleep here."

"You're welcome to."

He made an exaggerated expression of horror. "What would Nurse Aditi think?"

"Good point. Get out of here."

He stood up, leaned over, planted a gentle kiss on my forehead, and left the room.

Chapter Twelve

So that was our happily ever after. Aydın and I loved each other for the rest of our lives, and nothing we did pissed anyone off.

Kidding. Obviously.

In the morning Nurse Aditi cleared us to leave. Aydın and I stood facing each other outside the infirmary for a moment before he leaned forward and gave me a kiss on the cheek. Then he squeezed my hand and said, "See you later," before heading in the direction of Ben's cottage. I made my reluctant way back to the Orchard Oriole, half wishing we could've just stayed in the infirmary.

The only person inside was Sherry, who was clipping on a sleek gold chain-link necklace. "Rosaline!" She gave me a hug, then held me at arm's length for inspection. "How are you feeling this morning?"

"I'm alright. Have you... talked to my parents?"

Her lipsticked mouth twisted. "I have, sweetheart. I had to let them know."

Menacing organ music began to play in my head, warning me of my impending doom. "Are they mad?" What if they were on their way to Pine Bay right now to pick me up? That was the sort of thing my dad might do. I could picture him in the car, shaking his head and saying,

You have to learn some common sense. You can't do these things, especially not when someone else's family is so generously hosting you.

"Of course not! They're just happy you're alright."

I raised an eyebrow. "Are you sure? They're not coming to take me home?"

She laughed. "You're a riot, Rosaline. No, they were surprised you went to the infirmary at all. I believe your dad said, 'Ros could have two broken legs and still be running around, making trouble, insisting she was fine.'"

I couldn't help but smile. "Did you tell them I was forcibly marched there?"

"Let's let them think you went by yourself, hmm?"

"Sounds like a plan."

She sat down on the couch and patted the spot beside her. "Rosaline, while you're here, I want to ask you about Eleanor."

I took a seat, nervous. "What about her?"

"Is everything alright with you two?"

Not at all. "I…I think so?"

"Did something happen?"

Yes. "I'm not sure what you mean."

Sherry looked worried. "The truth is, when I told her about your accident and asked if she wanted to visit the infirmary, she said no and stormed off. I didn't want to tell you in front of your friends last night. I know she can be moody sometimes. I'm so sorry if she did something—"

"She didn't do anything," I said. "I promise. If anyone did anything, it was probably me." *Definitely me.*

"Well," Sherry said, "I hope you'll straighten things out. I hate seeing the two of you fight. You're her best friend, you know."

I nodded. "I'll talk to her." I would. And then everything would be alright. Back to normal.

———

Turns out, there was a hitch in this plan. To be more specific, a skinny, freckled, gorgeous hitch. A hitch named Chloe.

I spotted them as soon as I entered the dining hall. Eleanor and Chloe were sitting on the sill of a massive window, backlit by morning sunlight like a pair of angels. They were each holding a water bottle between their knees, with something tied to its handle. I immediately recognized the setup: they were making *friendship bracelets.* Literally what the fuck.

I walked right up to them. "Hey, what's up?"

Chloe smiled at me with her golden halo. "Hi, Rosaline," she said. "It's been a minute."

"It has!" I turned on my fake excitement—that weird thing that girls who don't actually know each other that well do when they talk to each other in public. "I didn't know you were coming here this summer."

"We always come. Although we were late this year. We were visiting my grandparents in California."

"How was California?" I asked.

"I love it out there," she said, tilting her head to the side with a smile. "It's so beautiful."

"I've heard great things." I glanced at Eleanor. She was studiously working on her bracelet, avoiding looking at me. "Eleanor," I said, "what's up with you?"

"Nothing."

I waited for something more, but it didn't come.

Chloe stepped in to fill the silence. "Eleanor and I went to bingo last night!"

"Oh?" I asked. I was sure my smile looked as strained as it felt.

She nodded. "It was super fun! The old ladies are hilarious. Especially that one... what's her name, Eleanor?"

"Sandy," Eleanor said.

"Yes, Sandy!" Chloe giggled. Ugh. "That's the type of old lady I want to be one day."

"That does sound like fun," I said, putting my hands in my pockets. "Meanwhile, I was in the infirmary."

Chloe's eyes went wide. "What happened?"

"I capsized a sailboat and ended up in the middle of the lake during the storm. They thought I might have hypothermia."

"That's wild! Are you okay?"

"I'm fine."

"Why were you on a sailboat in a storm? By yourself?"

"I—" I started, then hesitated. Maybe it would be better not to explain. I glanced behind me and pretended to spot someone. "Oh, I'm so sorry, I said I would meet—I've got to go."

"No worries," said Chloe. "See you around?"

"Yep!" I said.

I wound my way through the dining hall, searching for Aydın or Ben or literally anyone besides Eleanor and her new BFF. I was unsuccessful. When my stomach startled audibly growling, I gave up, grabbed a plate of pancakes, and settled myself in a far corner to scroll on my phone while I ate.

I couldn't stop thinking about Eleanor. She was clearly furious with me. And this was fair. But I hadn't *really* done anything wrong. Now, if I'd actually stolen Cameron from her, if she'd ever had a shot with him, that would be messed up. But I hadn't. So what could she stay mad about? Once I got the chance to explain, she would have to forgive me. Right?

A gnawing feeling in my stomach told me this wasn't true. I had done something really shitty. I tried to stifle the feeling by stuffing myself with more pancakes.

"Ros!" There was Aydın. The sour feeling in my stomach erupted into butterflies. He stopped in front of my table, sticking his hands in his pockets and giving me an almost shy, secretive smile. "How's your morning going?"

"It's going great," I said, beaming. And in the moment, it felt true.

"Have you seen Ben?" he asked.

"Um, no. Not since last night."

"Dang," he said, looking around the room. "I have no idea where he is. He won't answer my texts."

"Maybe he's having a tryst with his secret lover," I suggested.

Aydın laughed. "I don't think Ben is the type to have a secret lover."

"Or maybe he's exactly the type. People with secret lovers generally don't make it obvious that they have secret lovers."

"You make a good point."

"Breakfast?" I asked.

"Sorry, I already ate," he said. "Ben and I were talking about going waterskiing in a bit, though, if you want to join. I've just got to find him first."

I gave him a serious look. "Are you sure that's a good idea?"

His eyebrows scrunched with concern. "What do you mean?"

"You and me together on the lake. We don't exactly have a great track record," I joked.

He laughed. "I think it'll be a lot harder to capsize this one."

"You're probably right. That sounds great."

"I'll text you," he said.

———

I finally got Eleanor alone when I went back to the Orchard Oriole to change for waterskiing.

"Eleanor, please. Can we talk?" She said nothing, just set down her book, crossed her arms, and looked at me. But I didn't know how to start. "Are you mad at me?"

She laughed incredulously. "What do you think?"

"I'm sorry, okay? I'm sorry about Cameron. I didn't mean to—I wasn't thinking "

"It's not just about Cameron," said Eleanor.

I stared at her in disbelief. "Wh—what else is it about, then?"

She glared at me for a few seconds longer, arms still crossed, then got up and walked into the bathroom. She left the door open as she pulled out a makeup bag and started to put on mascara. "Tell me, then," she said. "What happened with Cameron?"

"It was an accident."

"An accident? You kissed the guy you knew I had a crush on!"

"I was trying to help, actually. I was getting intel. *Even though* I was mad because you sabotaged my chances with Aydın. Believe it or not, I was being a good friend. But...I'm sorry, Eleanor, I really am. Cameron's not interested; he has a crush on someone else."

"Oh, I've heard this story before," Eleanor said, getting louder. "Your pathetic friend likes a guy and thinks that maybe, *maybe* he could like her back, but instead, he has a crush on you!"

That stung. "It's not me," I said, softly. "He doesn't like me."

She threw her arms in the air. "Then *who?*"

"I don't...I don't know if he's okay with me telling anyone."

Eleanor rolled her eyes. "You're impossible! And you still kissed the guy I liked! There's no getting around that!"

I sat down on the couch and wrapped my arms around my stomach. "I know. I'm sorry." She leaned toward the mirror again. "I wasn't planning on it. But Aydın was there with Chloe, and—and I got jealous. Okay? And I was dancing with Cameron, and it was the perfect moment to try to make Aydın jealous in return, and I took it. I know it was stupid of me, and thoughtless, but you have to understand how much I needed to do it. And it worked, so...so everything worked out in the end."

Eleanor let out a little huff. "I have a few things to say about that."

"Go for it."

"One. The great Rosaline, self-proclaimed guy expert, got *jealous* of another girl?"

"Shut up."

"Two. Okay, you didn't 'need' to do it. You wanted to do it. Because you cared about making Aydın jealous. But guess what? I care about having friends who don't kiss their friends' crushes in front of them!"

I couldn't help myself. "So it would've been okay if I'd kissed him *not* in front of you?"

Her glare shut me up. "Three. About Aydın. If you saw him and Chloe happy together at the dance, *why* would you try to interfere with that?"

"He was trying to make me jealous," I said.

"This is what I'm talking about!" Eleanor shouted. "Why do you think everything revolves around you?"

"I don't!"

"You don't know everything, Ros. You're always telling me that I don't know the whole story, but in this case, you're the one who doesn't understand."

"What do you mean?" I asked. "They're not together, right?"

"Sure," said Eleanor. "But they had just had that conversation, and you threw yourself into the middle of it with your whole boat situation. Don't you think that chasing Aydın so soon after that is kind of insensitive?"

"I wasn't chasing him," I said, wrapping my arms tighter around my stomach. "He rescued me from Franklin Doss, and I needed to get away from everything, to cool off, so we went sailing."

"Well," said Eleanor, "I think it's slimy."

"On my part or Aydın's?"

"Both. They had that talk, what, like, a couple of hours before?"

"How do you know so much about it?" I asked, even though I already knew the answer. I didn't want to reveal that I'd eavesdropped on her conversation with Chloe.

Eleanor frowned. "Chloe told me. She's putting on a good front, but she's heartbroken."

"I'm sorry."

"Clearly not that sorry."

"I mean—" I threw my hands in the air. "We're not close. I don't think it's that shitty of me."

"She's a really good person," Eleanor said. "A good friend."

I could hear the pointedness in her words. "I didn't know you two were so close," I said half sarcastically.

Eleanor shrugged. "She needed someone to talk to, and I was there for her."

"I see."

"You sound jealous again."

"I'm not jealous of Chloe."

"Mhm. You stole her guy because you're *not jealous* of her."

"I didn't—" I huffed. "I give up."

Eleanor frowned. "What did Aydın help you calm down about, anyway?"

"I got into a physical altercation with Franklin Doss."

She let out a loud laugh. "Really? God, I wish I could've seen that."

"I had him pinned. I was about to let him have it."

"Why did Aydın stop you? That asshole deserves it."

"Don't I know it," I said.

"So, what did he do this time?"

I explained the whole thing: what I'd overheard, and then what Franklin had insinuated when I told him to stop.

Eleanor came and sat down on the couch as I spoke, her expression a mixture of anger, sadness, and disgust. "Wow," she said when I was finished. "That's just…" She shook her head. "I'm so sorry. I can't believe you're still dealing with his bullshit."

I shrugged, trying to play it off. But I could tell that she saw right through it.

My phone buzzed in my pocket, and literally half a second later, Eleanor's did too. I checked mine. "Aydın," I said.

Eleanor held her phone up. "Chloe."

"I've got to change into my swimsuit."

Eleanor stood up.

"I guess we'll see each other later?" I asked.

"Yeah, I guess."

I nodded. Eleanor turned to leave, but before she was out the door, I said, "I'm really sorry. Again."

She paused. "Thanks for saying that."

"Are we all good?"

I saw her hesitate. "Honestly? Not really."

"But—"

"I appreciate the apology. But you did something bad, and it's gonna take some time for me to get over that. You can't keep treating people like shit and thinking you can fix it with a quick apology. If you keep it up, you won't have any friends left."

I was speechless. Five seconds later, she was gone, and the door swung shut behind her.

———

Waterskiing was a blast, although the boat was *way* too crowded. Aydın and I sat together at first, our knees bumping against each other with every swerve of the boat, but then Ben pushed a fancy-looking camera into Aydın's hands and asked him to take photos while Ben took a turn on the water skis, and of course after that everyone else wanted photos too, so I didn't get to spend as much time with him as I'd hoped. But when we got off the boat, Aydın and I lingered for a moment, letting the rest of the group get ahead of us. He gave me a quick kiss on top of my head, which was unbelievably adorable, before we headed back to our respective cottages to shower and change.

There was a cookout on the main lawn that evening. I wandered into a sea of pastel blue and pink and white capri pants and polos. Guests perched in clusters of Adirondack chairs scattered across the lawn, sweaters tied around their shoulders like some sort of unofficial uniform: *I belong.* I glanced down at my own ripped jean shorts and crop top and felt very strongly that I did not.

I found Ben standing with his parents, a cup of water in one hand and a plate loaded with a burger and way too many potato chips in the other. He was in uniform—a sky-blue polo shirt and a white knit quarter-zip tied around his shoulders, with a smile that looked forced—while his parents chatted with another couple. The woman wore a pink-and-turquoise Lilly Pulitzer dress, accessorized with heavy-looking earrings and a matching necklace. The man wore white slacks and a blue button-down. I tried to imagine my parents here, putting them into these outfits like paper dolls, but the image wouldn't materialize.

Ben spotted me and excused himself from the conversation. "Thank god," he said.

"Who are they?" I asked.

"Family friends," he said. "Their daughter is our age, and our moms think we should meet up. We haven't seen each other since we were ten, but apparently we'd really hit it off."

"You sound so excited."

He rolled his eyes. "They made me follow her on Instagram." He unlocked his phone and showed me the profile of an attractive blonde girl whose wardrobe choices matched her mom's.

"She's cute," I said.

"I'm so not interested, you have no idea," Ben replied, slipping his phone back into his pocket.

"I figured. So just don't meet up with her."

"I wish. I'm sure my mom has already made a dinner reservation for the two of us and marked it on the family GCal." He glared back at her.

"You seem bothered."

Ben ran a hand through his light, curly hair. "My parents know I'm into guys," he said. "I came out years ago. And they've always claimed to be cool with it. But then they do things like this, and it just…it doesn't feel good."

"Maybe they really think you two could be friends?" I suggested.

He sighed. "Maybe."

My phone started buzzing in my pocket. It was a call from my dad. I motioned to Ben that I'd be right back, and picked up. "Hello?"

"Rosaline!" My mother's voice came through, high and loud. I held the phone a little farther from my ear.

"Hi, Mom."

"Merhaba, canım, how's it going?" asked my dad.

"It's going really well." I sat down on a bench at the edge of the lawn. "I'm having a good time."

"I'm so glad to hear that," said my mom. "It was a relief to hear from Eleanor's mom after so many days with nothing from you. We were starting to get worried."

I rolled my eyes, even though they couldn't see it. "I'm not ten years old. Did you think I'd call you every day?"

"Of course not," said my mom.

"But a little communication would be appreciated," said my dad.

"Sorry, I've just been busy," I said.

"Clearly," said my dad.

"We heard about your sailing accident," said my mom.

"It wasn't an accident," I said. "More of an incident."

"Mrs. Blake told us that you're okay. Is that true?"

"Absolutely," I said. "It was really no big deal."

"What were you doing sailing in a storm anyway?" asked my dad.

"I was giving someone a sailing lesson and the weather turned."

"Eleanor?" my mom asked.

"No," I said. "A new friend. His name is Aydın."

"Aydın?" asked my dad, sounding excited. "Is he Turkish?"

"Yeah, his parents are."

"That's wonderful!"

"Is he cute?" asked my mom.

My instinct was to say no…did I really want my parents knowing my personal business? But I was bursting with feelings, and I wanted to talk to someone about it. "Yeah," I said. "We're actually kind of seeing each other."

My mom squealed, and I held my phone farther away from my ear again.

"Too loud, Mom," I said.

"You have to send us pictures!" she said.

I glanced around to make sure no one I knew was in earshot. "This is embarrassing," I said. "Can we talk about it later? What have you been up to?"

"Oh, just the usual," my dad said. "Enjoying our freedom with you gone."

"Dad!"

"Just kidding. Seni çok özlüyoruz."

"I miss you guys too," I said, dropping my voice a little in case anyone was listening.

"We helped your cousin Abby move back into her dorm at

Princeton the other day," said my mom. "We had lunch with her and Aunt Astrid at the cutest little bistro."

"Is she still liking it there?"

"She loves it. She was so happy to be moving back in, you should have seen. She's in all these clubs, and she's tutoring high school students in the area. Isn't that lovely?"

Abby and I got along, but we hadn't talked much the past couple of years, aside from family holidays. She was just too close to being perfect at everything, and I found it exhausting.

"Speaking of college," said my dad, "do you already have your classes lined up for next year?"

"Dad, really?"

"You're going into eleventh grade—"

"It's summer!"

"I know it's summer, but this is when things really start counting for college."

"Don't be tiger parents," I grumbled.

"Rosaline..."

"I bet her kids turned out super weird."

"Who?"

"The Tiger Mom lady."

Silence.

"I'm serious. Her kids had no social lives because their mom was so controlling, and they probably grew up depressed."

My mom cut in, saving my dad. "I've heard they've been very successful."

"Successful, sure, but are they happy?"

A long pause. Then my mother's voice again. "Rosaline, honey, of course we want you to be happy. That's all we want. Giving yourself your best shot at getting into a good college is just a part of that."

"I know, I know." I sighed. I'd done that thing again, where I got wound up into an argument I didn't even care about, just for the sake of arguing. "I want to get into a good school too." The truth was, I had worked too hard for too many years to not care. "I guess I'm just feeling the pressure." I paused. "Sorry."

"It's alright," said my mom, and I heard relief in her voice. "I'm sorry you're feeling stressed. If there's anything we can do, let—"

"I'll be fine," I said. "And I do have my classes lined up. They make us pick in the spring, remember?"

"I was just checking," said my dad.

"*And*," I added, "I have a plan for something that will look great on my college applications."

"What's that?" asked my mom.

"I'm running for homecoming court this year. And I'm gonna win."

There was a brief silence. "What is that?" asked my dad.

"It's this tradition where they dress up and vote for king and queen and prince and princess at one of their dances," my mom said.

"Like prom queen?" my dad asked.

"Exactly." There was another pause, then my mom said, "Ros, sweetie, that's great. I'm glad you have something you're excited about."

"Will that really help your application?" asked my dad.

The truth was, I wasn't sure. "Probably!" I said. "It's a democratic process. It shows the student body's faith in my leadership capabilities."

"You don't lead anything, though. It's more about popularity, right?" asked my mom.

"I'm sure I can find a way to spin it," I said.

"You do have a talent for that," said my dad.

"Well, that's fun," said my mom. "I'm glad you're excited. Unfortunately, we've got to go now. We're meeting some friends for dinner at Lissa's."

"I'm jealous." I was surprised to realize that I was. A dinner out with my parents, spaghetti carbonara at Lissa's, our favorite restaurant, sounded perfect at that moment. Comforting and familiar.

"Seni çok seviyoruz."

"Love you guys too."

—

That night we had another campfire by the lake. I'd seen Eleanor briefly after dinner and asked if she wanted to come, but she shook her head and told me that she and Chloe already had plans to hang out. Since this plan would keep Chloe away from the campfire and Aydın, I didn't insist.

I was relieved to see that Franklin wasn't there either. What a blessing.

The setup was the same as last time: a circle of Adirondack chairs around a blazing fire pit, overlooking the glassy, dark lake. There was something different in the air this time, though. A new sense of comfort, and of adventure. We knew each other better than we had earlier in the week. We were willing to push the boundaries a little more.

I took a seat in the chair beside Aydın's and kicked off my sandals to dig my toes into the soft, cool sand. He reached out a hand, and I took it. Our clasped hands dangled between the arms of our chairs. Ben seemed to notice this, and he glanced curiously at Aydın's face.

Releasing my hand, Aydın stood up and asked me, "Want me to bring you a beer?"

"Yes please."

As Aydın returned carrying two cans, Garrett stood up, chugged his beer, then giddily crushed the can on his head. Aydın leaned in as he handed one to me, whispering, "What a dumbass." I laughed.

I was still pretty pissed off at Garrett and his friends, and Aydın seemed to be too, so for a while the two of us and Ben mostly hung out on our side of the circle.

At some point, Hunter, one of the nicer members of Garrett's crew, wandered over. "Hey, Ros," he said hesitantly.

"Hunter," I said, not particularly warmly.

He took a seat next to Aydın and took off his baseball cap, turning it around in his hands. "I just wanted to say sorry. About yesterday."

"You mean when you and your friends were laughing and egging on a disgusting bully's racist performance?" I asked.

"Yeah, and that stuff he said to you afterward. You seemed pretty upset."

"How observant of you," I said.

"Ros," Aydın whispered. "He's trying to apologize."

I sighed and leaned toward Hunter. "You know Franklin Doss is a piece of shit, right? He's, like, the human personification of a wad of gum that gets stuck to your shoe."

"Strong words," said Aydın.

"He's an *asshole*," I said. "Why were you guys even hanging out with him?"

Hunter spread his arms and shrugged. "Honestly, I don't even know. We were hanging out on the deck, having a predinner smoke, and he just came up to us and started making jokes. We were in the state of mind to find everything really funny, if you know what I mean."

"Bold to smoke right next to the dining hall," Aydın said.

"No one's caught us yet," Hunter replied with a shrug. "I guess the smell from the kitchen covers it up." He turned back to me. "Anyway, I'm sorry that you got so upset. We're not planning on hanging out with him again. No matter what Aaron says. Garrett's had enough of him too, I think."

It was a weird apology, but it was an apology nonetheless. And having been on the other side of one just a few hours earlier, I was in a forgiving mood. "Thanks," I said. Hunter nodded and returned to his friends.

When the beer was gone, someone pulled out a Nalgene water bottle filled with vodka, and we passed it around the circle, taking tiny sips. At some point, our divide was abandoned, and the whole circle started playing Never Have I Ever, which, I had to admit, was pretty fun.

The game became rowdier with every question asked, and eventually the idea of night swimming came up. The lake was glossy and black, reflecting the moon and the stars on its smooth surface. It looked beautiful and dangerous. It was calling to us. And who were we to refuse?

We rushed, barefoot, down to the dock, giggling and bumping into each other. The air was warmer than it had been during the storm, but my body shivered, remembering the inescapable chill of the water.

Ben was the first one to jump in, tearing his shirt off and barreling down the length of the dock into a forceful cannonball. He disappeared under the water and we held our breaths. After what felt like ages, his head popped up again. "Oh my god!" he bellowed. "It's cold!"

We took his survival as permission, and on the beach everyone stripped down to their shorts and bras and underwear. I was the second one to jump in, taking a running start like Ben, then hurling myself into a front flip off the dock.

I didn't quite make the full rotation, and the water slapped hard against my back, but once I was under, it was cold enough to make me forget the pain. For a long second, the world was perfectly silent and perfectly still. It was just me and the cold. Darkness. A freezing void. Then I surfaced and the world came rushing in again. "Holy shit!" I shouted. Ben had already found the ladder on the side of the dock and was climbing up, dripping, slipping on the rungs.

A large splash nearby sent a wave into my face and I spluttered, trying to wipe the water from my eyes with my wet arms. A figure swam toward me, then wrapped its sturdy, warm arms around me in the water. "You alright?" said Aydın.

"C-cold," I said.

He laughed, then released me, treading water to stay afloat. "I'm having some déjà vu," he said, thoughtfully. "No idea why."

"Maybe this will jog your memory," I said, and pulled him toward me for a kiss.

Instantly, the cold of the lake felt softer, gentler. It didn't bite, but instead enveloped our bodies. Our feet tangled as we kicked, working hard to keep our heads above water. The kiss only lasted a moment, but when we separated, I swear the stars were brighter and the sky was a deeper velvet black. There were splashes around us, and laughter, but all I could see was Aydın, his hair slicked back and his smile wide. He looked up at the sky. "The stars are unbelievable," he said.

In that moment, everything else melted away. Eleanor, Lydia, Franklin Doss, college, homecoming court…somehow, all the things that had felt so urgent just minutes before were reduced to after-thoughts. Inconsequential. For once, there was no game I needed to play, no move to make, no strategy to consider. I was simply there, and so was he, and in that moment, that was what mattered.

Chapter Thirteen

I floated through the next morning. Even Eleanor's obnoxious air of self-righteousness as she marched around the Orchard Oriole couldn't bring me down.

We walked to the dining hall together, which gave me some hope, but as soon as we entered, she split off to go find Chloe. Leaving me alone. I made my way through the massive room, weaving between tables and dodging toddlers, searching for Aydın, or at least Ben, or even Mary or Garrett.

After several minutes I hadn't caught a glimpse of anyone, so I grabbed breakfast and found an uncrowded corner table. While I picked at my bacon and eggs, I texted Aydın. **Where are you guys?** Then I set my phone down, face up, on the table, and stared at it for a while, waiting for the text bubble with three dots to appear. Nothing came. I knew I shouldn't, but I couldn't help myself: I picked up my phone and typed **I'm at breakfast. Alone!!!**

I hit send, then cringed. Had I turned into that kind of girlfriend already?

As I had this thought, I realized that I was calling myself Aydın's girlfriend, but he'd never called me that. We hadn't had *the talk*.

I closed my eyes. It didn't matter. We would have the talk

eventually, I was pretty sure, and for now, we were practically dating. There was no need to rush things.

Except there kinda was. When Aydın started at Bardet the next week, I desperately wanted to be able to call him my boyfriend.

After breakfast I went back to the Orchard Oriole and got dressed to go sailing. On the way down to the boathouse, my phone buzzed with a text from Aydın. **Just woke up, sorry.**

No worries, I wrote back. **I'm going sailing. Want to join?**

The typing bubble popped up, then disappeared. Then it popped up again. **I think Ben and I are gonna kick a soccer ball around. Have fun though. See you later?**

See you later. There was a small pit in my stomach, and I hated myself for it. **See ya**, I wrote back. I made my way to the beach, where the attendant helped me push a boat into the water. I strapped on a life vest, climbed in, pulled the mainsheet tight against the wind, and sailed toward the middle of the lake. It was a clear blue day, and the sunlight was a golden white, sparkling off the water. I adjusted my angle, coaxing the boat to go faster, faster, faster, skimming over the lake. It was tilting a bit with the wind, but it was perfectly in my control. As it usually was.

On the far side of the lake was a dirt bank with pine trees that looked almost close enough to touch. I slowed my pace and approached cautiously, unsure how deep the water would be. I waited to hear the hull scrape bottom, but it didn't, and I drifted closer. I glanced over the side of the boat, but I couldn't see through the water to the lake floor. There was a bush on the bank, covered in dark berries—blackberries?

I heard a rustle in the woods and looked up, expecting to see a deer or a rabbit. Instead, I saw something much less pleasant: Franklin Doss. He was walking with his gaze on the ground, apparently so lost in thought that he hadn't noticed me. *Good.* I grabbed the tiller, hoping to make a turn and get out of there before he did, but I heard that telltale scrape of the hull against rock and the boat lurched slightly to the right. Franklin looked up. "Rosaline?"

I wiggled the tiller, hoping the boat could free itself, but I felt it moving forward, getting more and more solidly lodged. *Shit.* "Doss," I said.

"What are you doing?"

"What are *you* doing?"

He gestured vaguely behind him. "Taking a walk."

"Is this what you do all day? How depressing."

I'd said it as a joke, but he didn't answer, which made me wonder if it was true. "Is your boat stuck?" he asked.

I almost lied, but considering the circumstances, I didn't think I could pull it off. "Yeah."

"Do you want help?"

"I'm good."

"Really, I can get in the water and push."

I knew that that was exactly what I was going to have to do to get the boat out of this mess, and I wasn't looking forward to it. But I didn't want to accept help from the Crown Prince of Evil. "No thanks."

He shrugged. His hands were in his pockets, and he stood facing the water. "Where's Aydın? I heard about your sailing adventure."

"He just woke up. Probably hungover."

"Hungover from what?"

"The campfire last night."

"Oh." The expression on his face told me that he had not, in fact, been invited. I glanced over the side of the boat again, wondering how deep it was and whether or not to take my shoes off. But when I looked up again, the King of the Shits was already barefoot. He grabbed a branch of a nearby bush and used it to hold his balance as he edged down the steep bank. The edges of his shorts dipped in the water, then immersed themselves, as he made his way toward the boat.

"I told you I don't need help," I said.

"It's not a big deal." He was now at the bow, pushing his hands against the boat while digging his heels in. I thought about getting into the water and helping, but instead I stayed right where I was, watching Doss grit his teeth and grunt with effort. The sun was hot, even with the slight breeze, and I was starting to sweat.

Finally, the boat budged. Doss dislodged it from the lake floor and gave it a shove toward the open water.

"Thank you," I said.

"You're welcome."

I hadn't yet pulled in the mainsheet, and the sail hung limp, flapping slightly.

"I'm sorry," Doss said.

"What?"

"I'm really sorry. I know I said some shitty things the other day. I didn't mean it."

I didn't know what to say.

"I went too far."

"Yeah. You did." I grabbed the rope and tiller and steered the boat away, toward the opposite shore. But the whole way back, I couldn't stop thinking about the look on Doss's face.

—

I met up with Ben and Aydın that evening for dinner. We ate and joked around, not talking about anything important, until Aydın got up for seconds and Ben seized the opportunity to lean across the table and ask, "Is everything alright with you and Eleanor?"

"Yeah," I said.

"You sure?"

"Um, yeah. Why wouldn't it be?"

Ben gave me a disbelieving look and leaned back in his chair. "She seems pretty pissed at you."

"What are you talking about?"

"Look, I wouldn't get involved, except that we miss having her around."

"Sure you do," I muttered.

"We do."

"She's not fun," I said. Then I immediately felt bad. Eleanor *was* fun, in her own totally-different-from-my-type-of-fun way. And I missed her, way more than I would ever admit. Aside from walking to breakfast together, we hadn't talked since our conversation the previous day about what happened with Cameron. Last night we'd slept on separate couches again, which were way less comfortable than the shared pullout, but I was trying to give her space, so I didn't complain. I kept telling myself that she would come around eventually. She had to.

"Ros." He sounded serious. "What happened? Is it because of…" He trailed off, then jerked his head in Aydın's direction, over by the buffet. "You two?"

I didn't say anything, so he continued. "I didn't know Eleanor and Chloe were such close friends."

I took this chance and grabbed it. "I think she feels bad for Chloe."

He gave me a searching look. I shrugged and took another bite of my dinner. "Chloe is upset?" Ben asked.

"I guess so."

"Does Aydın know?"

"I—" What was I supposed to say? "I don't know. Don't say anything to him."

"Why not? If he knew, he'd want to do something about it. That's just who he is."

"Why do you care if Chloe is upset?" I asked, suddenly suspicious.

"I just want to know what the hell happened with you and Eleanor."

I glared at Ben. He glared back.

Aydın appeared and set down his plate. "What did I miss?"

"Nothing," we said simultaneously.

"Cool."

My cellphone was sitting face up on the table, and it buzzed with a WhatsApp message from my babaanne.

Rosaline, canım, nasılsın? she'd written.

İyiyim, Babaanne, I replied.

She switched over to English—her English had always been way better than my Turkish. **I hear you're dating a boy.**

We're not really dating, I replied.

"Who's that?" asked Ben, leaning over.

I shielded my phone from him. "My grandma."

"That's sweet," he said. "Are you close?"

"Kinda, I guess."

His name is Aydın? my grandmother wrote.

Yes.

A Turkish boy?

Yes. He's transferring to my school this year.

She sent a string of smiling emojis, followed by prayer hands.

I hadn't expected my family to care so much that the guy I was semidating was Turkish. My dad and babaanne used to joke about setting me up with the sons of Turkish family friends, but I never thought they were serious. I would have resisted it. I didn't want to date someone just because we had something like that in common.

Which was maybe why my family being so enthusiastic about Aydın was bothering me, just a little bit.

"Earth to Ros," said Ben, waving a hand in front of my face.

"Sorry," I said, blinking. "What's up?"

"We were just talking about how we've only got like two days left."

I did a mental calculation and realized he was right. Today was Wednesday, and I was leaving with Eleanor's family on Saturday morning, so that we'd have two days at home to get ready before school started on Tuesday. "I can't believe it's almost over," I said.

"Right?" Aydın said. "The week has gone by so fast."

Ben spread an invisible rainbow over his head. "That's the magic of Pine Bay."

"Damn," I said.

"Here's the problem, though," said Ben. "We haven't done enough."

"Go on."

"Well, we've done a lot of the usual things, sure. But would I look back and call this an epic summer? I'm not sure."

Aydın nudged my knee under the table and rolled his eyes.

"What I'm saying is that there are certain things we can do to make sure that we *do* look back on this summer and say, 'Yeah, it was pretty epic.'"

"What do you have in mind?" I asked.

Ben leaned in, and so did Aydın and I. Aydın's knee was still against mine under the table. "Step one," Ben said. "We've got to break in somewhere and steal something."

"Dude," said Aydın.

"Nothing important! Something no one will miss. A pen or something."

"That seems high-risk, low-reward to me," Aydın replied.

"Where's your sense of adventure, bro?"

"'Bro'?" I asked.

"It's his new thing," said Aydın.

"Nice to meet you, Douchebag Ben. I'm Ros," I said.

"Guys, I'm serious," Ben pleaded. "It'll be more fun than it sounds, I promise."

"Oh, I'm in," I said. "There was never a question."

Ben fist pumped. Then he looked at Aydın, questioningly.

Aydın sighed. "I suppose I don't have much of a choice, do I?"

Ben and I both grinned.

———

That night our crew gathered on the lawn outside the dining hall. Ben had invited the other high schoolers to join in the fun, and we had pretty much everyone except Chloe, Eleanor, and Franklin. That was okay with me.

We'd set our sights on the rec center loft, with its stash of alcohol and ample supply of decorations—a treasure trove from which to select our prize for the night. After taking a head count and receiving a quick briefing in which Ben told us what to do if we were caught ("Don't get caught. Just don't. But if you do, don't be a narc"), we headed out.

Breaking in turned out to be extraordinarily easy: Mary picked the lock with a bobby pin and nudged the front door open. I waited for an alarm to go off. But nothing happened, and soon we were all tiptoeing inside. Ben closed the door behind us.

The rec center turned out to be super creepy in the dark. At first we couldn't see anything, and then someone swung their phone flashlight around, revealing folding tables stacked against the walls. Aydın moved closer to me. "This feels like a scene in a horror movie," he whispered.

I laughed softly. "I love horror movies."

"I hate them."

I grabbed his hand and squeezed it.

"What's the plan now, Benjamin?" Garrett asked.

Ben lifted a finger into the air. "To the stash!"

There was barely enough space for our group among all the junk in the loft. We waded through a sea of objects, picking through the piles in search of trophies. Ben pulled some liquor out of the stash, saying, "We shouldn't drain everything, but a little bit can't hurt, right?" We passed the bottle around.

"I've got an idea," I said. "Let's make it a competition. Whoever can find the best thing to steal gets to keep it, *and* they get a bottle of rum."

"Sick," said Garrett. "Who decides?"

"I'll judge," said Aydın, surprising me.

The search became more frenzied after that, with people digging through boxes and throwing wreaths and other decorations in every direction. Suddenly, Courtney screamed.

There was a loud thud as she dropped something.

"Courtney, what happened?" Hunter asked.

I could see her in the beam of someone's phone flashlight, holding her hand over her mouth, bent over. She looked terrified. I made my way through the mess toward her, and followed her horrified stare into an orange plastic box.

I grabbed a bloody, severed hand and held it up for the group.

"Oh my god," said Aydın.

"What the *fuck?*" said Garrett.

Mary squealed, pulling the sleeves of her oversized sweatshirt over her hands, and buried her face in Garrett's shoulder.

"It's plastic," I said, squeezing the hand to demonstrate. "A Halloween decoration."

"That is *way* too realistic," said Aydın.

Courtney stared at it. "That's…disgusting. Why would anybody make something like that?"

I shrugged. "It's fun to be a little scared sometimes."

That was when we heard footsteps outside.

Everyone froze.

"Shit," said Garrett.

Ben put a finger to his lips, then cupped his hand around his ear. *Listen.* I clicked off my phone flashlight, and everyone else did too, one by one. The footsteps circled the building, slow and deliberate. We saw the beam of a flashlight point through a window, then disappear. The seconds dragged on into what felt like minutes, although I couldn't be sure, and the footsteps continued to circle.

"It looks empty," a man's voice said. "I've been around the perimeter but it's dark inside. I don't see anyone."

"Are you sure?" a woman asked, her voice high and nervous.

Another man joined in, authoritative. "Can you tell me again what you heard?"

"A scream," said the woman. "It sounded like a girl."

"And you're sure it came from inside?"

"Yes," said the woman, at the same time as the first man said, "No."

There was a brief silence.

"I'll take a look inside," said the second man.

"Be careful," said the woman.

Even in the near-dark, I could see Ben gesturing wildly. *Everybody hide.* There was a brief scuffle, and a couple of too-loud noises that made me catch my breath, while everyone scrambled farther into the loft and dropped behind cardboard boxes. Aydın and I sat together with our backs against the wall, mostly blocked from view of the edge of the loft by a few boxes and a wicker chair. Aydın grabbed my hand. I scooted closer to him, resting my head on his shoulder.

The man's footsteps creaked through the main room, and then the flashlight beam appeared on the wall of the storage room as the man stepped through the door. We held our breaths as he paced slowly around the room, examining each corner and window. He made a full sweep of the room, and for a moment I thought he was about to leave. Then I heard the creak of the ladder to the loft as he placed his weight on it. I tucked my head into my knees, curling up into a ball, trying to make myself as small as possible. Beside me, Aydın did the same. I couldn't see the others, so I could only hope they were well hidden.

The flashlight beam appeared over the edge of the loft. For several seconds, there was nothing: no sound, no movement. And then the beam retreated. The man descended the ladder, and moments later, he was back outside.

"There's no one in there," the man said.

"Thank you," said the woman.

"No problem at all, ma'am."

Up in the loft, we let out a collective sigh of relief.

Aydın, beside me, reached his arm over my shoulders, gently tilted my face toward his, and kissed me.

Mary ended up winning the competition, thanks to the bright blue sequined tuxedo she found in a box of tablecloths. She went back to her cottage to tuck away her prizes, while the rest of us lingered by the rec center, not ready to end the night. We talked for a while, laughing about our adventure and already starting to exaggerate details, turning it into our own legend, until members of the group started to yawn and everyone dispersed to head back to their cottages. Aydın said, "I'll see you tomorrow," and gave me a hug before leaving with Ben.

As I headed toward the Orchard Oriole, I heard footsteps and the rolling of suitcases down the dirt path, and then voices. "That was a bit of a drive, wasn't it?"

"I'm sorry, sweetie. You know I would have left work earlier if I could. But we're here now, so let's enjoy this time. One last bit of summer vacation."

I would have thought nothing of it. People arrived at Pine Bay all the time. But I knew the two voices that we had just heard. Very well, in fact. From memories of family dinners, ice cream runs, even that one summer that they brought me on their vacation to the Cayman Islands.

The voices belonged to Lydia's mother and father.

Chapter Fourteen

When Lydia and I were kids, our parents used to joke that we were psychically bonded. Starting in kindergarten, we did *everything* together. We were always thinking the same thing at the same time, speaking in sync, showing up to school in the same outfit. We joined the track team together and both ended up quitting a month later. We performed in our middle school's annual musical, although neither of us was particularly musically gifted, so we both ended up with ensemble roles—which was fine with us, because we didn't have to navigate any imbalance and could rehearse together. We had the rest of our lives planned out together too. We were going to find hot twin guys to marry, and then we'd be sisters-in-law and we'd live in houses next door to each other and our kids would be friends and we would all hang out at the pool every day.

We were equals, always. And sometimes maintaining that balance meant that one person had to make a sacrifice.

The summer after eighth grade, having survived six miserable months at school with the fallout from the Franklin Doss rumor, I begged my parents to let me go to Lydia's sleepaway camp. I didn't want to go to sailing camp again. I wanted to be with my best friend.

My parents talked to Lydia's parents, and they decided to let me go to camp. My mom told me I was lucky that she trusted Lydia's mom's judgment so deeply. I tried to push the issue and go to Pine Bay with Lydia's family too, but that was a step too far and my parents almost rescinded their agreement on the summer camp thing. Almost.

When I told Lydia the news, she squealed and said we had to go to the Silver Scoop to celebrate. It had been our favorite spot since we were little, where we went whenever anything big happened in our lives. Over eclectically topped bowls of ice cream (that was the summer we decided sour gummy worms went wonderfully with cookies 'n cream, for some reason), she told me in a low voice that she'd heard from one of her friends that Zane was coming back again this year.

I knew all about Zane. Lydia had had a crush on him since her first year at camp, the summer after fifth grade. Zane was a year older than us, and based on Lydia's description, he was a beautiful god walking amongst mortals. He was quiet, she said, but not in a shy way. In a way that indicated wisdom beyond his years. There was something sad and infinite about his soul. And also, she wasn't sure he knew her name.

So, we went to camp. I couldn't stop smiling the whole drive there. I was excited to spend a month with Lydia at one of her favorite places, and moreover, I was excited for a fresh start, away from the drama of that school year. We got out of the car, said goodbye to Lydia's parents, and dragged our duffel bags to our assigned cabin. And that's when I got the first hint that things were going to go south.

As we opened the door, five girls screamed and descended on

us with ecstatic hugs. Or, more accurately, they descended on Lydia. I stood by and watched her jump up and down, holding hands with each of them in turn, screaming incoherently about how much she'd missed everyone and ohmygod it was so nice to be back!

She only remembered me when it was time to choose beds. At least she remembered that I liked the bottom bunk because I got nervous about being left out—everyone knows that all the juicy conversations happen on the bottom bunks. Lydia, to her credit, had no issue taking the top bunk.

The rest of that first week was okay. I met Lydia's friends. We went canoeing. We did crafts. Sometimes I felt like she wasn't paying enough attention to me, and sometimes she abandoned me—alone, the new kid at camp, friendless—to hang out with her friends. But it was fine. I started hanging out with this group of guys, a mix of boys in our year and the year above, whom I met through sailing and archery practice, neither of which particularly interested Lydia's friends. And to top it all off, the legendary Zane was in this group.

I have to admit, the first time I met Zane, I had to keep myself from blurting, "*You're* Zane?" The mysterious, godlike figure turned out to be a skinny fifteen-year-old boy with messy black hair and braces. I was absolutely baffled, but as the days went on, I started to see what Lydia liked about him. There *was* something alluring about his smile. Like he knew something you didn't, but if you stayed quiet long enough, he'd tell you.

We became friends. And when Lydia realized I was hanging out with Zane, she demanded that I introduce her to him.

That's when the real downhill spiral began.

Zane started slipping notes under our cabin door. Sheets of paper torn out of a spiral notebook, with little messages. *You have a lovely smile. -Z.* Or else: *The moon in the midday sky reminds me of you.* Or: *I had a dream about you last night.*

You can imagine the excitement this caused in our cabin. When the first note arrived, I walked in on a circle of girls holding it up, speculating wildly about both the identity of Z and the identity of the note's recipient.

"It's Zane," I told them, just as Lydia walked in.

Her expression changed to one of alarm. "What's Zane?" she asked.

One of the girls held out the note to her. Lydia's eyes moved quickly back and forth, reading the words: *I don't know how else to tell you that I think about you all the time. -Z.* Lydia's expression transformed from concern to confusion to rapture within the span of a few seconds. She looked up at me, her eyes shining. "Rosalie," she said (her nickname for me: an inside joke from back in kindergarten, when we first became friends and she couldn't pronounce my name right), "he noticed me."

"Are you sure it's for you?" one of her friends asked.

Lydia scoffed. "Of course it is. Everyone knows I've had a crush on him for *years*. Who else would it be for?"

The girl shrugged.

Lydia turned to the rest of us. "I mean, do any of you have reason to think it would be for you?"

No one said anything.

"See?" Lydia asked her friend.

It seems disingenuous, after a bad thing has already happened, to claim that you knew it was going to happen all along. But I did. In that moment, I could feel the ground crumbling under our feet, giving way to an avalanche.

I should have told her then. But how could I?

I let her go on believing it.

Every day I ran with her to the cabin after afternoon activities to check if Zane had left another note. I smiled when she grabbed each one and read it out loud to her enraptured audience of five other fourteen-year-old girls. I didn't want to ruin it for her. Here was her long-unrequited crush of four years, leaving her what were essentially love letters.

But I spent less and less time tagging along with Lydia and her friends when they went to make elaborate, color-coded friendship bracelets. I spent less and less time with them at meals, listening to their gasping, giggling recall of events of summers past. I spent less and less time with them on their favorite rock in the woods, where they braided flowers into one another's hair and told secrets. Who had lost her virginity, who had promised herself to Jesus, who had helped her older brother hide his weed stash from their parents once by putting it in her ballerina jewelry box, where she knew they'd never look.

Instead, I spent more and more of my time with the boys, swimming in the lake, exploring in the woods, working on my archery aim. And there was always Zane, with his mysterious, sweet smile, and his eyes that flicked away from mine the moment I thought I had caught them. He was looking at me whenever I turned away, I knew, and I overheard his friends teasing him more than once. But while I loved the attention, I wasn't sure I liked him that way. Plus, there was Lydia.

She thought about writing back to him, when the notes first started appearing. But her friends shut down that idea.

"You have to let *him* chase *you*," one said.

"Don't give him too much," said another.

So she stayed aloof and depended on me for reports on what Zane was doing from week to week, what his friends were talking about.

And then it was the week of the camp dance. The dances always had a theme, and this year it was ancient Greece, so the girls had decided that they would dress as the goddesses of Olympus. They each wore a matching tunic (made of bedsheets) and something that symbolized their particular goddess. Hera, Athena, Aphrodite, Artemis, and Demeter.

Lydia had refused to pick a goddess, because she was so sure Zane would ask her to go together. But as the date drew closer, and no note arrived, she relented. She would be Hestia, goddess of the hearth and domesticity. The other girls turned to me with hesitant smiles and said they could expand the theme beyond Olympians to the other, minor goddesses if I wanted to join. I could be Persephone, they said. Or Iris, goddess of the rainbow.

But I had my own plan. I'd happened to bring a black dress to camp that was perfect for the theme: tight, sparkling just around the hem, and one-shouldered, like a toga. I did a Google search and decided I would be Eris, goddess of chaos and strife. One girl said, "You're going to look so much hotter than us."

The evening of the dance, while the others were pinning their baggy tunics into place, I applied a dark smoky eye, using the single eyeshadow palette I owned. I let one of the other girls put my hair in an updo that she assured me was Grecian. I put on black platform sandals. I was feeling older than my years, and *hot*.

Then a note slipped under the door. The girls rushed over in their tunics and bare feet to grab it. It was a miracle it wasn't torn to pieces right then, I thought. Someone read it aloud. *"Will you go to the dance with me? If yes, meet me by the Love Tree. -Z."*

Anyone who knows me knows that I've never been good at keeping my emotions bottled up. My heart was beating so hard, I thought the other girls were bound to hear it. But Lydia just looked at me with wide, shining eyes. "I'm going to the dance with Zane!" She looked down at her tunic, and at her friends, who were practically biting their nails with excitement. "Is it alright if I…?" she asked them.

There was a chorus of "yes, yes, go," and she started toward the door. And in that moment, it hit me. Her narcissism, her self-centeredness to just *assume* that Zane was interested in her and not someone else. And not me. Me, the girl who had been hanging out with him and his friends *every day* while Lydia was playing make-believe with her friends and putting flowers in her hair. What did it say about what she thought about herself? About what she thought about me?

I took a step toward her, ready to say all of this and more, to tell her the truth, but then she turned to face me. "Rosalie," she said quietly, "I'm nervous. Will you come with me?" She held out her hand, her wrist stacked with friendship bracelets in various patterns and colors—each the signature of a different member of her little coven.

Despite everything, I felt a burst of satisfaction at the fact that *I* was the one she asked to come with her. None of the other girls. Our bond wasn't dead, after all.

Then one of the girls said, "Wait." She was staring at the back of the note.

"What's wrong?" asked Lydia.

Wordlessly, the girl held the note out to her. Lydia took it, her expression growing confused. Then she looked at me.

I saw it then. The back of the note said, in Zane's clean handwriting: *To Rosaline*.

It's hard to remember what happened next, who started talking first, or when exactly Lydia sank to the ground, burying her head in her arms. Her friends gathered around her, rubbing her back, telling her that it was okay, that he was an idiot and not good enough for her anyway. Then one of them said, without looking at me, "Honestly, Lydia, I bet he just likes her because she's easy. She's probably been hooking up with him behind your back."

"Makes sense, knowing her history," said another.

For a moment, I was too stunned to speak. I managed to say, "Excuse me?"

"Ros," said Lydia, but it was too late. I knew that Lydia had told her friends about the rumor, that she'd brought the drama I was trying to escape here to camp. That even Lydia—the one person I really thought was on my side—believed Franklin's word over mine.

"How could you?" I asked her.

"I shouldn't have told them," she said.

"Why did you? You know it's not true!"

Lydia had been avoiding my gaze, but now she looked me straight in the eyes. "Look, Ros. I stuck by your side because I didn't care if you were hooking up with Franklin. No matter what you did, it wasn't fair of the girls at school to treat you like that. But how could you betray me like this after all that I've done for you?"

I turned and stormed out the door, leaving her with her horrible friends, heading straight to the Love Tree.

The Love Tree was the campers' name for this old, knotty tree a ways into the woods. It was covered in carvings: initials, hearts and arrows, even some full names. Tributes to camp romances past. I'd spent an afternoon sitting in the branches of the tree with Lydia's clan earlier that month, tracing the carvings and speculating about what had happened. Were any of these couples still together?

As I approached the Love Tree, I saw Zane standing beneath it, leaning against the trunk. He looked up when he heard me. He was wearing dark jeans and a black T-shirt. His hair was just as messy as usual, but he'd put on a cord necklace with a stone pendant for the occasion. I let him take in my outfit—the sandals, the dress, the updo. "I'm Eris," I said.

"Discord," he said. "Love it." There was a moment of silence. "You look stunning."

He was the same awkward teenage boy he'd always been. My feelings toward him hadn't changed. But the situation had.

He held out his arm and said, "Shall we go?"

I nodded and closed the gap between us, slipping my arm through his.

The Main Hall had been decorated with Ionic columns made out of construction paper and crepe paper streamers. The lights were turned down, and Zane hardly let go of my arm all night. Some of the other boys had brought dates, and the rest had gone as a group, wearing ridiculous bedsheet togas. Someone with a name tag reading HELLO! MY NAME IS: *Dionysus* was carrying around a massive bunch of grapes. The music was loud and good, and I found myself swept up in the excitement. I forgot about Lydia. Or at least I told myself I did.

Sometimes, when Zane was spinning me around on the dance floor, I caught glimpses of her out of the corner of my eye, glaring at us. Her group, in their white tunics and signature accessories, was easy enough to spot. And when the music for a slow dance came on, and Zane settled his hands on my hips, I had a moment of doubt. I saw her on the edge of the dance floor, watching us, and for a second I felt terrible. What was I doing? Then I remembered: Lydia had assumed that he was interested in her. It didn't even occur to her that it might be me that he wanted instead.

And she had broken my trust. She had betrayed me, and she had the nerve to suggest that *I* was the one who had betrayed *her*.

That fact, combined with the heat of Zane's body so close to mine and the knowledge that Lydia was watching, was enough to push me to cup the back of his head with my hand, lean forward, and kiss him as hard as I could.

For a moment he stiffened—in surprise and not horror, I hoped—and then he softened into it. He knew how to kiss, it became evident, and I did not. I turned it down a notch and let him take the lead. There were moments that were sort of nice, and then his tongue would stick into my mouth, which was gross, and his braces would scrape my lips so hard I had to resist the urge to pull away and check if they were bleeding. After what felt like several long minutes, a hand on each of our shoulders pulled us apart. We found ourselves facing a vaguely amused-looking counselor. "Leave room for Jesus, kids," he said.

"Sorry, man," Zane said.

"Please don't tell my parents," I said.

"You're not in trouble," the counselor said. "We're just required to stop it when we see it." Then he left.

Zane whispered, "Do you want to go outside?"

I couldn't breathe, I suddenly had a pounding headache, and I didn't know what to do. I shook my head. "I'll be right back." I needed to be out of that room, to have a moment by myself to think, to breathe.

As I headed for the restroom door, I passed Lydia's group. They were dancing together in their own tight circle, looking like a single unit. But one pair of eyes followed me. Lydia's. And I could swear I saw hellfire in them.

———

Maybe she didn't come with them. That's what I kept telling myself in the morning as I got dressed. I had only heard Lydia's parents—maybe they were taking a Pine Bay vacation with their friends.

Throughout breakfast there was no sign of Lydia or her family. I began to wonder if maybe I'd imagined their voices last night.

A voice came over the loudspeaker. "We've received a report of a break-in at the rec center." The room broke into excited murmurs. "If you have any knowledge of the perpetrators, please come to the front desk after breakfast. Thank you."

Our group broke into simultaneous, secretive smiles.

After we finished breakfast, Aydın and I walked together ahead of the group, chatting as we headed for the exit. Just as we were about to reach it, the door swung open, and there was Lydia. Beside her stood Jeff, a classmate of ours who had been in Eleanor's and my AP Bio class freshman year.

It was like my body had momentarily shut off. My brain, however, had the courtesy to notice that Lydia looked good. She was wearing makeup and was dressed in a pair of crisp white shorts and a white collared button-up tank top, like she was about to go play tennis or something. Her blonde hair was chopped to shoulder length, shorter than I'd ever seen it. Jeff looked the same as he always had. Short brown hair, snub nose, slightly oversized ears.

"Rosaline?" said Lydia. "Oh my gosh, hi!"

"Hey," I said weakly, and glanced at Jeff. He gave a wave.

"It's been so long! Are your parents here?"

"No, I'm staying with Eleanor's family. What about you?"

I wished I could un-ask the question as soon as I'd asked it. Lydia smiled at Jeff, then grabbed his hand and leaned her head on his shoulder. "Our families are here together. You know Jeff, right?"

Before I could say anything, Jeff said, "Ros and I took AP Bio together."

"Aw, fun," said Lydia in a fake, cutesy tone. "Jeff's mom and mine have become *such* great friends since we started dating. It's sort of disgusting."

"Wow," said Aydın, "that's…unusual."

Lydia looked at him for the first time and stuck out her hand. "Lydia." Then she frowned. "You look familiar."

Aydın reached for her outstretched hand and opened his mouth to speak, but I interrupted. I grabbed his hand and said, "Lydia, this is Aydın. My boyfriend."

I could feel him tense up in surprise as Lydia's eyes traveled from my face to his and back. "You two are so cute together! I love it," she said.

"So do we!" I said, with my brightest *fuck you* smile.

"Well, we've got to be off. Tennis lesson after breakfast." She waved her fingers and pulled Jeff toward the tables.

Aydın turned to me, but I tightened my grip on his hand and pulled him through the front doors. Once we were safely outside, I released him. I waited for him to ask why I'd done that, for him to ask me not to do it again, but he just asked, "More Bardet people, I take it?"

"Yeah," I said, slightly relieved.

"That's *the* Lydia, isn't it?"

180

I grimaced. "That's her."

"Damn," he said. "I guess you didn't expect to see her, huh?"

"Her family comes every summer, but I expected them to have come earlier. Not, like, the last weekend before school starts."

"Fair enough."

"Do you want to go on a hike?" I asked.

———

The forest was peaceful. The sunlight took on a greenish-gold tint, filtering through the canopy of leaves above us, and for a moment I managed to forget about Lydia and Eleanor and Chloe and my parents and my babaanne—everything that was stressing me out.

Then my phone buzzed. I checked it, put my phone back in my pocket, then did a double take and checked it again. "Holy shit," I said.

"What's up?" asked Aydın.

"Lydia just texted me."

"What did she say?" He leaned over my shoulder to look.

Hey! Any interest in getting coffee tomorrow?

"What the fuck?" I asked.

Aydın shrugged. "Sounds like she's trying to be nice."

"I'm sure there's some ulterior motive."

"What if there isn't?"

"Lydia hates me."

"Maybe you should meet up with her and see," he said. "Maybe she wants to apologize."

"You don't know Lydia. There's no way she wants to apologize," I muttered. Then an idea struck me. "Do you want to go with me?"

Aydın frowned. "That would be weird, wouldn't it?"

"We could make it a double date. That way I'll have a layer of protection."

"I mean, if you think it'll help."

I typed out my response quickly. **Make it a double date? I'd love for our guys to get to know each other.**

As I slid my phone back into my pocket, a movement on the path in front of us startled me, and I jumped back with a gasp. Aydın jumped too. It was a small green frog, hopping away. I started to laugh.

"Jesus, Ros."

"Sorry," I said between laughs. "I don't know why that freaked me out."

He cracked a smile too. "You're cute," he said, and wrapped an arm around my shoulders. I planted a kiss on his cheek.

"So, um," I said. "I feel like we should talk. About…us."

"What's there to talk about?"

"You know."

He rubbed the back of his neck. "You introduced me as your boyfriend."

"And?"

"And I guess that's that."

I was starting to get that tingly feeling of irritation. "Well, I'm sorry, I didn't know what else to say."

"Hang on, are you mad at me?"

"You should've just told me you weren't okay with it!"

He held up his hands. "Chill! I didn't say that!"

"Fine," I said. "Can you just tell me what you're thinking?"

He crossed his arms. "What do you want us to be?"

"Don't turn this around on me."

"Okay. You said we were dating, let's stick with that."

I didn't know how to respond, so I just kept staring at him.

"Or not?" he said. "Ros, you've got to give me something to work with here."

"Yes," I said. "Yes, let's do that."

He let out a sigh. "Glad we got that cleared up. Now, can we continue our walk?"

I gave him an angelic smile. "Yes, we may."

My phone buzzed again. **Sure. 10 work for you guys?**

Yes. I sent back. Then, on second thought, I added a chipper **See you then! :)**

———

That night I dreamed about standing onstage at homecoming and having that tiara placed on my head. I was in an emerald dress that shimmered in the bright stage lights. The crowd was cheering. I gave a royal wave and turned to my companion, who had just been crowned homecoming prince. His eyes were the exact same shade of green as my dress. As the music started, we began to dance, and the cheers grew louder. He pulled me closer, into a long kiss, and I closed my eyes. But when I opened them again, just for a moment, I was looking into a pair of pale blue eyes under a mop of blond hair. Franklin Doss was smiling back at me.

I woke up with a start, heart racing. I sat up, taking care not to wake Eleanor, and chugged the glass of water on the side table, trying not to think about my dream, which was now burned into my brain.

After four nights apart, Eleanor and I were finally back in the shared couch bed. This seemed like progress, but she still wasn't spending any time with me during the days. She'd spent yesterday with her BFF Chloe. I kept telling myself that she'd get over it, but there was a seed of doubt in my mind that kept growing. What if Chloe actually was better than me in every way, including as a friend? What if Eleanor decided to replace me entirely?

Maybe we were just too different for our friendship to work. Maybe I should've known better than to trust her.

Besides, I just needed to make it through one more day here before we headed home, and then I could focus on my real goal. As I lay down again, I focused on picturing Aydın next to me on that stage, beaming, his green eyes matching my dress. And our kiss.

With Aydın by my side, it could happen. We just might have a shot at winning. And the closer it felt, the more badly I wanted it.

Chapter Fifteen

"Where's Jeff?" I asked, sliding into the booth across from Lydia. We were at the Pine Bay coffee shop, and it—of course—was absolutely adorable. Dark wood countertops and green seat coverings and leafy plants spilling out of the cubbies that lined the edges of the ceiling and a row of gleaming silver espresso machines.

"Men," she said, rolling her eyes. "You know them. Always late. He went fishing with our dads, but he said he'd be here."

"Cappuccino for Lydia!" the barista called. Lydia raised one hand—fingers bedecked in delicate silver rings, I noticed—and the barista ducked out from behind the counter, carrying a foam-topped cup to our table.

"Thank you!" she said, smiling brightly up at him.

"My pleasure," he said, setting the coffee down with a wide, smitten smile. As he walked away, he glanced back over his shoulder, but Lydia didn't look at him. She was taking a careful sip of her coffee.

"Mm," she said. "Did you order anything?"

"Were you just flirting with that guy?"

"Of course not!"

I raised an eyebrow, but her innocent expression didn't crack.

"You have to go up to the counter to order," she said.

I slid out of the booth and headed over. The same barista asked, "What can I get for you?" Just a regular smile, nothing like the one he'd given her. I ordered a drip coffee, black. No sugary, foamy things for me.

When I got back to the booth, both Jeff and Aydın were standing there. Jeff was standing on Lydia's side, his hands awkwardly in his pockets. Aydın looked more relaxed, leaning against the other side of the booth. The juxtaposition made me secretly happy. With the two of them side by side, it was clear who between the two of us—me and Lydia—had won.

"You guys have to go to the counter to order," I said, slipping past Aydın and into the booth.

The boys looked at each other. "Alright," said Aydın. He headed toward the counter. Jeff followed behind, hands still in pockets.

Lydia watched them go. "He's cute," she said.

I nodded in agreement.

"Thanks for coming," she said. "It's good to see you."

It's good to see you? I snorted. "Sure," I said.

"Excuse me?" she asked.

"Nothing," I said. "It's *great* to see you too." I colored my voice with all the sarcasm I could muster.

"Look, Ros," Lydia said, lowering her voice. "I'm trying here. Do you really want to go into junior year still stuck in this stupid fight?"

"What fight?" I asked.

"You tell me."

Aydın appeared next to the booth. I slid over, grateful for his presence, and he sat down, placing a cup of black coffee on the table.

"We're matching," I said, gesturing to my own cup.

"Adorable." Lydia's smile was not just fake, but pointedly fake.

"What were you guys talking about?" Aydın asked.

I looked at Lydia.

"Oh, you know, just girl things," she said. "So how did you two meet?"

"Aydın is friends with Ben Whittington," I said. "He introduced us."

Lydia's eyes flicked to Aydın and widened slightly with recognition. "That's right," she said. "You were here a couple summers ago, weren't you?"

Aydın nodded. "I thought I remembered you."

Lydia looked back and forth between the two of us. "Cute," she said. "Another Pine Bay romance."

"Dirty chai!" called the barista. Over at the counter, Jeff picked up his drink and made his way back toward us.

"What's a dirty chai?" asked Aydın.

"You don't want to know," Jeff said, winking at Lydia.

"Jeff!" Lydia elbowed him. I wanted to vomit.

Aydın brushed it off. "What have you two been up to this summer?"

"Our families have been spending a lot of time together," said Lydia. "My dad convinced Jeffrey's dad to join our country club, which was genius."

I remembered the country club. Lydia's family used to bring me there sometimes. White-and-yellow-striped deck chairs everywhere, a turquoise pool, mothers in tasteful bikinis and oversized sunglasses sipping drinks while their kids ran wild, to the annoyance of the lifeguards.

"Sounds like fun," said Aydın. "What do you do there?"

"Tennis, mostly," said Lydia.

"There's a pool," added Jeff. "Also been doing a lot of fishing. You fish?"

"Nope," said Aydın.

There was a moment of silence. I sipped my coffee.

"You guys are leaving tomorrow?" Lydia asked.

"Yep," I said.

"Sad."

"Very." I took another sip of coffee. "How long are you all staying?"

"Monday. Getting back just in time for school."

"Exciting stuff."

"Ugh, I am so not excited for school to start again. The only things keeping me going are homecoming court and the new theatre season. I've already started prepping for auditions."

"Since when are you serious about acting?" I asked.

She gave me a look. "I was in the spring play last year. Actually, I was the lead. I'm pretty sure you came to see it."

Of course I remembered; I just didn't want to admit it. I'd auditioned and didn't even get a callback. In middle school, it was so easy: everyone who auditioned got a role. Now things were different. Last spring's play was *Our Town*, a high school drama classic, and the way I understood it was that I didn't look American enough to play one of the characters in the classic, all-American town. Maybe that was unfair, but if you'd seen the cast taking their curtain call that night, you'd understand.

"Right," I said. "So now, what? You're really into acting?"

"I like doing things I'm good at," Lydia said with a shrug, then took a delicate sip of her cappuccino.

"And homecoming court? Why are you excited about that?" I tried to sound casual, but I knew she could hear the tightness in my voice. Her eyes met mine, cold blue. She *knew*.

"Jeff and I are running for homecoming prince and princess." She put her hand on top of his on the table and gave it a squeeze. He smiled at her. "I've already planned out everything."

"What's there to plan?" asked Aydın.

"The campaign."

"The *campaign?*" I asked, not even trying to hide my annoyance.

"A good politician never goes into a race unprepared. And homecoming court, despite the name, is far more democracy than monarchy, don't you think?"

Aydın slipped his arm around my shoulders and gave me a squeeze. Was he trying to calm me down? "Ros has been teaching me how to sail."

"Oh, really? How did that go?"

"Not so well. We ended up in the water."

"Weird, I thought Ros was a good sailor," Lydia said, then turned to me. "You always said you'd teach me."

"Oh, she is," said Aydın. "It wasn't her fault. Some mix of mine and the weather's."

Jeff and Lydia and Aydın continued to make small talk while my mind spun in circles. She knew that I wanted to be elected to homecoming court. She must've known. I don't know how she would've known, but she must've. Why else would she be doing this?

At some point Lydia excused herself to use the restroom, and I followed shortly afterward. I waited by the sinks until she came out of her stall.

"Ros," she said, looking caught off guard for the first time since she'd arrived. "What are you doing here?"

"It's a restroom," I said. "I'm allowed to be here."

"Sure." She washed her ring-bedecked hands and wiped them off on a fancy, cream-colored paper towel from a stack between the sinks. "Clearly you want to talk. What is it?"

"Homecoming court?" I said. "*Really?*"

She rolled her eyes. "It's fun, okay? There's no need to sound so condescending."

"I can't believe you'd stoop so low."

"What are you talking about?" Lydia checked her makeup in the mirror, then pulled a lip gloss from her bag and started to reapply.

"You're just doing this to sabotage me!"

She looked straight at me. "You're running too?"

"Of course I am. You *knew* this was, like, the one thing I wanted!"

"Since when?"

"I've been planning this since freshman year."

"How was I supposed to know that? We haven't talked in, like, two years."

"You knew," I said. "You have to have known."

"Anyone can run for homecoming court," Lydia said. "You know that, right? Just because you want something doesn't mean that you're entitled to it."

"Of course I know that! I just want a fair shot."

"You still have one."

"Not with you trying to sabotage me."

She shook her head. "I can't deal with this right now." She stalked out of the restroom.

I splashed cold water from the sink on my face, then patted it dry with one of the paper towels, which was surprisingly soft. I took a few deep breaths, collecting myself, then headed back to the table, where I pulled out my phone and pretended to look at the time. "Would you look at that?" I said. "We've got to go. I haven't packed yet and I'm leaving early tomorrow morning with Eleanor's family."

"That was quick," said Jeff.

"I know," I said, standing up and gesturing for Aydın to follow. "I'm sorry. But it was nice catching up with you guys! See you at school?"

"Mhm." Lydia looked like she could barely hide her fury, which made me sort of happy as I hurried away, shepherding Aydın along with me.

"That was far from subtle," he said as soon as we were out the door. "I didn't even get to finish my coffee. It was like four dollars."

"I'm sorry," I said. "I just couldn't do it. She's horrible. And she hates me."

"Do you ever wonder if some of that feeling that she hates you is just you projecting? It seemed like she was trying to be nice."

"Are you really going to take her side?"

Aydın scrunched up his face. "I'm not taking anyone's side. I'm just saying."

"She hates me, Aydın. Trust me."

"Whatever you say, Captain."

"Don't call me that."

He grinned. "I think I just found your new nickname."

⸻

That evening Aydın met me outside the Orchard Oriole to walk to the campfire. Neither of us knew what sort of shenanigans we'd be walking into, and as we made our way there, we joked about what type of trouble Ben had in mind this time. Honestly, though, I was pretty exhausted and was still trying to process my conversation with Lydia. I only half wanted to go to the campfire. The other half of me wanted to curl up under a blanket and hide from everyone.

As soon as we got within eyesight of the campfire, the latter feeling intensified tenfold.

"Shit," I said.

"What?"

"Lydia's here."

Aydın followed my gaze to the fire. "Do you not want to go?"

"I mean…" I thought about it. "Not really." It wasn't just Lydia. I could see that Eleanor and Chloe were there too, sitting next to each other and whispering about something.

"We don't have to."

"It's just… with our coffee earlier, and everything…"

"It's been a long day?"

I nodded. "Yeah."

"Let's not go, then. We can go back to my place."

"Ben's family won't mind?"

"Nah, they're chill. And they might be out, anyway. Mrs. Whittington keeps dragging Mr. Whittington out to ballroom dance classes in the evenings."

"Ballroom dance? How many classes does this place have?"

He laughed. "No clue."

It was our last night at Pine Bay, and of course I didn't want to waste it, but I also couldn't deal with Lydia. Or seeing Eleanor and Chloe laughing like they'd just discovered the funniest joke in the world. As much as I didn't want to admit it, it stung to see that Eleanor was having a good time without me. It was like she didn't even care that I wasn't there.

"You should go to the campfire if you want to," I said. "I'll just hang by myself."

Aydın shook his head. "I won't have any fun if you're not around."

"Gross," I said.

"Too much?"

"So *sweet.*"

"I'll try to tone it down."

"Appreciated."

Mr. and Mrs. Whittington were, in fact, out at their ballroom dance class. Aydın gave me a cursory tour of the cottage, which looked pretty similar to our own. He and Ben were sharing a bunk bed in the second bedroom, and the floor of their room was basically unnavigable. Dirty socks galore.

"Bit of a mess," I said.

"Yeah." Aydın closed the door to the bedroom and led me back into the living room area. "Let's forget you saw that."

"It's burned into my mind."

He sat down on the couch. "What now?"

I sat down next to him. "We could watch a movie."

"Sure." Aydın grabbed the remote and turned the TV on. "Is there anything new on Netflix?"

"There's that ski documentary."

He frowned. "Which one?"

"It's in…Nepal, I think? On a mountain? It's supposed to be really good."

"Sounds good, Captain," he said. Then his face lit up. "That reminds me!" He pulled his phone out of his pocket and leaned in closer. I snuggled up next to him, hoping he couldn't feel how fast my heart was beating.

"Reminds you of what?" I asked.

He typed in his phone passcode: 1235. Very secure. "Have you seen that video of the skiing dog?" he asked.

"I don't think so…"

"It was on a bunch of people's stories this morning. Hang on. It's so funny." He opened Instagram and tapped the search bar. A list of recent searches appeared below it. At the very top of the list was a familiar handle, and a familiar gorgeous profile picture.

Chloe.

Aydın didn't seem to notice me noticing, and he found the post he was looking for. It was a funny video, although I sort of had to remind myself to laugh—I was still processing the fact that Aydın's most recent search was Chloe.

During the ski mountaineering documentary, the questions kept circling. What did it mean? Was Aydın still in love with Chloe? Was I not good enough? Not pretty enough? Maybe (I didn't want to admit to this thought, but it was there) what he really wanted was a girl who was less Turkish than me. After all, I'd had my own mini-crisis about being too predictable by liking him, like dating him meant I was giving in to a familial pressure that I hadn't even realized was there. What if he felt the same way? It hurt to think that maybe I wasn't what he wanted, but it hurt ten times more to think that maybe I could never be, that my not-enoughness was built into my DNA.

I was only pulled out of this spiral of doom by the film: a breath-taking drone shot of the peak, and the four mountaineers standing on the summit in front of a brilliant pink dawn sky. I got out my phone and jotted down a quick note. *Think about ski movie directing as a career. Or drone cinematography? (Do you have to be a good skier to make ski movies?)*

In the last half hour, Aydın paused the film. "I've gotta use the bathroom. Be right back."

"No worries."

He got up and walked into the bathroom. I stretched, turned, and lay down lengthwise on the couch. I told myself that I was being paranoid. After all, I was the one who was here with Aydın, right? Chloe didn't even want to be with him. She'd told him that. They weren't together. And he had been the one to break up with her in the first place.

But what would happen now that we would all be at the same school?

I *needed* to walk in on the first day and be able to call Aydın my boyfriend. I *needed* us to cement our reputation as a perfect couple so we could win spots on the homecoming court.

My toe touched something that didn't feel like a pillow. Aydın's phone. The bathroom door was closed. My brain spun through a set of quick, involuntary calculations, and before I knew what I was doing, I had entered his passcode and pulled up Instagram. I went to the search bar, found Chloe's profile lingering there, and clicked on it. Nine perfect squares of Chloe. Well, eight plus one group photo, but even in that one, she was glowing. How could you even look at the other girls when Chloe was there, in a gold dress? She looked like she was on her way to some glamorous party, the type that I didn't get invited to. The harder I stared, the more I started to hate her. Aydın had clearly searched for her account recently. With her name right up at the top, he'd probably be tempted to do it again. And again. What if she distracted him from me? From *us*? I knew then what I had to do.

I unfollowed Chloe from Aydın's account.

Then, for good measure, I blocked her.

Maybe she'd assume he'd deleted his Instagram. Or, better yet, she'd realize he'd blocked her and would never speak to him again.

I heard the toilet flush and the tap turn on, and I exited out of Instagram and threw Aydın's phone back toward the other end of the couch. By the time Aydın returned, I was stretched out again and had my eyes closed, feigning sleepiness.

Aydın slipped onto the couch and lifted my head onto his lap. "Tired?" he asked.

I shook my head, stifling a fake yawn. "Movie?" I asked.

"You want to finish it?"

"Mhm."

He laughed. "Alright." I sat up, leaning into him. He reached over me to the coffee table and pressed the play button on the remote, then snuggled in close. I watched the rest of the movie with the warmth of Aydın's chest against my back and the weight of his arm over me, making me feel safe and perfectly, perfectly content.

Chapter Sixteen

Eleanor continued to ice me out on the drive home from Pine Bay the next day. This time, she didn't volunteer to take the middle seat; instead, she told her parents that it was Mason's turn. She immediately opened her book and held it pointedly in front of her face. Whenever I tried talking to her—about Ben, about school, about Pine Bay in general—she responded to each of my statements with a sarcastic-sounding "Mhm." I noticed Sherry's eyes moving between the two of us in the rearview mirror, and eventually I stopped trying.

I arrived home to find that my parents had made a welcome-home feast with all my favorite foods. Arugula salad with goat cheese and pears and walnuts, Mom's grilled pork chops and dad's green bean fasulye, followed by a pile of chocolate cupcakes decorated with silver star-shaped sprinkles.

As we dug in, I told them the stories I'd planned to tell. They listened, and although they weren't as impressed by the magical world of Pine Bay as I'd hoped they would be (thinking that maybe they'd be willing to try it out themselves next summer), it was nice to be home again.

"It sounds like there were a lot of kids from Bardet there," said my dad.

"That's what I've been telling you!" I said. "It's practically a school tradition."

"The other kids were nice?"

"Very." Then, remembering, I wrinkled my nose. "Except Franklin Doss."

"Oh, I remember that jerk," said my mom.

"Honey! We don't talk about high schoolers that way," my dad replied.

"That's the only way to talk about this one," she said.

I laughed. "She's right."

"He was awful to the other kids back in elementary school. A real bully," my mom said. "And his parents refused to do a thing about it. They said it couldn't possibly be his fault. 'His classmates must have been instigating it.'"

"Some people don't change," I said.

"Is he still bad?"

"He's horrible. He did this whole racist thing—" I broke off, not sure I should explain. I was worried they might make a big deal out of it, when it was over and done with already.

"A racist thing toward you?" my dad asked slowly.

"No, not toward me, toward this other guy...."

"Who?" asked my mom.

"The guy I told you about. Aydın."

They exchanged a look. "What happened?" asked my dad.

"It was dumb. Honestly, I don't really want to rehash it."

There was a pause, a brief moment of consideration. Then my mom asked, "So when do we get to meet this boyfriend of yours?"

"Mom!"

"You're right, you're right," she said. "It's too early for that."

"I don't think it is," said my dad.

"Can we stop talking about this too?" I asked. "It's embarrassing."

"Fine," said my mother. "But invite him over for dinner soon?"

"I'll think about it."

"How's Eleanor?" asked my dad. "Did she have a good time?"

I shrugged and stuffed another bite of fasulye into my mouth. "Probably."

"Probably?" asked my mom.

"I mean, I think so."

"Weren't you with her?"

"Yeah, but not the whole time. We hung out with other people."

My parents exchanged another look. Annoying.

"What happened?" my mom asked.

I huffed and set my fork down. "She's being immature," I said. "Like, I made a little mistake, but then I apologized for it, so I don't know what more she expects me to do."

"What did you do?" asked my dad.

"I don't want to talk about it."

"Maybe she needs some time."

"That's all I've been giving her! Time and space!"

"And Lydia? Was she there?" asked my mom.

Of course she'd ask that. I'd spent years trying to convince her to take me to Pine Bay, citing Lydia's adventures as evidence of its magic. And even though I'd told her an abbreviated version of what went down between me and Lydia two years ago, she still seemed to be holding out hope that we'd reconcile.

I didn't want to deal with talking about it again. "Nope," I said.

—

That night, lying in bed, I texted Aydın. **Miss you.**

The typing bubble appeared, lingered for a few seconds, then disappeared. Then it reappeared, and finally, a text came through.

It's been eons. How much longer must we wait to reunite?

Weirdo, I replied.

How's the fam?

They're good. Nosy as usual.

Lol same here.

That made me wonder if his parents were asking about me, the same way that mine were asking about him. Before I could write back, my phone buzzed again.

Hey, I have a question, Aydın wrote.

My heart jumped into my throat. **What's up?**

Are you free Monday night? Want to come over for dinner?

To your house?

Lol, he replied. **Yes, to my house.**

It was too soon, wasn't it? Was it? **Of course!** I replied. **I'd love to!**

Great, he wrote back. **I'm cooking.**

I searched for the most skeptical-looking emoji and sent it.

Hey now, Aydın replied. **I happen to be an excellent chef.**
I'll believe it when I see it.

You'll believe it when you taste it, he wrote, along with three chef emojis.

———

Two days later I stood facing the turquoise-colored front door of Aydın's house, wondering whether this was a good idea. My mom had dropped me off, and I half wanted to call her and ask her to come back and pick me up.

Aydın had told me that his parents would be there for dinner, and given the way that he'd described them, I wasn't sure what to expect. So I dressed in a way that I hoped would win them over: a navy cardigan and matching headband over a white skirt—not too short. Parents liked preppy, right? I shook off the doubt, straightened my shoulders, and rang the doorbell.

Almost immediately, the door swung open. Aydın's mother was older than I'd pictured, with kind green eyes like his and thick, dark hair. She smiled and opened the door further, ushering me in. "Rosaline!" she said. "It is *so* nice to meet you." She took my face in her hands and kissed each of my cheeks, momentarily reminding me of my babaanne. "Come in!" she said.

I followed her in, then unbuckled my sandals and set them next to one of the neat rows of shoes beside the door. She waited patiently, still smiling. "Hoşgeldin," she said. "Türkçe biliyor musun?"

"Hoşbulduk," I replied, grateful for the few words my dad had taught me. I held my index finger and thumb a centimeter apart. "Biraz."

"Çok iyi," she said, nodding her approval. Then she called, "Aydın! Rosaline is here!" She gestured for me to follow her out of the entryway. "Come, let's go to the living room."

I padded barefoot down the hallway, along a long Turkish carpet patterned in red, navy, and white, into a bright living room that had all the familiar trappings. A large nazar boncuğu hanging over the doorframe, another richly toned rug, a beautiful turquoise-and-red bowl sitting in the center of the coffee table.

A man appeared and introduced himself, with a firm handshake, as Aydın's father. He was tall, with a strong nose and cheekbones that looked just like his son's. After a brief exchange, he excused himself to make a work call.

"Please, sit," Aydın's mother said, and I obliged, taking a seat on a long sofa. "Would you like some coffee?"

"I would love some," I said.

"Sugar?"

"No, thank you. I'm a black coffee kind of girl."

She nodded and gave another approving smile before disappearing into the hallway. While I waited for her to return, I examined a framed family photo that sat on the side table. It showed Aydın—maybe ten or eleven years old—next to his mother, his father, and a teenage girl with dark, curly hair and green eyes just like Aydın's and his mom's. He'd never mentioned he had a sister.

Aydın's mom reappeared, carrying a tray with two intricately patterned coffee cups. She held it out to me and I took one, breathing in the thick scent of the strong coffee.

"Thank you, Mrs. Muhtar," I said, and then I sipped it. It was perfect.

She took a seat on the sofa across from me and sipped from her cup. "You're very welcome, dear."

Aydın appeared, dressed to the nines in his usual rumpled, just-rolled-out-of-bed way. A white button-down rolled up past his elbows, the collar slightly crooked, and his hair messy. And…an apron. Aydın was wearing an apron.

"Hey," he said.

"Come sit with us," said his mother, patting the sofa cushion beside her.

"I'm cooking. Do you want me to burn the dinner?"

She made a clucking sound and shooed him away. "Go on, then. Back in the kitchen."

He shot me a grin before leaving.

"Do you drink Turkish coffee at home?" Mrs. Muhtar asked me.

I nodded. "My dad loves to make it for us. Especially on weekends. I think it's comforting for him—reminds him of home."

"It reminds me of home too. We'll have to meet them, your parents."

"Mom!" came Aydın's voice through the open door.

"Do you know where you want to go to college?" she asked me.

"I'm not sure," I said. "I'm trying to keep my options open. My parents and I started going on college visits last year."

"Aydın has his heart set on Princeton."

Aydın popped his head back into the living room. "Mom, you know that's not true."

"I thought you were cooking," she said.

"I am."

I sipped my coffee, observing their back-and-forth.

"And you loved Princeton," his mom pointed out.

"I did, but that doesn't mean you can go around saying I 'have my heart set' on it. There are plenty of places I'd be happy to go."

She turned her attention back to me. "Aydın wants to be a doctor."

He sighed and disappeared again.

"So, Mrs. Muhtar," I said, trying to change the topic for Aydın's sake, "do you still have family in Türkiye?"

She nodded. "My parents are there, and my brother. My two sisters are both in the U.S."

"Where do they live?"

"İdil lives in Greenwich with her family, and Pelin is in L.A."

"I love L.A.!" I said.

"Pelin writes for television shows there."

I lit up. "Really? What sorts of shows?"

"Aydın, canım," Mrs. Muhtar called through the open door. "Do you know what Auntie Pelin writes?"

"Didn't she do that really complicated sci-fi show, with all the different timelines?" Aydın's voice replied.

"I can never remember," his mother said. Then she asked me, "Do you like to write?"

"No, I'm not much of a writer," I said. "But I love movies. I've thought about trying to direct."

Mrs. Muhtar's eyebrows lifted, just a bit.

Feeling awkward, I went on, "I'm into old movies. Not like *old* old, but eighties movies. The Brat Pack and all that."

Her face was blank.

"*The Breakfast Club*?" I offered.

"I've never seen it," she said. "You want to make movies like that?"

"Well, I don't know," I said, feeling my face starting to heat up. Why did I say that? I never talked about these things out loud. "Maybe. I mean, I don't really know what I want to do yet."

Thankfully, Aydın interrupted our conversation to tell us that dinner was ready. Mr. Muhtar reappeared, and the three of us sat down at the table in the dining room. Aydın brought us plates piled high with Turkish food—some dishes I recognized from my dad's cooking, and some new ones.

I took a few bites. "Oh my god, you weren't kidding. This is actually amazing," I said, looking at Aydın. "How did you learn how to cook so well?" I asked.

Aydın shrugged, smiling sheepishly. "My mom is a fantastic cook."

"When he was a little boy, he used to lurk in the kitchen while I made dinner," Mrs. Muhtar said. "I didn't intend to teach him. In Türkiye, boys don't usually take an interest in cooking. But there he was, and before I knew it, he'd become my helper."

I glanced over at Aydın, who was blushing.

The rest of dinner was pretty fun, actually, despite my stress over making a good impression. His mom seemed to like me: she asked a lot of questions about my dad and his family, and some about my interests. Aydın's dad was quiet and stoic, but that seemed to just be the way he was, so I didn't take it personally.

After dinner Aydın took me on a tour of the rest of the house. The kitchen, which smelled familiar and comforting; the family room, which was a less stuffy version of the living room, with a TV and bookshelves; the powder room; the primary bedroom. And, finally, Aydın's room. I pushed open the door and walked in.

Aside from a bed and a desk, the room was full of cardboard boxes, stacked to form precarious towers. "Sorry it's such a mess," said Aydın. "I haven't had time to properly move in yet."

I moved farther into the forest of boxes. "The rest of the house is so put together, it's like you've lived here for years."

"Yeah, that's my mom for you. She spent the whole time we were at Pine Bay unpacking and making everything beautiful. She's all about the way things look." He grabbed a small box and used it to prop the bedroom door open.

"What are you doing?" I asked.

He raised an eyebrow. "Are you allowed to be alone in your room with someone of the opposite gender? Because I'm not."

"Whoa, really?" I asked. But as I said it, I realized I didn't know my parents' stance. The situation had never arisen. The fact that we were, indeed, alone in his room together suddenly hit me, and I felt heat rising in my cheeks again.

I turned away and tore off the tape on a box labeled POSTERS

AND STUFF. Opening it, I reached in and pulled out three posters. They were old and wrinkled, and they depicted people who I assumed were famous soccer players, all kicking soccer balls with intense expressions on their faces.

Aydın came to stand next to me.

"I knew you liked soccer, but I didn't know you were such a fan-boy," I teased.

"Doesn't every American kid have to be obsessed with a sport?"

"Soccer's big in Türkiye too, right? Futbol?"

"True," he said.

I reached back into the box and pulled out an elementary school soccer team photo, with Aydın in the front row, dressed in a blue-and-white jersey. He was adorable. It was easy to see the charmer he would grow into.

"Do we have to do this?" Aydın asked.

"I'm doing you a favor, really," I said, setting the photo down on his desk. "You've got to start unpacking sometime."

"I guess," he said. He reached into the opened box and pulled out a framed photo of him and the same girl I'd seen in the family photo in the living room.

"Who's that?" I asked.

"My sister."

"You never told me you had a sister."

"Huh. I guess it never came up."

"How old is she?"

"Twenty. She's off at college. Yale, of course."

"Of course," I said. It irked me that Aydın hadn't told me about her. "Why don't you like to talk about her?"

"I never said that."

"But you never mentioned her to me. And we talked about our families."

He sighed. "She's kind of an additional pressure. She's perfect, and she's done everything perfectly, so it's that much harder to live up to my parents' expectations, following in her footsteps."

I wanted to say that I was sure that she wasn't *actually* perfect, but I didn't. Instead, I let it go and tore off the tape of another box, this one labeled BOOKS. To my surprise, the books inside looked worn, like they'd been read over and over. "A reader," I said.

"I guess," he replied.

"I'm surprised."

"Really?"

"I'm learning a lot of secrets about you today. The cooking, the reading, the sister…"

"They're not exactly secrets," he said, looking uncomfortable.

"So why didn't you tell me?"

"You never asked."

That hit me. Had I been so focused on myself, and on what being with Aydın could mean for me, that I didn't care to get to know him? I brushed away the thought. I was falling in love. Wasn't I?

Reaching down into the box, I lifted out a stack of books. Something at the bottom of the stack fell to the ground: a bundle of handwritten letters, tied together with string. I picked them up and saw

Aydın's eyes go wide. He reached for them. I held them away. "What are these?" I asked.

"Nothing," he said.

"This is like something out of Jane Austen," I said. "Who even writes letters anymore?"

"They're from a few years ago," he said. "Really, they're nothing."

Clearly, they weren't. I knew, deep down, that I shouldn't snoop, but I needed to know what other secrets he was keeping from me.

I untied the string and opened the first letter while Aydın winced. It was written in Turkish. I could pick out a phrase here and there, but mostly it was indecipherable. A letter from a relative, I figured.

Until I saw the sign-off. *Seni seviyorum,* it said. *I love you.*

And it was signed *Chloe.*

"Chloe?" I asked. "Like, *Chloe Choi* Chloe?"

Aydın nodded. He'd taken a seat on the edge of his bed.

"Are these all from her?" I asked.

He hesitated, then nodded again. "But Ros, you have to understand—"

"I'm sorry," I said quickly. "I didn't realize—"

"It was a long time ago."

"I don't even know what it said," I said. "My Turkish isn't great."

Aydın wasn't looking at me, I noticed. I turned to see if he was looking at something behind me, but the wall was blank. When I turned back, his gaze refocused. "Well," he said, with something like his normal grin, if a little halfhearted, "this is awkward."

"I didn't know Chloe knew Turkish."

"She studied it for a while."

"For you?"

"When we were...together, yeah."

"Wow," I said. "That's cool. That's...dedication."

"We were thirteen. It doesn't...it wasn't a real relationship, you know? Like, it wasn't serious."

I shrugged, trying to look nonchalant. "Sure."

"I broke up with her," he said.

"Why?"

"What?"

"You've mentioned that before, but you never explained why."

His hands were clasped tightly in his lap. "*Because* we were kids. Because we lived in different towns and would never get to see each other. Because...I thought she deserved better." His voice broke on the last sentence.

"What are you talking about?" I asked. "You're amazing."

He shrugged. "I've come into my own since then. I told you, I had a lot of anxiety as a kid. And not a lot of self-confidence. Anyway, why continue a silly thirteen-year-old romance if you're never going to see each other?" He adjusted his seat on the bed. "So I told her that my parents were religious and that they would only let me date a good Muslim girl."

"*What?*" I was taken aback. "You didn't tell me any of this before—"

"It's not true," he said, almost laughing. "I made it up because I knew that my explanation wouldn't be enough, that she'd say that we should try and stick it out anyway."

I put a hand against my heart. "I was gonna say, if that was the case, I'm not sure I would've made the cut."

He smiled, and it felt like a little bit of the tension between us eased.

But I had more questions. "What happened back at Pine Bay? On the boat you said something about how the timing wasn't right."

"I..." He rubbed the back of his neck. "I'm not going to lie to you about this, Ros. I asked if she would consider getting back together."

"And?"

"She said no."

"But why?"

"I don't know," he said. "But isn't that proof enough that it's over? There's nothing there anymore."

Right then, his mother called down the hallway. "Aydın! Will you come here for a second, please?"

He grimaced. "Do you mind if I—"

"Not at all," I said.

Aydın stood up and left the room, with a quick glance back at me. I sat, trying to process what I'd just learned.

It wasn't serious. That's what he said. They were kids. It was three years ago.

But then why did he still have the letters? He'd kept them, put them in a box to move into his family's new home. There was intentionality here. And he'd asked her to get back together. This summer!

It was then that I realized that Aydın's phone was on the bed next to me. He probably hadn't noticed what I'd done on his Instagram, or else he would've been careful not to leave it with me again. Right?

I paused, making sure I couldn't hear his footsteps returning, then grabbed his phone, typed in his passcode, and pulled up Instagram. Chloe was still unfollowed and blocked. I let out a sigh of relief, then closed the app and set the phone back on the bed. Then I pulled out my own phone. Thirty seconds later Aydın walked in. "My mom wants us to come back down for dessert," he said.

"Dessert sounds great." I sat up.

"Are we good?"

"Yeah," I said. "Why wouldn't we be?"

Chapter Seventeen

Tuesday was the first day of school, and that morning, I dressed to kill. The way I saw it, junior year marked a new phase of life. We were almost old enough for college. Almost old enough to move out and live away from home and make big decisions about life. Naturally, it followed that the way I looked on the first day would set the tone for this whole period. I put on a power outfit: a black denim skirt and forest-green turtleneck with black, over-the-knee heeled boots. A leather jacket. And a new backpack. I even put on mascara.

I sauntered into school with a forceful, intentional confidence. The confidence of a girl who was entering junior year not only with a boyfriend, but with a boyfriend who happened to be the hot new guy—probably one of the hottest guys in the school.

This was going to be my year.

First-period AP U.S. History and second-period calculus were pretty uneventful. My third-period class was the one I was actually looking forward to: scene study. Even though I hadn't had any luck getting cast in Bardet school plays, I loved being onstage, and I missed it. The lights, the glamour, the attention…I felt like I was basically made for it. Plus, I figured that if I ever tried to make a career for myself in the film industry, it would be useful to have some perspective on the process from different sides. Know how it feels to be an actor, so that you can be a better director, or whatever.

Scene study was in the school auditorium. I strode in confidently, feeling ready to take on the world—or at least the drama nerds. Mr. Davids, the teacher, directed us to leave our backpacks in the audience and sit in a circle of chairs onstage. I chose one, smoothing my skirt, as a lacrosse team guy named Lawrence entered the back of the auditorium, shouting, "Yo, Mr. D!" Lawrence really leaned into the lacrosse thing—shoulder-length hair and everything. Good-looking and he knew it. Still, I thought, as he walked through the aisle toward the stage, not as hot as Aydın. *Aydın.* My boyfriend. My exceptionally attractive, well-mannered, homecoming-prince-material boyfriend.

The scrape of the chair next to me jolted me back into reality. I glanced up and saw a stunning dress—black, overlaid with a sheer layer of jewel-toned embroidered flowers. A white rounded collar. A little Wednesday Addams, but the ensemble wouldn't have looked out of place at NYFW.

"Hey," Lydia said, smoothing the floral skirt under her legs as she primly took her seat.

I straightened in my seat. "Hey." Of *course* she was in this class too. It was the only performing arts class the school was offering this semester, and since she was such a hotshot actress now, I should've known she would be taking it.

"How's it going?" she asked.

"Good. You?"

"Same here."

Lydia turned her attention to her phone, and we sat in silence until Mr. Davids said, "I think that's everyone. Phones away, and let's get started."

Lydia didn't so much as look at me the rest of class.

———

Fifteen minutes before lunch, I texted Eleanor. **Meet at our usual table? I miss you.** I'd been planning this since we got back from Pine Bay. I'd gotten the message that she needed space, so I'd given it to her. But it was time to reconcile. And I figured the cafeteria would be the perfect meeting ground. We'd sat at the same table in the corner by the windows for the past year and a half, and as everyone knows, high school cafeterias are rife with politics and unspoken rules. There was no way timid, polite Eleanor would try to sit somewhere else.

I felt my stomach grumble as I strode into the cafeteria, sweeping my gaze across the rows of tables. I was so hungry, I was almost looking forward to the greasy pizza slices and limp romaine lettuce salads that our cafeteria offered.

My heart sank when I saw that Eleanor wasn't at our usual spot. But then I spotted her at a different table near the windows and quickly made my way toward it.

"Eleanor!" I called, sliding around the end of the last table in the way. She looked up, a spoonful of Greek yogurt raised halfway to her mouth.

"Ros—" she began, but I stopped short. The football douches at the table right in front of them had been blocking my line of vision, but now I could see who Eleanor was sitting with. It was Chloe.

The golden girl of our school turned her gaze on me too. She smiled and gave a friendly wave. Her other friends were there too—her *usual* friends. Girls just like her, who maybe shone a little less brightly, but were happy to bask in her rays. Pretty, athletic girls with straight hair and small, stubby noses. Girls who wore fluffy velvet scrunchies around their wrists and had the same quilted backpack in different jewel tones.

"Do you want to sit with us?" Eleanor asked. She scooted over on the bench and moved her backpack to the floor. I waited for Chloe to protest, but she didn't.

Instead, Chloe said, "Join us!"

An image appeared in my mind: the letters in Aydın's room, with Chloe's perfect signature at the bottom. Her profession of love.

"I can't," I said, swiveling to look around the cafeteria. I'd been so sure that Eleanor would agree to sit with me that I hadn't even thought about texting Aydın about sitting together. In fact, I hadn't texted him all morning. The last thing I'd sent him was a message last night wishing him good luck on his first day at Bardet. "I told Ay—" But there he was, just a couple of tables over, surrounded by Ben's friends, who were spilling over each other, loud, raucous, jock-y. Aydın himself was turned away from the table, talking to...Franklin Doss.

"What were you going to say?" Chloe asked.

I realized I'd been staring at Aydın and Franklin, simultaneously bewildered and furious. "I just remembered, I told someone else we'd get lunch together today. So sorry! See you later!" I turned and made a quick escape before anyone could say anything, heading toward the cafeteria door. I didn't have to answer to my traitor of an ex–best friend who had replaced me with my archnemesis. *Okay, that's not quite fair,* I said to myself as I walked away. *But she did,* the other half of my brain protested.

I ate lunch alone in a secluded corner of the courtyard, watching videos on my phone and hoping no one would walk by. *What a stupid way to start junior year.*

I was determined not to repeat the experience the next day. At lunchtime I strode into the cafeteria and walked straight toward the table where Aydın and Ben sat with Ben's friends. I tapped Aydın's shoulder and motioned for him and Ben to stand up and come with me.

"What's going on?" Aydın asked.

"Important business," I said. "Don't question it."

"Yessir," said Ben, with a solemn nod.

I led them out into the courtyard and positioned Aydın under a large oak tree, straightening his white T-shirt and pushing a stray lock of hair off his forehead. Then I opened my phone's camera, set it to portrait mode, and handed it to Ben. I stood next to Aydın and put on my brightest smile. "Look regal," I told him.

"Aye aye, Captain."

Ben lifted my phone and began snapping photos. I immediately knew I'd put my trust in the right photographer—he switched up the camera position confidently, even getting down on one knee to get a low-angle shot. "So," he said. "I'm always happy to play photographer, but what's this about?"

"Our campaign flyers," I said, angling my body toward Aydın's and tilting my head, adjusting the way my hair spilled over my shoulder. "For homecoming court."

"Oh," said Aydın.

Ben laughed. "I'm gonna have to delete that last photo, because you do *not* want to see the look on Aydın's face right now."

I elbowed Aydın lightly in the side. "We have a real shot," I told him.

"Do we have to do this?" he asked.

"Yes," I said. "This is what I want." Then I met his gaze, trying to look sweet and pleading and adorable. "Please."

The corners of his mouth twitched upward. "Fine," he said.

"Excellent." I grabbed his arm and wrapped it around my waist, turning back to the photographer and lifting my chin in what I hoped was a gracious smile worthy of a princess.

———

On Friday I decided to get a head start on homecoming court. The dance was only five weeks away, after all. I came to school an hour early, carrying the hefty stack of flyers that I'd made the previous evening using one of the photos Ben had taken, and started taping them up in the hallways. They were minimalist, with black backgrounds and neon lettering surrounding the photo, which I'd filtered black and white, and I thought they looked good.

I wandered into the visual arts wing, with its brick walls lined with artsy student photographs and charcoal sketches. It felt different from the rest of the school—separate, a little more relaxed. I hadn't spent much time there. The department offered one film class, and it was supposed to be a ton of fun, so it was always over-registered and seniors got first pick. I couldn't wait to take it myself.

Most of the classrooms were still empty and dark, but light spilled out of one doorway. As I got closer, I heard voices.

"I think it's beautiful," a student said.

"Of course it's beautiful," said someone else. "But it's also sad."

Someone with an older voice, a teacher, said, "I think that's exactly right. But what makes it sad? Chloe, do you want to talk about the process behind your piece?"

A sign next to the door said ART CLUB. I peered around the corner into the classroom, trying my best to stay invisible. A group of students was sitting around a large art table, presided over by a young teacher with a long brown braid. In the center of the table was some sort of sculpture made of wire and translucent shapes in shades of turquoise, blue, and green. The shapes were made out of something thin, and they shivered, shimmering, anytime anyone moved.

"Um, yeah," said Chloe. She wore a puffy black coat, and there was something different about her demeanor. She wasn't her usual ray-of-sunlight self. It was like she had taken a step back, to blend in, to let others share the spotlight. "I mean, I was thinking of it sort of as a sculptural representation of sadness. Like, if sadness was a physical thing, what would it look like?"

The teacher nodded. "It's a bit Calderesque."

Chloe nodded. "He's one of my favorites."

"But it also feels like there's some real emotion here," the teacher continued. "If you don't mind sharing, did something inspire you to make this?"

"I guess…" Chloe stuck her hands in her pockets. "I don't know, I've just been going through some stuff. Nothing world ending. I'm fine." Then she brightened. "Oh, and of course, Annaliese's work-in-progress that she posted on Instagram last week. I meant to say that. It's so gorgeous. Obviously a different medium, but it was the colors in your painting that made me think about the blues and greens. They looked so perfectly and exactly like the ocean, and it made me realize that the ocean is a perfect metaphor. For what I'm trying to do."

Another girl, presumably Annaliese, smiled. "Oh, thank you so much!"

Just then, someone on the other side of the table locked eyes with me. *Shit.* I ducked out of the doorway and hurried away as fast as I could, embarrassed to have been caught eavesdropping. I slowed down once I made it to the performing arts wing. There were bulletin boards outside all the classrooms and rehearsal rooms here, for advertising upcoming shows and concerts, but also perfect for my flyers. I started pinning them up, one or two on each board.

"Rosaline?"

I was so startled that I dropped the thumbtack and flyer I was holding. Bending down to grab them, I muttered, "Hey, Lydia."

"What are you doing here?" she asked.

"Putting up posters. For my campaign. I assume you're doing the same." I gestured to the stack of flyers under her arm.

"Oh," she said, with a fake expression of surprise. "You're still running?"

I clenched my jaw to keep from saying anything and pinned up the flyer that I had dropped, then moved on to the next board.

Lydia clearly didn't know what to do with my silence, and after a moment she let out an irritated huff of breath and walked away, pinning up her own flyers farther down the hall. I slowed my pace. Once she'd rounded the corner, I grabbed each of the flyers she'd just put up and threw them in the recycling bin.

———

The doorbell rang just as I was applying a layer of shiny red lip gloss. "Rosaline!" my mom called from downstairs.

"Coming!" I shouted back.

"Should I open the door?"

"No!" I smacked my lips together, then stood up and gave myself a rushed look-over in the mirror. A white dress patterned with red cherries, matching the lip gloss. My hair was in a half up, half down style, tied with a red ribbon. I looked like a starlet in a cute movie from some other era, about to meet the love of her life at a diner while they sipped on strawberry malts.

When I got downstairs, my mom had totally ignored my instruction and had opened the door. She was leaning on the doorframe and chatting with Aydın, who stood on the doorstep, holding flowers. "Mom, don't scare him away," I said.

"Honey, you look lovely!" she said to me. Then, gesturing to him, "You both do!"

"So, what is this mystery date?" Aydın asked now.

I grinned. "Come inside and you'll find out."

"I can take those," my mom said, reaching for the flowers.

"Thank you," said Aydın, handing them over and taking off his shoes. With a smile over her shoulder, my mom flitted away into the kitchen with the flowers.

"Did she talk your ear off?" I asked.

"She's sweet," said Aydın. "And you look amazing."

I did a little curtsy. "Thank you."

"Are you going to tell me what we're dressed up for?"

"You'll find out." I held out my hand and he took it. I led him down into the basement, where our family movie nights happened—we liked to call it the Screening Room. The projector and movie screen were set up, and the couch was draped with cozy blankets. On the table in front of it were two large bowls of popcorn and about a dozen small bowls filled with every topping you could think of. M&Ms, chocolate chips, chocolate-covered raisins, crushed Oreos, pretzels. Extra flaky sea salt.

"What is this?"

"It's a popcorn bar!" I said. "Unlike you, I'm not a chef, but I *can* provide the ultimate popcorn experience and give you a walkthrough of the best eighties movies of all time."

"'The best eighties movies of all time' is sort of redundant, since they were all made in the eighties."

"Just sit down," I said. "Anything to drink? We've got an excellent slushy fruit punch. Or soda pop."

"Soda pop feels more fifties than eighties to me."

I rolled my eyes. "I wasn't really going for historical accuracy. But I'd recommend the punch. It's ICEE-inspired, and I think I did a damn good job."

"Alright, alright," he said. "One punch please."

I brought two slushy fruit punches down from the kitchen, then turned off the lights and settled myself next to Aydın. "We're starting with the ultimate classic, *The Breakfast Club*."

"You know, I think I've seen this. When I was younger."

"That doesn't count."

"Why not?"

"You've got to be old enough to *appreciate* its craft."

"Well then, if you're the expert…"

"I am," I said, dumping dark chocolate chips into my bowl of popcorn, followed by a pile of salty pretzels. Aydın leaned forward and added toppings to his as well. Then we settled back, bowls of deliciousness in our laps, to enjoy the movie. I rested my head on his shoulder, feeling satisfied. It was a perfect date.

But perfect, of course, never lasts forever.

Chapter Eighteen

In class Mr. Davids assigned partners for our scenes. "I don't want any complaining, now," he said. "Don't come crying to me after class because you didn't get paired with your best friend."

I knew what was coming even before he said it.

"Rosaline and Lydia," Mr. Davids announced, handing us each a packet of photocopied pages. I sighed.

We were learning an acting technique called Practical Aesthetics. It involved a specific four-step analysis process: breaking down a scene into the "literal," the "want," the "essential action," and the "as if." When Mr. Davids finished assigning scenes, he told us to read through them and start on our Practical Aesthetics analyses. I curled up in one of the red auditorium seats with my script and a pencil in hand.

The first step in the technique is to come up with the "literal," a description of what's *literally* happening to your character in your scene. Lydia and I were going to play a pair of twin sisters who had had a falling-out. Our parents had died in a car crash when we were eighteen, and while Lydia's character had gone away to college on the other side of the country and gotten married, my character had stayed behind to take care of our younger brother. Now our brother was going off to college himself, and Lydia's character had come back to help him pack and to drive him to school. It was the first time our characters had spoken in years. (How fitting.)

The second step is the "want": What does your character want from the other character in the scene? I decided that my character wanted Lydia's character to admit that she'd been selfish, and that it had been generous of my character to sacrifice so much of my life to take care of our brother.

The third step is the "essential action": a sort of universal want that sums up the character's general goal for the scene. Mr. Davids gave us a list of sample essential actions: "to get someone in my corner," "to lay down the law," "to get a confession," etc. I figured my character's essential action was "to make someone feel guilty."

The final step in the analysis is using the essential action to come up with an "as if": a scenario that could theoretically happen in your own life, in which you would have the same essential action as your character. This is the trickiest part. You don't want your "as if" scenario to be too close to what happens in your scene, and you also don't want it to be something that you've actually done. Mr. Davids emphasized that it should be *hypothetical*.

I got stuck on my "as if." I needed to come up with a hypothetical situation in which I'd be trying to make someone feel guilty, but every situation I envisioned was too close to reality. The problem, I decided, was that there were too many people around me who ought to feel guilty for one reason or another.

"Remember," said Mr. Davids, interrupting my train of thought, "when coming up with your 'as if,' you don't have to tell your scene partner or anyone else what it is. As long as you can act it out, it can be as private as you want."

I wrote, *As if I were making Eleanor feel guilty for abandoning me for Chloe this summer.* It was close to reality, sure, but I figured Eleanor and I were past that now. We were back in school, and their little summer BFF-ship would be over soon enough. Chloe had plenty of other friends to hang out with.

Then I changed my mind. If I was going to get so close to reality, I might as well pick one that would really hit home. I crossed out the sentence I'd written and replaced it with *As if I were making Lydia feel guilty for trying to take my spot at homecoming court.*

I glanced over at Lydia, who was glaring at her notebook with focused intensity. I wondered what her "as if" was, and if it happened to have anything to do with me. I had a feeling it might.

———

That Friday Aydın and I went into town after school and got frozen yogurt at the Silver Scoop, heaping our cups with chocolate syrup and Reese's pieces.

By the time we reached the checkout, both of our cups were spilling over. We sat on the bench in front of the store to eat, wiping drips from the sides of the cups with paper napkins.

"How are your parents doing?" I asked.

"They're good," said Aydın. "I think they really like you."

I gave him a skeptical look. "Really?"

"Why wouldn't they?"

I shrugged and focused on scooping a melting glob of frozen

yogurt before it dripped onto me. "I felt kind of self-conscious around them."

"Why?"

"I guess it just made me realize how not-Turkish I am." My next spoonful was more toppings than froyo. Ideal, honestly.

He laughed, once, then got quiet, like he wasn't sure how serious I was.

I continued, "Like, I don't think I've ever thought of myself as particularly Turkish, but it's also part of my identity. I've spent so much time running away from it, trying to distance myself from it, but I guess I think it's inescapable, because people always ask me where I'm from anyway. You can't really hide something that's written on your facial features."

"You don't look *that* Turkish."

"But I don't look *that* white either. Or like, *white* white. You know. European white."

"*Technically,* we're both white."

"Yeah, but…" I rested my froyo cup in my lap.

"I know," Aydın said. "I know."

"I know you do." The breeze was soft and cool against my face. I closed my eyes. "I appreciate that about you."

We sat in silence for a moment.

"How much time have you spent in Türkiye?" Aydın asked.

"A lot. My babaanne lives there, and so do my cousins."

"How many?"

"Three. But one is a baby."

"All in Istanbul? I remember you mentioning your dad's family is there."

I nodded. "We went there, like, every summer when I was a kid."

"I didn't know." He paused. "You never talk about it."

"Did you go often as a kid?" I asked.

"Still do. Every summer for at least a month."

"You must speak pretty good Turkish."

"Yeah, I'm not bad. Why did you stop going?"

"Less time, I guess? I started going to summer camps instead?"

"Does your dad still go?" Aydın asked.

"Once in a while. Maybe he stopped missing it so much."

"Huh." Aydın swirled his spoon around, mixing the chocolate syrup into the froyo. "I don't think my parents will ever stop missing it. I don't think *I'll* ever stop missing it."

That made me curious. "What do you miss?"

"Everything. My family, of course, but also the food. Simit, döner…"

I nodded. "Pide."

"Lokma."

Just the mention of the syrup-soaked fried dough made my mouth water. "That stuff is dangerous."

He laughed. "Also Istanbul itself. All the historic sights, the Kapalıçarşı—"

"The Grand Bazaar? Really? You're such a tourist!"

"I guess I have to be, sort of, since I grew up here and not there. Don't you think? Although," he said thoughtfully, "my mom loves that stuff too."

"What about the cats?" I asked.

"What about them?"

"I loved the cats as a kid. Just…hanging out everywhere. They're so cute."

"They're strays," Aydın said.

"But they're sweet!"

He laughed. Then his phone buzzed, and he checked it before setting it down on the bench beside him.

I hadn't thought about Istanbul in a while, and I was surprised by how easily the memories came back. The heat, the mosques, the fruit vendors on every corner. The call to prayer, resounding through the city over grainy loudspeakers. It felt good, recovering these details with someone who maybe sort of understood my complicated relationship to it, at least a little bit.

"Oh shit," said Aydın, looking down. Froyo had dripped onto his pants and stained the knee.

"Oof," I said. "Want me to run in and grab some napkins?"

He shook his head. "There's a restroom inside, right?"

I nodded. Aydın set his cup on the bench and went into the Silver Scoop. I couldn't help but notice that his phone was on the bench too, just inches from my leg.

I told myself I wasn't going to snoop again. I trusted him. Right? That was what couples were supposed to do.

But then his phone buzzed. I swiped on the notification and entered his passcode.

It opened to a conversation with his friend Jorge. A childhood friend, someone who had moved to a different state in elementary school. Aydın had said they were still close.

At the top of the screen, Aydın had sent three texts in a row:

I'm pretty sure I'm in love with her.

It sounds sappy, I know.

But I can't stop thinking about her.

My heart skipped a beat. We hadn't even come close to saying "love" out loud in this relationship.

But I thought back to night swimming in the lake at Pine Bay, under the stars. I thought back to our sailing accident, and the night in the infirmary, and a shiver passed through me. Maybe *love* wasn't a word that I was ready to say, but if I was honest with myself, it was a word that I had thought. Aydın was beautiful, yes, and he was also sweet and funny and probably the smartest guy I knew. He was much more than just a means to an end, a tool to get onto homecoming court.

I looked down at the rest of the text conversation. Jorge had replied: **Do you know if she feels the same way?**

Aydın had written: **I don't think she does. She won't even look at me.**

My eyebrows came together. What did he mean, I wouldn't even look at him?

The most recent text was from Jorge. **Dude, you have to tell her.**

It only took a split second for the world to come crashing down around me.

It wasn't me Aydın was talking about in his texts.

It was Chloe.

Chapter Nineteen

To my credit, I did an excellent job of wrapping up the date, acting like nothing was wrong. Aydın smiled his perfect smile at me, and I had to fight not to glare at him. *Charming bastard.* You'd never have known what was really going on in his head.

Except that I should have. The clues were there. The expression he'd had every time Chloe was mentioned at Pine Bay. The way he talked about her when we were sailing. And, of course, the fact that he'd kept her love letters.

But it hadn't fit with my plan. So I'd blocked it all out.

That night I sat in bed and weighed my options.

1) I could break up with Aydın right then and there. I probably shouldn't tell him that I'd been going through his phone, but I could come up with some sort of excuse.

2) I could let things be. Pretend nothing was wrong. That seemed to be what Aydın was doing, anyway. That liar. Who else had he told? Who else knew that our relationship was a sham?

The problem with the first option was that I wouldn't get on homecoming court. To win, you had to be one half of a serious couple. Everyone knew that. People want to vote for a pair, not just the individuals. And what's cuter than two people in love dancing in crowns, staring dreamily into each other's eyes?

Aydın was still an essential part of my plan.

He was beautiful, with that smile and those eyes and that perfect skin—more beautiful than any high school boy should be allowed to be. And he was romantic, and smart, and thoughtful. He stood out like a sore thumb from the crowd of immature jerks at our school.

Maybe he had thought he could love me, when we were out on that boat in that storm, or when he snuck into my room at the infirmary. Maybe he had thought, like I did, that if we held each other tight enough we could become something beautiful, something unshakeable.

But the truth of it was that he was already in love. I had wanted to believe it was history. But it wasn't. And he and I both knew that.

Options one and two. My pride versus my pride. Was I willing to date a boy who was in love with someone else, just so I could prove myself (and spite my ex–best friend) by winning homecoming princess? Or was I going to end the relationship and admit defeat?

I didn't know if I could give him up after going through so much to get him in the first place. I'd already lost Eleanor, at least for now. If I gave Aydın up, I realized, I'd be more alone than ever.

If I'd been smart, I would have let him go. It would have saved us all a whole lot of trouble. But I wasn't, and I didn't.

———

At our next scene study class, Mr. Davids explained how we would apply the Practical Aesthetics technique to our scenes.

He called up a pair of volunteers to demonstrate. Once they were standing onstage facing each other, and he instructed them to start acting out their "as if" scenarios by taking turns saying one sentence that would be a part of their hypothetical conversations. Of course, since each of them had a different "as if," and neither knew what each other's was, they were talking at each other instead of to each other. One of them seemed to be begging a parent to let him buy a dog, while the other was trying to negotiate a better grade on a test. It was pretty fun to watch. Some of the more absurd back-and-forths sparked laughter from the class.

In the middle of the exercise, Mr. Davids shouted, "Now switch to your scene!"

They switched from their one-sided conversations into their characters' lines, but kept the same tone and attitude that they'd had for their "as ifs." And there was something magical about it. I hadn't thought it would work, but they were super convincing. I exchanged an impressed glance with the classmate sitting beside me.

"Alright," said Mr. Davids, "now I want everyone to get into their pairs."

Lydia and I found our way to an empty spot on the stage and stood across from each other. We avoided looking at each other.

"As if," Mr. Davids said, and the room broke into a cacophony of voices.

I took a deep breath and imagined what I would say to Lydia if I were to confront her head-on about homecoming court. "Do you realize how it makes me feel? How much this means to me?" I asked, looking Lydia straight in the eyes. Her stare back at me was cold.

"Look, the evidence is right there," she said.

"This is everything to me!" I said.

"You just need to be rational."

"I've been planning for years!" I said. "I can't believe you'd do this to me!" My heart was already racing, and my hands balled up into fists.

Lydia's voice was calm and her eyes were steely. "There's no need to get so worked up about it."

Mr. Davids's voice cut through the noise. "Switch to your scenes!"

Lydia had the first line. "Cecily," she said, in that same cold voice. "You look tired."

My breathing was heavy. "That's because I am," I replied, and the line came out more angrily than I had rehearsed it.

"Can I make you a coffee?"

"That's my coffee," I said. "In *my* kitchen." I was in character, without having to try. My lines were coming out differently than I'd imagined, and somehow it *worked*.

"Great," Mr. Davids said. "Everyone, pause your scenes here!" Across the stage, pairs froze and turned to look at him, some still half-caught in their expressions of rage, confusion, despair, joy. "How did that feel?" Mr. Davids asked.

Lydia raised her hand.

"Yes, Lydia?" Mr. Davids asked.

"It felt amazing," she said.

Aydın and I were supposed to go shopping for homecoming outfits the next day after school. Really just for my dress, but I figured Aydın might have some useful input. He had some style, at least. And he had a car, which was important, since I didn't have my license yet.

As I hurried to the front of the school, my phone buzzed twice and I pulled it out of my pocket. There were two texts from Aydın.

The first: **Hey, I'm so sorry to do this, but I think I have to cancel today. Are you gonna be okay to shop without me?**

And the second: **I have stuff to wear anyway.**

I typed, **No, I can't shop without you, because I don't have a car, you asshole.** Then I took a deep breath and hit backspace. Instead, I wrote, **Why so busy haha.**

He called me. I picked up immediately.

"Hey," he said.

"Hey. What's going on?"

"I'm sorry to cancel."

"It's fine," I said, trying to keep my tone light. Ever since I'd discovered those texts on his phone, it had been hard not to take everything he did as an insult, as proof that he didn't actually care about me—at least not in the way I wanted him to. But I had gone with option two. I was trying to keep us together, at least through homecoming, so I had to pretend nothing was wrong.

"You do know that homecoming isn't for another three weeks, right? We can go another day," he said.

"Three weeks is soon! I want to be prepared. What if I wait until the last minute, and then I can't find anything I like?"

I thought I heard him sigh.

"What came up that made you have to cancel anyway?" I asked.

"Ben and his friends are playing basketball this afternoon, and they invited me to join," Aydın said. When I didn't reply, he continued, "I know we had plans, but I *am* the new guy here and I need to make friends."

"I'm your friend," I said. "And so is Ben."

"Of course!" he said. "But you get it, right? I don't want you guys to be my only two friends at Bardet."

My mind immediately jumped to wondering whether he was planning to break up with me. Why else would he need to make sure he had other friends? But I pushed that thought down. "Totally," I said. "Have fun."

"Thanks for understanding," Aydın said. "I really appreciate it."

I hung up and called my mom.

"Rosaline! What's up?"

"Hey, Mom." I picked at a loose thread on the edge of my denim skirt. "Can you give me a ride home from school?"

A pause. "Weren't you going to go shopping with Aydın?"

"Yeah. He canceled."

Another pause. "I'm sorry, sweetie."

"It's fine," I said quickly.

"Why don't we go shopping together? You need a dress, right?"

"Aren't you busy?"

"I can make time for some mother-daughter bonding. If you're up for it."

"Uh, sure," I said. "I mean, yeah. Please. Thank you."

I could hear her smiling as she said, "I'll be right there."

"I know things are a little rough between you and Eleanor at the moment, so have you been hanging out with Lydia at all?" my mom asked, pulling a sequined silver dress off the rack. "How about this one?"

"I would look like a disco ball."

"Disco balls are hip."

"The fact that you just said 'hip' means that you have no right to tell me what to wear." I took the hanger from her hand and put it back on the rack.

"Hold on, I might want to try that one on." She took it back with a grin.

"We had that fight," I said.

"What fight?"

"Me and Lydia."

"You haven't gotten over that yet?"

I tried to sound calm. "*I* have." As I said it, I knew that it wasn't quite true. But I wasn't about to say that out loud. "She's the one who's still stuck on it. I think it's about time we stopped fighting over something that happened when we were kids."

"Oh, you're still kids, honey," she murmured.

"Excuse you."

"Once you're a real adult, maybe you'll understand just how cool this silver dress is."

I rolled my eyes and kept walking down the rack, pausing to feel a few fabrics.

"Well, I'm sorry that you and Lydia haven't made up yet," said my mom. "You two used to be attached at the hip."

"I'm not sorry," I muttered. "She's the worst."

My mom made an *mm* sound and kept moving along the rack.

"Slip dresses are really in," I said, pulling out a satiny black slip for her to see.

"That's lingerie."

"It's not. It's fashionable. People wear them with T-shirts underneath."

"Are you planning on wearing that with a T-shirt underneath?"

"Well, no, but—"

"Let's maybe try something that looks a little less like it belongs in the bedroom. Do you really want Mrs. Kimpel seeing you in that?"

She had a point. Mrs. Kimpel, the French teacher and perpetual school dance chaperone, connoisseur of granny sweaters and opaque stockings, would probably have a heart attack.

I put the slip back on the rack and kept moving.

"Are you…" She paused, examining a dress that I knew she would find horrifically ugly if she was actually looking at it and not distracted by whatever it was that she wanted to say.

"What?"

She smiled at me, apologetically. "Are you having fun? In school? Are you happy?"

"Yeah," I said. Instinctively, I glanced around to make sure no one I knew was nearby to hear my mom being embarrassing. "Why wouldn't I be?"

She shrugged. "I just know you had a fun summer and sometimes coming back to the real world can be a bummer."

"I'm doing well in school, I have a great boyfriend—"

"I was just asking!" she said. "How is Aydın? He seems like such a sweetheart."

For a moment I thought about telling her all of it. It would be nice to confide in somebody, to not have to bottle it up. But I knew what my mom would say. She would tell me to let it go. That Aydın and I weren't going to work out if he was hung up on someone else. And I didn't want to hear that. "He's great," I said. "He's absolutely perfect, actually."

"From what I've heard, he seems head-over-heels for you. As your father would say, I wonder if he's your Majnun."

"My what?"

She waved a hand, dismissing it. "It's a joke. About Layla and Majnun?"

"Never heard of them."

She held a hand to her heart as if in shock. "You've never heard the story of Layla and Majnun?"

"What kind of a name is Majnun?"

"It means 'crazy' in Arabic. You should read the poem about them, because you'll get much more out of it than my summary."

"It's a love story, I'm guessing."

My mom nodded. "In the story, a man falls in love with a girl named Layla. He writes love poems for her, and he's so wildly in love that people start calling him 'Majnun.' He wants to marry her, but her father refuses to let him, and instead her father marries Layla off to another man. Majnun is so devastated that he wanders into the desert and essentially disappears. And Layla dies of heartbreak."

"Well, that's a terrible love story."

She smiled. "Your father used to call me his Layla."

"Gross."

As we looked through more dresses, I thought about how things can look so different from the outside. Aydın was *not* Majnun. At least not mine. But I must have been doing a good job of keeping up the image of our perfect relationship if I'd convinced my mom that he might be. Hopefully everyone at school saw me and Aydın the same way she did.

She pulled another dress off the rack to show me. "How's this?"

It was a deep, silky red—the material was like the slip dress I'd shown her before, but instead of spaghetti straps, this one was off-the-shoulder—and the dress was cinched around the waist with a red band. I knew immediately that it was perfect.

"Yes," I said. "Oh my god, yes."

My mom smiled. "Go try it on."

The next morning I convinced my dad to drive me to school early, and I arrived with a folding table, posters, flyers, and the crown jewel: six boxes of doughnuts with vanilla frosting and neon-colored sprinkles, which I'd ordered to match the color scheme of my campaign materials. It's all about the details.

I set up the table just inside the front door of the school, taped the posters up on the wall behind me, and opened a box of doughnuts.

Aydın hadn't arrived yet, and I was struck with a wave of anxiety. Sitting here alone, waiting to ply my classmates with doughnuts in exchange for the promise of their votes, I felt vulnerable in a way that I hadn't expected to. I was really doing this, I realized. I was putting myself out there, presenting myself and my relationship for the scrutiny of the entire school. The last time I'd gotten attention from the entirety of my peers was in the aftermath of the Franklin incident, and, well, look how that had gone.

I closed my eyes and took a deep breath, picturing Hailee Benson wearing the homecoming princess tiara. It was all going to be worth it, I reminded myself. This was my chance to undo the damage that Franklin's rumor had caused.

I heard hurried footsteps and opened my eyes. Aydın appeared, looking more disheveled than usual. "You texted that I had to be here early? What's up?"

I spread my hands, presenting our campaign station. "It's time to get serious," I said.

"Oh." He looked at the posters, then at the table, with its stack of flyers and box of doughnuts. "Do I get a doughnut?"

"No," I said. "These are for our voters."

Aydın pouted. "I haven't had breakfast yet. You made this sound urgent."

"It is."

He came around the table to stand next to me, under the black-and-white images of our smiling faces. He dropped his backpack to the floor.

The front door swung open, and a few students trickled in. I put on my brightest smile and leaned forward. "Hi!" I said. "Vote Ros and Aydın for homecoming princess and prince! Would you like a doughnut?"

The word *doughnut* was the key. As I'd expected. More students shuffled in, and they joined the mass around our table. I made conversation, handing out flyers and opening each new box of doughnuts as the previous one was emptied. Aydın stepped up as well, swapping his pout for his usual winsome smile.

In the lull between when the early crowd went to the cafeteria for breakfast and when the school buses arrived, I turned to Aydın. "Don't you want to ask me how dress shopping went?"

He was eyeing the remaining two doughnuts in the open box. "How did dress shopping go?"

"It went great. I have my dress."

"Awesome."

"You're supposed to ask me what color it is so you can match your pocket square."

He stared at me. "I'm not wearing a pocket square."

"Why not?"

"Ros, this is homecoming, not prom. I wasn't even planning on wearing a jacket."

"What the hell were you going to wear?"

"Khakis and a nice shirt."

"Seriously?"

"What's wrong with that?" he asked.

"There's nothing special about that for you."

"It's *homecoming*," he said.

"*Yes*," I replied icily, "and you're going to be *homecoming prince*."

"Do you really care about this?"

"Ugh." I leaned back against the wall and stared at the ceiling. "You're going to single-handedly destroy our chances of winning with your indifference."

"I just don't get why you want it so much," Aydın said.

"What do you mean, 'why'? There's no 'why' about it."

"I'm not sure I follow."

"It's just, like, duh. Of course I want to be on homecoming court. Who wouldn't?" I said.

"Plenty of people?"

I rolled my eyes. "Maybe because you're a guy. All the girls I know would *die* to be homecoming princess."

"Even Eleanor?"

"Especially Eleanor."

"How is she, anyway? I haven't seen her much."

"She's fine." I tried to think of something more to say, but the truth was, I'd barely seen her since we'd gotten back to school, let alone had a real conversation with her. "Been pretty busy."

"Gotcha."

"Have you written your acceptance speech yet?"

He stared. "Have you lost your mind, Ros?"

"What? Acceptance speeches are an essential part of any awards ceremony."

"Have you been watching Oscars clips or something?"

"...Yes."

"Seriously?"

"If I'm going to win an Oscar for directing one day, I want to be prepared."

He looked startled. "Did I just hear the great, indifferent Rosaline Demir suggest that she actually *does* know what she wants to do with her life?"

"Oh, come on, you knew this."

"I don't think I've ever heard you say it that definitively."

"I didn't say anything definitively."

"You want to make movies! That's awesome!"

"I didn't say that." I felt protective of my weird little dream, which I wasn't even sure was my dream.

"Ros, come on, own it. It's great that you have something you love." The front door swung open and we both straightened up, switching back into campaign mode, to offer doughnuts and flyers to these students. I went to grab the next box, but they were all empty. The students who hadn't gotten doughnuts walked away, disappointed.

Aydın turned to me again. "I'm just saying *maybe* instead of pretending you don't care about anything except things like homecoming court, you should embrace the things you like."

"I *care* about homecoming court," I said.

"I still don't understand why."

"Jeff and Lydia are running."

"So what? Jeff and Lydia are Jeff and Lydia. We're Aydın and Rosaline."

"You don't get it," I said.

"Yeah, that's what I said."

"Ugh. It just—" I cut myself off. Everything I could've said to explain it sounded stupid. Was I supposed to tell him that I'd hung all my hopes and dreams of salvaging my social standing on winning homecoming princess, based on some other girl's experience almost two years ago?

But I knew it wasn't just about that. It was also about proving that I *could* win. I was always coming in second place. I was good at school, but not as good as Eleanor. I was a decent actor, but Lydia ended up with the roles I wanted. And then, of course, there was Chloe. I wasn't even thinking about the Aydın situation. I was thinking about her as the middle school loner, stuck with one foot in each culture, just like me. I'd thought that out of the two of us, I was the one who would end up figuring it out. And somehow, despite everything, she'd ended up *more* everything than me. Prettier, more popular, more creative. More Korean than I was Turkish.

Instead of explaining any of this, I changed the subject. "Do you have any ideas for getting more people to vote for us? Like, what if we hired an ice cream truck?"

"We are not hiring an ice cream truck." Aydın's phone buzzed and he pulled it out of his pocket. "Oh god," he said in response to something on the screen, and he grabbed his backpack. "Sorry, Ros, I've got to go."

"But we're not done!"

He gestured to the empty boxes. "We're out of doughnuts."

"So? We still have flyers!"

"Look, Ben needs a friend right now. Can you hand out flyers on your own?"

"Is Ben more important than me?"

Aydın frowned and tilted his head. "Right now, yeah, he is. Because he needs me. And I know for a fact that you can handle this on your own." He leaned in and gave me a quick kiss on the cheek before jogging away.

Chapter Twenty

Whatever had happened with Ben, he'd apparently recovered enough by the weekend to throw a rager while his parents were away. Predictably, the Whittingtons' house was straight out of the pages of *Architectural Digest*. Huge and white, with a roundabout driveway encircling a fountain—a goddamn fountain! Inside, kids from our grade and the grade above us were lounging on white sectionals and loitering around the marble-topped island in the open-concept kitchen-slash-dining-room-slash-living-room.

"Welcome!" Ben appeared beside me and Aydın, wearing a wide smile and a navy shirt buttoned only halfway up his chest. He handed Aydın a Bud Light and jangled a set of keys. "Shotgun?"

"Maybe later," said Aydın. "I need to be a little less sober for that."

Ben shrugged. "Ros, can I get you anything to drink?"

"Seltzer?"

"You got it." He disappeared into a massive refrigerator.

"This place is insane," I said to Aydın.

"Welcome to the world of the Whittingtons."

A can slid neatly into my hand. "Here you go," said Ben.

"Thanks!" I said.

Ben put an arm around my shoulders. "Ros, I need to ask you something. It might be weird—"

"Ben! Get out on the porch *right now!*" someone shouted.

"Damnit. I hope no one's fucking with the grill again." He craned his neck over the crowd. "I'll be back for you," he said to me, and darted away.

"What was that about?" I asked.

"No idea," Aydın replied. He turned away from me, surveying the party. *Looking for Chloe, probably.*

That was when I spotted the beer pong table. "Let's go play!"

"Pong?" Aydın said.

"Yeah!"

"I hate that game."

"Why?"

He shrugged.

"You're in a mood," I said.

"I'm not in a mood. I just don't like beer pong."

"Fine," I said. "I'll go play by myself." And I stalked over to the table. A game was just wrapping up. "Who's playing winner?" I asked.

"All yours," said some blond guy in a Hawaiian shirt.

"Need a partner?" someone asked. I turned and found Jeff standing behind me, holding a red Solo cup.

"Sure," I said. *Why not?*

Together, we set up the next round. He seemed clumsy, like maybe he'd had one too many.

"Where's Lydia?" I asked, pouring beer into the cups.

"Not here," he said. His breath stank. "Boring."

"True," I agreed. "She is boring."

The other team shot first and made one cup. Jeff shot and missed by about a mile. I shot and hit one of the cups toward the front. Jeff gave me a high five.

The next round, he missed again. I hit another cup. "Heating up," I said.

"How did you get so good at this?" he asked.

I shrugged and glanced around, searching for Aydın. Instead, I spotted Chloe walking in through the front door, arm in arm with Eleanor and trailed by her horde of copycat friends. Chloe was laughing at something that Eleanor said.

And there, of course, was Aydın, leaning against a wall with his hands stuck in his pockets, watching Chloe. I couldn't see his expression, but I could imagine it.

I wanted to shake him. *Look at how happy she is without you,* I wanted to say. *She's moved on. Didn't she tell you she didn't want to get back together? When will you move on too?*

Eventually, Jeff and I lost the game (but it was close!), and I left to find Aydın. "Hey," I said. "Are you okay?"

He hesitated, then nodded slightly. "Yeah, I don't know," he said. "I'm just feeling down today."

"Anything I can do to help?" I asked quietly. His gaze met mine, and there was something subdued about it. It was hard to see him like this. Even if I had a feeling that I knew why.

Someone grabbed my shoulders. "There you are!"

Ben looked more disheveled than the last time I'd seen him.

"Hello, you," I said. "You were mysterious earlier."

"I know, I know." He glanced around. "Can we go outside?"

I looked to Aydın, who said, "Go ahead."

Ben grabbed my hand and pulled me through the crowd out onto the patio. My heart was in my throat. This seemed serious. Something about Aydın? About Eleanor? It was crowded out there too, so Ben led me through a gate and down a set of stor steps set into a hillside, toward a bench by the edge of a glassy, dark pond. There was a lantern on the ground next to the bench, illuminating us in yellow-orange light. It was quieter out here—the voices and music of the party became a dull wash of background noise. The air smelled like freshly cut grass, with a faint marshy scent hiding beneath it.

"Ros—" he began.

"What is it?" My heart was beating out of my chest. A hundred possibilities for what he was about to say ran through my mind, none of them good.

"Can I trust you not to tell anyone?"

"Of course." *Get to it.*

He was twisting his watch on his wrist. "I've been texting this guy."

This was not one of the scenarios I'd had in mind. "Like, *texting* texting?"

"Yeah. And he's so funny and sweet and cute and I think I like him a lot."

"That's great!"

"Yeah." Ben paused. "It's still early, which is why I don't want to make it public. But I think I want to ask him to be my boyfriend."

"Ben, this is great news! He sounds amazing. Do I know him?"

"Yeah, that's the thing."

A pause. A frog croaked on the other side of the pond. "What?"

"You've sort of…had a…thing with him. And I don't want to do anything without your permission."

"Who?"

He grimaced. "Cameron."

I couldn't help myself. I started laughing. "I'm so sorry," I said, "I just…that's great! Cameron is so sweet!"

"You're not mad?"

"I thought for a second that you were going to say Aydın, and *then* we might've had a problem."

He started laughing too.

"You have my blessing," I said. "My blessing times a bajillion. I did sort of a shitty thing to him."

"Yeah?" Ben said, curious. "I have no idea what went down between you two. He won't tell me anything."

Cameron was an angel who was too good for this world. "He… may have told me that he had a crush on you. And then I kissed him." Ben's eyes went wide. "Don't tell him I told you!" I said.

"But why did you…?" Ben asked.

"I was trying to make Aydın jealous?" I said, cringing.

Ben raised his eyebrows, then shook his head. "Yikes."

"I was shitty. That's all there is to it." Another thought occurred to me. "When are you going to get to see him? Doesn't he live, like, hours away?"

"That's the wild part," said Ben. "He lives, like, thirty minutes away. Just works summers at Pine Bay."

"That's lucky."

"I was thinking about inviting him to homecoming, actually," he said.

"You should!"

"It would be a big step. I mean, it would make the whole thing so official. But ugh, I like him so much!"

I laughed and grabbed his hand. "You have my support all the way. Anything I can do."

Ben smiled. "You're a good friend."

His words momentarily knocked the breath from my lungs. I hadn't realized how important it was to me to hear that, and how long it had been since I had. I looked at the fully dark surface of the pond—there was no moon in sight—so he wouldn't see as I blinked to clear the moisture from my eyes. "Thank you," I said.

—————

Aydın and I had planned to spend the night at Ben's house, so Aydın wouldn't have to drive us home. I'd told my parents that I was sleeping over at Eleanor's, and luckily they were so happy to hear that we were hanging out again, and they thought so highly of her (straight-laced, straight-A student that she was) that they didn't feel the need to confirm this with her parents. Ben had said we could use one of the guest rooms, and despite everything, I was excited about the prospect of sharing a bed with my boyfriend for the night. Not that I thought anything was going to happen—I didn't think I wanted it to. We hadn't gone any further than that night in the infirmary, and that was fine with me.

But when the party cleared out, I found Aydın soundly asleep on a sofa in an upstairs office. I thought about trying to snuggle in with him, but the sofa was small and didn't look comfortable. So I made my way to our room, fell onto the bed, and promptly fell asleep, exhausted and alone.

Chapter Twenty-One

I missed Eleanor. Freshman and sophomore years, we'd go over to one of our houses and do homework and we'd watch ridiculous reality TV shows until dinnertime. Now, trying to replicate those afternoons on my own, I kept finding my hand drifting to my phone before opening Instagram and checking Eleanor's and Chloe's stories to see if they were hanging out. I thought about texting her, but I was too proud. *She* was the one who was being childish, wasn't she?

So the weeks flew by in a blur of classes and tests and family movie nights and dates with Aydın, and before I knew it, it was Spirit Week.

The theme days were pretty much the same every year: Sports Day, Pajama Day, etc. Personally, I was looking forward to my favorite, which fell on Thursday: Character Day, when you were supposed to dress up as your favorite book or movie character. I loved it because it was silly, and there was so much more room for creativity than in the other categories. *And* I loved it because every year, there was a school-wide trivia tournament in the gym. It was chaotic and intense, with the questions projected onto huge screens and the competitors screaming their answers. Most of the categories were about books and films—to fit the theme of the day.

Eleanor and I had competed in the trivia contest together twice now. Freshman year, we were still getting to know each other, but based on our AP Bio quiz competition domination, I had the feeling that we would crush it. That year we'd gotten eliminated in the quarterfinals, because we were up against the team of seniors (all Ivy League–bound) that ultimately won, but last year we'd made it to the final round and placed second. Between my film knowledge and Eleanor's love of books, we made a rock-solid team. This was going to be our year.

I texted Eleanor on Wednesday night: **You ready to crush it tomorrow?**

By lunch the next day, Eleanor still hadn't replied. As I walked to the cafeteria, dressed as Veronica from *Heathers* with a stack of home-coming campaign flyers in hand, I texted her a third time. **Hello??** I slid my phone into the pocket of my blue blazer and approached the nearest table, which was filled with kids with earbuds in, studying.

"Hey, guys!" I said cheerfully, sliding a flyer onto the table.

Four of the five people at the table looked up; the fifth had his eyes closed and was nodding along to whatever music he was listening to. One of the others, a girl who I vaguely recognized but whose name I didn't know, with glasses and dark hair in long braids, slipped off her chunky black headphones so they hung around her neck. "Hey," she said. "Rosaline. What's up?"

I leaned over the table. "I just wanted to let you all know that Aydın and I are running for homecoming prince and princess. Can I count on your votes?"

I was met with blank stares. One guy shrugged and said, "Sure."

The girl with the braids said, "I'm probably not going to homecoming."

"Why not?" I asked.

She shrugged. "Not really my thing, I guess." Then she added, "But if I do go, I'll vote for you."

I gave her a thumbs-up and a smile and walked away, silently cringing. I needed to be more targeted with my campaigning. I looked around and spotted a table with a group dressed like *Mean Girls* characters. I approached and slid a flyer into the center of the table. The girls paused their conversation and looked up at me.

"Rosaline!" said a girl named Giselle, who was dressed as Regina George. "What's up?"

I smiled and tapped the flyer. "Aydın Muhtar and I are running for homecoming court tomorrow."

"You and Aydın are like, couple goals," said a girl named Annabel.

Giselle nodded. "You two are so cute."

"Like, the most gorgeous couple ever," said Annabel.

"That's sweet," I said. "So, can we count on your votes?"

"Of course!" said Giselle.

Another girl said, "I mean, if Aydın wasn't *born* to be homecoming prince, I don't know who was."

Feeling a bit giddy, I said, "Thank you all so much! See you there tomorrow!" and blew the table a kiss, which Giselle returned.

I was walking on air. For the first time, my dream felt fully within reach. I floated through the next cluster of tables, dropping flyers in front of students who were busy on their laptops. Barely looking down, I placed one in front of a blond kid who seemed to be absorbed in a book he was reading. Until he looked up.

"Ros?" asked the Worst Person on Earth.

Ugh.

I turned to leave, but Franklin had already picked up the flyer. "What's this?"

"Aydın and I are running for homecoming court," I said.

He furrowed his brow. "Huh."

"What?"

"I'm just surprised."

"Why—" I started to ask, and then realized that I knew why. "You know what, of course you are. I know what you're going to say. That I'm not the 'typical' homecoming princess or whatever. Well, you know what? I don't give a shit what you think."

"That's not—"

"Can we just agree that we saw enough of each other this summer and that we never need to speak again?"

For once, he seemed to be at a loss for words. Then he said, "All I was going to say was that campaigning for homecoming court doesn't seem like the Rosaline I know."

"That's because you don't know me, asshole," I said, and stomped away before he could continue the conversation.

A moment later my phone buzzed with a text. It was from Eleanor, and it just said: **??**

Trivia, I wrote. **This afternoon.**

Oh, she replied. **Sorry. I already have a team.**

I stared at her message, not comprehending. She had a team? How could she have a team? *We* were going to be a team.

I stepped out of the cafeteria and called her. She picked up on the second ring. "Hi," she said.

"What do you mean, you have a team?" I asked.

"I'm with Chloe and Rissa and Kaylie."

"And you didn't tell me?"

"I didn't realize I was supposed to."

"We agreed that we were going to be a team this year!"

"I didn't think that was still a thing," she said.

"Why would you think that?"

"I figured you'd team up with Aydın."

"Aydın doesn't do things like this. And he's my boyfriend. You're my best friend. Best friends do stupid things like sign up for trivia together."

There was a moment of silence. "Am I?" she asked.

"Are you what?"

"Your best friend."

"Of course you are!"

"I don't think anyone watching from the outside would think that."

My head felt like it was full of static. I saw a bench and sat down. "What do you mean?"

"I mean that you haven't exactly acted like a best friend this summer."

"Is this still about the Cameron thing? Because I told you, he wasn't even—"

"It's not just Cameron," she said. "It's more than that. It's about how you have this image of me and nothing I do can change it, and how you think that what you like to do is more fun and better than what I like to do, and how you think that you always know better than me. It's like you don't even want to get to know the real me. And the fact that you can't see it, well..."

My heart was beating fast and the static in my head was buzzing louder. "Eleanor," I said. "Come on."

"I don't know, Ros," Eleanor said. "I don't know if I can call someone who doesn't seem to give a shit about me my best friend." And then she hung up.

———

I didn't go to trivia. I went home and lay in bed, watching the endless stream of Instagram stories of the event, liking my classmates' photos of their costumes that they thought were sophisticated and clever and funny and whatever.

Eleanor and Chloe's team got out early, after a stupid error from Kaylie, which I could've predicted. I felt vindicated, but only for a moment. I turned on one of Eleanor's and my stupid reality shows to keep myself from thinking too hard about the fact that I was literally at home, alone, in bed, while everyone else was laughing and cheering and having fun and would probably go out to the diner for milkshakes and French fries later to rehash it and talk about plans for homecoming tomorrow.

I couldn't stay focused on the show, so I threw on my running shoes, put my angry workout playlist on shuffle, and went outside.

It had been a while since I'd gone on a run, but I felt good. Strong. I'd stepped out with the plan to run just a mile or two, but two miles passed, and then three, and I was feeling better. I turned the volume all the way up. My legs were filled with electricity, my brain mercifully blank. Finally, at mile five, my adrenaline-fueled energy ran out, and my lungs started to hurt. I slowed to a walk in a neighborhood I didn't recognize. I switched my music over to something softer and started to walk back in the direction of home.

I checked Instagram again. Everyone was still hanging out, as I'd expected, grabbing milkshakes at the diner or froyo in town.

The sun was starting to sink toward the horizon, casting everything in a golden early autumn light. The neighborhood that I'd found myself in was full of trees, the houses swimming in a sea of green with bright patches of yellow and red where the leaves had started to turn. A light breeze came through and ruffled them, like ripples on water. I closed my eyes, feeling oddly peaceful. I couldn't name the scent in the air, but it felt like autumn, conjuring memories of bobbing for apples at my cousins' house in New Jersey and picking out matching Halloween costumes with Lydia. We'd been princesses and mermaids together, then rock stars and witches, then Batman and Robin (I was Batman; she was Robin). And we'd always gone trick-or-treating in her neighborhood, which was full of big houses that went all out on the decorations: fog machines and flashing lights and scarecrows that moved when you walked past them. Bucketfuls of candy. Some houses even handed out whole goodie bags to kids, instead of making them take just one piece. Those were the best.

I suddenly realized I was smiling, thinking about how scared Lydia had been at one especially scary house, and how I'd acted brave and marched ahead. I paraded past spooky ghosts and open graves, letting Lydia follow behind, never showing how scared I was, no matter how fast my heart was beating.

Back then things had been simple. One of us was scared, so the other one stepped up to be brave. When had we stopped looking out for each other? When had everything gotten so complicated?

I missed her, I realized.

And, of course, I missed Eleanor. Was it true, what she'd said to me? Did I really not know who she was? I was hard on her, I knew that. I'd never shown her how much I admired her honesty, her kindness, the openness with which she communicated her feelings.

I missed that friend, the one who called me out when I needed to be called out, for going too far or for being too selfish. The one who made a whole community out of a bingo game. The one who gave her brother the bedroom on vacation. The one who let people put their needs above hers.

She deserved better. I needed to make things right.

Chapter Twenty-Two

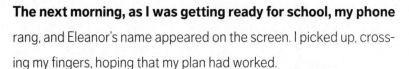

The next morning, as I was getting ready for school, my phone rang, and Eleanor's name appeared on the screen. I picked up, crossing my fingers, hoping that my plan had worked.

"Um," she said. "What is this?"

"Do you like it?" I knew she would. I'd spent my whole month's allowance on a *huge* basket of flowers from the local florist, making sure that all of Eleanor's favorites were in there—because I was a good friend, and I knew what my best friend's favorite flowers were. I'd arranged for the basket to be delivered immediately.

"What are these for?" She sounded less pleased than I'd hoped.

"Have you read the note?"

"There's a note?" I heard some shuffling as she dug for the envelope and tore it open. Then there was silence. I waited as she read. "Um, thanks," she said finally.

The note was a heartfelt apology for being such a bad friend this summer, and a promise that I'd make it up to her if she'd let me. "Did you read the whole thing?" I asked.

"Yeah," she said.

"And?"

She sounded exasperated as she said, "And I don't know, Ros! What's the point of this?"

"The point is to tell you that I'm sorry, and that I realize how self-centered I've been, and that I really, really miss you."

Eleanor huffed. "This is classic."

"What?"

"You think you can just talk your way out of everything. You can't just put a Band-Aid on all the hurt you've caused and think things are going to magically get better."

"I'm not—"

"I just don't believe it, okay? Why should I trust you, just because of some nice words, when you've chosen yourself over and over again?" And then she hung up, leaving me totally speechless.

———

It was Friday. The homecoming dance was that evening. I was distracted all day, unable to think about anything else. Luckily, when I showed up to my last-period French class, there was a note on the door informing us that Mrs. Kimpel wasn't feeling well, and class was canceled. Most kids left immediately, but I had to stick around because Lydia and I had scheduled a rehearsal after school. We were supposed to present our scene in class the following Monday, and Mr. Davids had told us that we were required to have at least one rehearsal on our own, outside of class. As much as I hated being alone with Lydia, I liked our scene, and I liked the technique we were practicing, and I really wanted to impress Mr. Davids. I hadn't auditioned for the fall musical—I wasn't musically gifted—but I was thinking I might audition for the spring play again. Maybe this time I'd have better luck. And as much as Lydia hated being around me, it seemed that her priorities were similar. So we'd agreed to meet in the performing arts wing at the end of the school day.

I wandered slowly toward the cafeteria, killing time. I figured I could sit and do some homework or something until the end of the day. With everyone else either in class or already on their way home, the halls were like a ghost town.

As I passed by the hall that led to the visual arts wing, a movement caught my eye. There was a large wire sculpture hanging from the ceiling, right in the middle of the hallway. I walked over to get a closer look, and discovered that the sculpture was composed of photographs printed on transparent plastic hanging from the wire—a shifting mobile structure. I caught a glimpse of what looked like the Empire State Building on one, a lush green park with a dirt path leading over rolling hills on another. A kid holding a hot dog in front of a street vendor. A little girl in a brightly colored long-sleeved dress with a huge skirt. As I examined it more closely, I noticed that the mobile had two main branches. One was filled with what looked like pictures of New York City sometime in the 1970s or '80s. The pictures on the other branch had a slightly less familiar setting. I studied them and noticed street signs in Korean, as well as a city skyline with mountains rising up behind it. There was a contrast among the photos between gorgeous greenery and bustling, bright streets. Seoul, maybe?

Any slight breeze in the hallway caused the mobile to shift, sending the pictures spinning, sometimes lining them up in front of each other, creating double-photographs that you could look straight through.

I heard footsteps behind me and turned to see Chloe, dressed in Spirit Day red and black, holding a piece of plastic attached to a wire, just like the ones that made up the sculpture. She paused when she saw me.

I'd known it was hers. The structure was similar to the turquoise wire sculpture I'd seen. Still, I asked, "Did you make this?"

Seemingly recovering, she strode past me and started attaching the new segment to the sculpture. "It's not finished yet," she said.

I stepped around to the other side to give her space. I saw her face, focused, through the layers of photographs, and I immediately understood what she'd been trying to do.

"I love it," I said, and I meant it. "It's beautiful."

She didn't say anything, still hanging the piece.

"How did you get the school to let you put it up here?" I asked. "Or did you?"

She looked straight at me then. "I designed it as a concept for my art class. The teacher really liked it, so she asked the school if I could turn it into an installation. Build the whole thing." She shrugged. "I don't know, I'm kind of nervous about it being out here."

I nodded. "It's personal, isn't it?"

She brushed a strand of hair behind her ear, looking at the sculpture uncertainly. "Yeah," she said. "I don't know, I'm not sure it does what I wanted it to do."

"I think it does," I said, more forcefully than I meant to. She gave me a strange look. "Do you need help?" I asked.

She thought for a moment, then nodded. "Sure, I could use some help carrying the pieces out, if you're not busy."

"Nope," I said. She led me into one of the art classrooms, where more of the plastic photographs were laid out, attached to pieces of wire, across a large gray table. I grabbed a couple and carried them out behind her, so she could attach them to the sculpture. "I heard you did trivia yesterday," I said.

"We did," Chloe replied. "Our team was terrible."

"It's tough," I said.

"Did you compete?" she asked.

"Not this year," I said.

She nodded. We were quiet for a while as she hung up the pieces. Then we went back into the classroom to grab more.

"Eleanor told me," she said suddenly.

"Told you what?" I asked.

"That you were upset. I didn't know that you guys were planning to sign up together this year. I wouldn't have signed up with her if I'd known."

Why was she being so nice? "Oh," I said. "No. It's okay. I didn't care that much."

She didn't look like she believed me, but she didn't say anything else about it.

After another pause, I said, "I really do love this sculpture. I feel like...it just makes sense to me. Where are the pictures from?"

"They're old family photos," she said.

"The two branches," I said, "and the transparent photographs—lenses that people see you through. Sometimes separate, sometimes overlapping. It's *so cool*."

Chloe gave a little smile. "Huh," she said. "That was exactly what I was going for. I didn't think anyone would get it."

"I don't think everyone will," I said. "But some of us. I mean, I know it's not the same, but I kind of know what it's like."

She looked at me. "Yeah," she said slowly. "I guess you do."

She took the last photograph that I was holding and started attaching it to the sculpture. There was a long pause.

"We actually have a lot in common, don't we?" she asked.

Of course we did. We always had. But one thing in particular. I could tell she was thinking about it too, from the sad look on her face.

The words tumbled out of me: "Why did you tell Aydın you didn't want to get back together?"

Chloe's eyes widened in surprise. "I...why do you ask?"

I wished I could take it back. But the words were out. "It's just... I know you two had a...thing...once." It was much more than that, I knew. "And I just...I don't know, I've been wondering."

She crossed her arms. "You don't have to worry about me," she said. "I'm not going to try to steal your boyfriend."

I shook my head emphatically. "No, that's not what I meant!"

"Then what did you mean?" Her expression was guarded.

I took a deep breath, trying to get my thoughts in order. They had been such a foggy mess lately. But now, I felt like the clouds were finally starting to part, and the thing that I'd been avoiding was shining through. "I think he might be in love with you," I said slowly.

She looked away from me, like she couldn't meet my gaze. "Even if that is true," she said, "it doesn't matter."

"Why?"

"Because we can't be together," she said with an unexpected ferocity. "His family won't accept me. They want him to be with someone more like them, like him. He told me that himself."

She still believed Aydın's lie?

"And besides," she continued, "at this point, he wants nothing to do with me. He blocked me on Instagram. I don't know how much clearer he could be."

"That doesn't necessarily mean..." I trailed off.

Chloe said, "He seems happy. With you." A pause, and then she started to say something else but cut herself off.

I crossed my arms.

"If he's happy, then that's that," she said.

"Are you still in love with him?" I asked.

She turned away.

"Chloe," I said. She didn't move. "I just need to know. Please."

She let out a forceful breath. "Fine," she said, and she sounded angry. "Yes. Is that what you want to hear? That I've been in love with him since we were in middle school? Does that make you happy?"

Taken aback, I asked, "Why haven't you told him?"

"Because it would never work out!" she said. "And because you're together, and I would never, ever, do that to another girl." She finally turned to face me. "That's not who I am."

"I—" I said, then stopped myself. I was going to say *I'm sorry*. But instead, I said, "He didn't block you on Instagram. I did." Then I turned and ran down the hallway, leaving Chloe alone with her shifting sculpture.

Chapter Twenty-Three

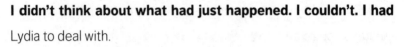

I didn't think about what had just happened. I couldn't. I had
Lydia to deal with.

We found an empty classroom in the performing arts wing and
set down our backpacks, barely looking at each other. Lydia pulled a
water bottle out of her bag and took a long drink while I moved some
chairs aside to clear a space in the center of the room.

When I turned, she was standing across from me, looking ready
to fight, even in her ridiculous red-and-black Spirit Day tutu. "Shall
we?" she asked.

I nodded.

"I just can't believe you're still deluding yourself," she began,
jumping into her "as if."

"Do you understand how much it hurts that you'd try to take this
one thing from me?" I asked.

"It's so obvious."

"It's selfish of you! Selfish and mean!"

Lydia rolled her eyes. My blood boiled. "I can't believe you're
being so childish," she said.

"How dare you!"

"We're not kids anymore."

"Yeah, but you still behave like one!" I said.

Surprise registered on Lydia's face. I had broken a rule: I had responded directly to what she had said, rather than continuing my own separate monologue. But it had made sense, in the moment. It felt right. "Well, that was uncalled-for," Lydia said.

"*That* was uncalled-for?" I replied.

"What the hell does that mean?"

She was wearing a pair of silver hoop earrings with three small diamonds hanging from the bottom. I knew those earrings. They were Lydia's mom's, and we had been obsessed with them as kids. We would borrow them and dress up, trying to look like old-timey Hollywood starlets, and make short films of murder mysteries using the camera on her desktop computer.

"We used to be best friends!" I said. "I can't believe you'd just—throw that away like it was nothing! I made a mistake, okay?"

"*I* threw it away?" Lydia asked, sounding incredulous.

We were really doing this. "You stopped talking to me. It's been years now, and you still won't have a real conversation with me."

"You've made it very clear that we're not friends. That's fine; I don't give a shit."

"You're blaming this on me?"

She shrugged, wearing an expression of careful indifference. But I had seen this face on her enough to know that there was something else underneath it. She was hurt.

"I tried," Lydia said. "I *tried* to make up with you, and you didn't let me."

"What are you talking about?"

"That coffee in Pine Bay was me trying!"

"You mean that fake 'Let's catch up!' coffee? The one that was just an excuse for you to brag about how great your life was going?"

"That's not what I wanted it to be! I genuinely wanted to catch up, but then you asked to bring the boys along, and I knew what that was about: you needed a shield so you wouldn't actually have to talk to me," Lydia said. She looked up at the ceiling, like she was trying not to cry. "I just feel like I tried so hard, and you were nothing but hostile. So I decided I wasn't going to try anymore."

"*I* was hostile?" I asked, shocked.

"Don't pretend."

"You decided to run for homecoming court just to spite me!"

Lydia threw her hands in the air. "Ros, I had *no idea* you were running. When and how could I possibly have learned that you were planning on it? We hadn't spoken in *two years.* And you have to know that I'm not that petty!"

For the first time, I realized that she might be telling the truth. But I was angry, and I forged onward. "You're the one who stopped talking to me after the Zane thing!"

"Okay, fine," she said. "Yeah. I was really fucking mad about that. You were a shitty friend. And you acted like you hadn't done anything. Of course I was going to be mad."

"You were the one who told everyone about that stupid rumor! *You* betrayed *me* first!"

Her expression shifted. "I didn't realize—"

"You didn't realize what?" I shouted. "How much it would hurt me that my *best friend*, the *only person* who believed me and stood by my side through all of that stuff, would bring that rumor with us to camp? When it was exactly what I was trying to escape?"

"I thought it was true, okay?" she said.

"What?"

Lydia took a deep breath. "I really, truly thought it was true. Eighth grade was such a weird time. Everyone was changing, so much and so fast, and I guess…maybe I thought you were growing up faster than I was. And, yeah, that made me a little insecure. Plus everyone else believed it. And honestly, Ros, the rumor itself wasn't that bad. So what if you were hooking up with a bunch of guys? Like, go you."

"But I wasn't."

"I figured that out later," she said. "The point is that the way people treated you afterward was awful. So shitty. It totally changed the way I looked at most of our classmates."

"Okay," I said, crossing my arms and trying to sort through the chaos of thoughts and feelings. "But then why did you tell your camp friends?"

She looked at the ceiling. "I thought maybe if they felt bad for you, knowing what you'd been through at school that year, they'd… I don't know, try harder to make you feel included? You spent that whole summer running off and hanging out with the guys instead of them, you know."

"You all knew each other so well. I felt out of place."

"I know," said Lydia. "But I was trying. I wanted them to see a glimpse of the real, vulnerable Ros instead of just that hard exterior that you're always putting up."

For some reason that hit a nerve, and I felt tears welling up in my eyes. I brushed them away quickly. "That was dumb of you," I said.

"They were my friends," she said, and her voice was soft. "I had no idea that they'd use that story against you."

I sat down on the floor. Lydia sat facing me. "You believe me that it wasn't true, right?" I asked.

"Of course I do," she said.

"I'm sorry," I said, and I felt the tears welling up again. "I mean, you hurt me, but I shouldn't have tried to hurt you back. I didn't even *like* Zane in that way, but I went to the dance with him to get back at you. I wanted to believe that you were the bad guy. But deep down, I knew I was at fault too."

Her eyebrows drew together.

I continued, "And I'm realizing now that I've felt guilty about it. For a long time." I just hadn't wanted to admit it to myself.

Lydia was quiet.

"I know it was a while ago, but I recognize that it was so ridiculously selfish of me. And catty. And…I did something similar again. Recently. To another person I really care about." The next words came out easily, so much more easily than I'd ever imagined them being. "I'm so, so sorry. Will you forgive me?"

Lydia stared at me for a moment. Then she did something unexpected. She laughed.

"What?" I asked. Was she laughing at me? After I'd apologized?

She stopped laughing and shook her head slightly. "Ros, I forgave you for the Zane thing, like, forever ago."

I didn't know how to respond to that, so I just said, "I know I'm a shitty person."

Suddenly, Lydia leaned forward and gave me a hug. It was weird and awkward and lasted about half a second, but when she released me, she said, "You're not a shitty person." There was a firmness in her voice. "You just do really stupid things sometimes."

I nodded.

"And for what it's worth," she continued, "I'm sorry too. I'm sorry for telling everyone about it, and I'm sorry for not believing you. And I shouldn't have stopped talking to you for so long. I should have tried to fix it a long time ago."

"That's not only on you," I said.

Lydia shrugged, and we stared at each other. I asked, "Can we talk sometime? Or hang out? I miss you."

After a moment Lydia nodded. "Yes," she said. "I'd like that."

Something had shifted—the tense silence had morphed into something else, something hesitant but warm.

"Should we get back to rehearsing?" Lydia asked.

"That sounds great," I replied. And for the first time, as we ran our scene, playing a pair of sisters, it actually felt like we *were* sisters. Frustrated with each other, going through a rough patch in our relationship, but sisters nonetheless.

As we got ready to leave, I told Lydia what had happened with Eleanor, and I asked for her advice on what to do.

Frowning, she told me that she wasn't sure there was anything I could do. I'd kissed Cameron *just* after assuring Eleanor that I'd never betray a best friend like that again. In doing so, I may have irrevocably broken Eleanor's trust. Words wouldn't fix it.

If Eleanor didn't want to be friends with me anymore, I couldn't force it.

She was her own person, and it was up to her whom she wanted to call her best friend. The only thing that I could do was try to set right the other things that I'd screwed up.

It wouldn't be easy, but I knew what I had to do.

Chapter Twenty-Four

The homecoming dance looked like a scene from a dream. The walls were lined with silver balloons. Silver fringe hung nearly to the floor and dissected the gym into a collection of smaller, sparkling rooms, through which you would sometimes catch a glimpse of a brightly colored dress, a tall figure, a couple dancing. Blue lights swept across the scene, painting us in shades of cerulean, periwinkle, navy. It felt like we were underwater, swimming deep in a cenote somewhere tropical, illuminated in shafts of light from the world above.

Aydın wasn't there when I arrived. Big surprise.

I wandered past the table where the homecoming committee had set up a sparkling silver box to collect ballots for the court. One of the girls smiled at me. "Good luck, Ros!" she said.

"Thanks," I replied.

I walked deeper into the room, wading through the curtains of silver fringe. No sign of Aydın. I pulled out my phone and texted him. **Where are you?**

Someone tapped me on the shoulder. I turned.

"Hi, Ros." He was smiling. I tried to take a snapshot with my mind, to remember this moment exactly as it was, the two of us alone in this silver room. Blue lights danced across his features.

I had spent the past few hours turning a question over and over in my head. But I always came back to the same conclusion.

"Aydın," I said, smiling back. "Hi."

"Want to go find our friends?" He turned to venture through a silver curtain, but I grabbed his hand.

"I have to tell you something first," I said.

Concern flashed across his face. "Is everything alright?"

"Everything's fine." I took a deep breath. Then I said it. "I know you're in love with Chloe."

His expression was unreadable. His eyes looked turquoise in the blue light, like precious stones.

"And I know you have been for a long time," I continued.

"Ros—"

"It's okay. Really."

I'd been worried that he would try to deny it, but he didn't. Instead, he said, "That doesn't mean that I don't have feelings for you."

"I know." On the way to the dance, I'd practiced what I was going to say. But now the words were escaping me. "I—I care about you a lot." He started to say something, but I interrupted him. "And that's why I need to say this. I want you to be happy, and I realized how self-ish I've been. Not just with this, with you, but with other people too. And I don't want to be that way anymore."

He was quiet, listening.

"I care about you, and I think you're a wonderful friend, and I hope that you like me too. But this isn't working. You're not happy with me."

"I—" He cut himself off. There was a pause. "I think you're wonderful, Ros."

"But I'm not Chloe."

Another pause, and then he said, "My feelings for Chloe don't matter. She's told me herself that it's over. She's not interested."

"That's the thing," I said. "You're wrong."

"She's been avoiding me since we got back from summer break. Trust me, she wants nothing to do with me."

This, somehow, struck me as funny. I laughed.

His brow furrowed. "What?"

"You don't know girls as well as you think, do you?" I said.

"You're not making sense."

"She loves you too," I said.

Aydın frowned, his eyes searching mine. He was silent for a long moment. Then he asked, "How do you know?"

"She told me," I said.

"But at Pine Bay . . . why did she say—"

"Remember what you told her when you broke up?"

His thick eyebrows drew closer together. "That my parents wouldn't approve. But that was a lie. I figured she knew that by now."

"She doesn't. And I think she thinks that it would be too painful to try, knowing that you could never end up together."

"She still believes it?"

I shrugged. "No one told her otherwise."

"Oh." He frowned, rubbing his brow.

"I need you to go talk to her," I said. "Tell her the truth."

He still didn't look like he believed what I was saying. "Why are you telling me this?" he asked.

"I'm tired of standing in the way," I said truthfully.

The music got quieter, and a voice came over the loudspeaker: "Last call to submit your votes for homecoming court! The coronation ceremony will take place in thirty minutes!"

"I have to go do something," I said.

He nodded. His eyes didn't leave mine.

"Talk to her," I said. "Please."

"Okay," he said. "Okay."

I stepped forward and wrapped my arms around him in a hug. He tensed up for a moment, then wrapped his arms around me. We stood there for several long moments, and I was surprised to find that I wasn't sad. This felt right.

When I pulled away, I said, "I want you to be with your Layla."

His nose wrinkled in confusion.

"Because I don't want you to end up like Majnun," I added, suddenly unsure he'd get the reference.

To my surprise, he laughed. Then he nodded. "Alright." As I turned to go, he said, "Ros?"

"Yeah?"

"Thank you. For everything."

I gave him one last smile. "You too." Then I turned, not letting myself look back, as I slipped away through the silver curtains toward the homecoming court table. I had another important task.

Chapter Twenty-Five

As I was leaving the homecoming court table several minutes
later, I spotted Chloe emerging from a silver curtain fifteen feet away,
dressed in deep forest green, her hair in a sleek ponytail that shone
blue in the lights. Our eyes met, and she looked slightly terrified. Then
she threw her shoulders back and marched toward me.

"Hi," she said.

"Hi," I replied.

She crossed her arms. "Aydın told me what you said," she said.

Had I done something wrong? My heartbeat sped up. "I'm sorry,"
I said.

"Why would you do that?" she asked.

I *had* done something wrong. I'd screwed everything up for her.
And for him.

Chloe continued: "I couldn't help myself earlier. It was really
impulsive of me, telling you that. And trust me, I am *not* an impulsive
person."

"I shouldn't have told him. I'm sorry."

She shook her head. "No, that's not what I'm saying." She took a
deep breath. "I am a terrible, horrible person for telling you that even
though I knew you two were happily dating. I don't want to break you

up. I really, truly just want him to be happy. I want both of you to be happy."

"Chloe," I said, "he's in love with you."

She looked at the ground. "That's what he told me."

"Do you still love him?"

She met my gaze, her eyes uncertain. "I do," she said. "But it was wrong of me to get between the two of you. If you want me to stay away from him—"

I threw my arms up. How many times was I going to have to explain this? "Chloe! I told him because I want you two to be happy together!"

"Really?"

"Yes! One hundred percent."

Chloe tilted her head as she looked at me. "You're an angel, Rosaline. A strange angel."

I curtsied jokingly. "I do have something I'd like to ask in return."

"What's that?"

"Can we get coffee or something?" She stared at me, so I continued, "I know I haven't been the friendliest to you, or made any effort. But honestly, I was jealous. You seemed so perfect, and then when my best friend started hanging out with you instead of me, I just… didn't know what to do."

"Eleanor cares about you a lot. That's always been clear," Chloe said.

I didn't know what to say to that. So I asked, "Will you give me another chance? At friendship?"

She smiled. "Yes," she said. "A hundred times yes."

The music got softer again, and the voice came over the loud-speaker. "Everyone, please gather for the coronation of our home-coming court!"

Chloe and I made our way to the front of the gym, following the river of other students, passing through the silver curtains toward the makeshift stage. I had been dreaming of this moment for weeks—years, really—and now that it had arrived, I felt nothing like I'd imagined I would. I'd pictured sweaty hands and paralyzing nerves. Instead, I felt perfectly peaceful.

I spotted Lydia in the crowd. As the committee announced the names of the homecoming prince and princess, I watched her eyes go wide in shock. She stood frozen for so long that people started actually pulling her toward the stage, where Jeff was already stand-ing. The expression of surprise didn't leave her face the whole time that they stood there, while the sashes were placed on their shoul-ders and the crowns on their heads, and while the homecoming king and queen, a gorgeous pair of seniors, were crowned.

When the court's first dance song came on, Jeff turned and extended a hand to Lydia. She hesitated, then took it. They danced awkwardly, stiffly, I noticed. The other couple, by comparison, were wrapped in each other's arms, lost to the rest of the world. And when the song ended, Lydia hurried off the stage. She found me almost immediately and came running over.

"Did you withdraw?" she demanded.

"Why would you think that?"

She tilted her head. "Come on, Ros, I'm not dumb. Everyone knew you and Aydın were going to win."

"What are you talking about?"

"They conducted a poll in the cafeteria last week. You guys were ahead by a landslide."

"I didn't know that." I'd had a feeling we were going to win, but I hadn't known about the poll.

"Why did you pull out?" she demanded.

I shrugged. "I didn't want it anymore."

"Oh, come on."

"Aydın and I broke up."

She blinked. "Really? Why?"

"It's a *long* story. Actually, our talk helped me figure some stuff out."

She looked at me for a second, processing. Then she started to laugh.

"What's so funny?" I asked.

"I didn't want it either! I would've withdrawn, except I thought you guys were going to win so it wouldn't matter anyway!"

"What do you mean? I thought you really wanted this!"

"I did!" she said, still laughing. "But Jeff and I broke up two days ago."

"No!" My hand flew to my mouth.

"Yes! Did you see how awkward that was? Can you imagine? Having to dance with your ex in front of the whole school?"

I started to laugh too. "Oh my god. And here I thought I was doing a nice thing for you!"

Lydia hugged me. "It's the thought that counts."

I hugged her back. It felt nicer than I wanted to admit.

"Who is *that?*" she whispered. I glanced over my shoulder to see who she was looking at. Ben had appeared, dressed to the nines, with a lanky, redheaded boy on his arm. A *familiar* lanky, redheaded boy.

Cameron spotted me and gave a small wave. I waved back. Ben caught sight of the exchange and, grinning mischievously, turned to Cameron and kissed him. I laughed, cringing just a little at the reminder of what I'd done, and gave them a thumbs-up.

As the happy couple disappeared in the crowd, Lydia asked, "Doesn't that guy work at Pine Bay?"

"Yep."

"And you guys are friends, I take it?"

"Also a long story," I said. "We're going to have to catch up about this summer." I paused, considering. "Actually, we probably need to catch up about the past two years."

She laughed. "I would love that."

Someone tapped my shoulder. I turned, expecting Aydın again, maybe, but instead found myself face-to-face with Franklin Doss. "How's your night going?" he asked.

Lydia slipped behind him, grimaced at me, and mouthed "Good luck" before disappearing into the crowd.

"It's alright," I said. What was he up to?

"I guess you and Aydın broke up. I'm sorry to hear that."

"How did you know?"

He nodded to the left, and I followed his gaze to see Aydın and

Chloe slow dancing, Chloe's head resting on Aydın's chest, her eyes closed. Something in my chest twinged.

"Ah," I said.

"Are you doing okay?"

I nodded. "Better than ever, actually." It was true. Yes, seeing Aydın and Chloe in their seemingly perfect, no-longer-star-crossed love hurt a bit. But I knew I had made the right decision. And that felt good.

"I'm glad," Franklin said.

There was a long period of awkward silence until I said, "I should be going," at exactly the same moment that he said, "I'm so fucking sorry."

I paused, processing. "What did you say?" I needed to make sure I'd heard right.

"I said I'm sorry. I've been an asshole."

"What brought you to that conclusion?" I asked.

He shoved his hands in his pockets and looked away, his mouth twisting. "Honestly? It's going to sound stupid, but it was a book I've been reading. It's sort of about… well, a lot of things, but like, racism and misogyny, and I never would have read it, but I was starting to realize… after you beat me up at Pine Bay…" He trailed off.

"I didn't know you could read," I said.

Franklin half smiled. "Funny," he said. Then he shrugged. "Aydın gave it to me, actually. The book. He said he thought I could use it. And, well, he's the type of person whose advice I guess I need. Because…" He trailed off again, but I waited for him to continue.

"Well, I've felt sort of excluded for a long time. A lot of people hate me, and I know that, and that's why I don't get invited to things. So when I'm around groups of people—like the kids at Pine Bay—I kind of panic and do whatever I can to get them to like me. And I'm realizing that sometimes the things I do are just…asshole-ish. And not the way to get people to like me. Or to get the girl I like to like me."

While part of me wanted to dismiss this apology as the last-ditch effort of an asshole to not be canceled, part of me was impressed that he'd actually read the book.

"Do you…" he began, then broke off. He rubbed his nose. "Do you have any other recommendations? For me to check out?"

I was stunned silent for a moment. When I regained my voice, I said, "I—I'll think about it."

He nodded. "Okay. Well, that's all I wanted to say. I'm a fucking asshole, and I'm sorry. And I'm trying to be better, so if you have any advice—"

"Thank you, Franklin."

He nodded again. He took a step away as though he was leaving, then paused. "And maybe this is inappropriate, but I have to ask: Since you and Aydın aren't a couple anymore, is there any chance you want to go on a date?"

It was all I could do to stop myself from bursting out laughing. I choked back the impulse, trying to keep a straight face. "I—I don't think so, Franklin. Not right now." He looked disappointed. "I'm flattered."

"Right. Of course. Sorry, I had to ask. See ya around."

"See ya," I replied as he walked off.

And then someone beside me said, "Never in a million years did I think I'd hear Franklin Doss repent for his asshole-ness." It was Eleanor, wearing a short gold dress and layered gold necklaces.

"I'm weirdly…proud of him?" I said. "Also, you look amazing."

She crossed her arms. "Thanks." Then she leaned toward me and said, "You dropped out of the homecoming race, didn't you?"

"How'd you know?"

"I figured the poll couldn't have been *that* wrong."

"How did everyone know about this poll but me?"

Eleanor shrugged. Then she nodded toward where Chloe and Aydın were dancing. "You did the right thing," she said.

"I think so too."

"I'm still mad at you," she added quickly.

"That's fair."

"You can be absolutely infuriating, you know?"

I nodded.

"But I also care about you a lot."

"I care about you too. More than you know."

"And I realize that I'm not perfect either. I've made mistakes too." Then she smiled, just slightly. "I don't want us to stop being friends."

I took her hand and squeezed it. "I don't want that either."

"Let's try again?"

"I would love that."

"Can I ask you just one favor, though?"

"Name it."

"Will you give Chloe a chance? I know you've sort of written her off, but I think if you spent some time with her, you two could be really good friends."

I smiled. "I'm two steps ahead of you on that one."

The music turned upbeat, and we both started dancing, just a little. I took Eleanor's hands and started a waltz. She hesitated at first, then laughed and got into it. Our waltz got faster and more frenetic until we were galloping around the room at an inappropriately fast clip. Almost colliding with a group of Chloe's friends, we slowed to a halt. The circle opened to let us in, and we all danced together, although Chloe was noticeably absent. At some point Lydia joined us, and she and Eleanor were friendly as they said hi to each other.

Watching my friends' faces among the blue lights and the colorful dresses and the silver curtains and balloons, I felt unbelievably happy, like I was filled with helium myself and might just float away toward the ceiling.

I knew that everything wasn't fixed. That's not how things work. I wasn't about to start blindly trusting everyone—after all, I'd been in a couple of shitty situations, and I needed to recognize that without letting the resentment consume me. But I had also done some stupid things in my friendships. And while Lydia and Eleanor might be willing to forgive me, I understood that building our relationships back would still take a lot of work.

The magic of the dance was working on us for now, and everything could look and feel beautiful and easy just for the moment, even if the reality was that we still had a ways to go.

I knew that I could and would put that work in. Because it was worth it.

———

Eleanor, Lydia, and I left the dance linked arm in arm, laughing, giddy with the night's energy, and headed toward Lydia's car in the parking lot. We heard the sound of clicking heels behind us, and someone called, "Wait! Rosaline!"

I turned. There was Chloe, running toward us. She slowed and finally came to a stop in front of me. "Sorry," she said, panting. "I just wanted to say, again, thank you. Before you left. You don't know how happy you've made me." She wrapped her arms around my neck in a tight hug.

I hugged her back. "Of course."

When she released me, she noticed the other two, as though for the first time. "Are you all headed home?"

I shook my head. "We're going to the diner for milkshakes and fries."

"We're going to do a photoshoot in our homecoming dresses," said Eleanor.

"Do you want to come with us?" I asked.

Chloe glanced back toward the gym, where the dance was nearing its end, but the music was still playing.

"Please come with us!" said Eleanor.

"Aydın will still exist tomorrow," I said.

Chloe laughed. Just then, Aydın walked out of the gym, looking for her. His eyes briefly met mine, and he smiled, hesitantly. I smiled back and waved.

"Next time?" Chloe asked me.

"Of course," I replied.

She pulled off her heels and ran, barefoot, back to Aydın. She wrapped her arms around his neck. He beamed down at her, and then leaned in for a kiss. Eleanor, Lydia, and I all turned away, giving them their privacy.

The stars were bright above us, and the air held the chill of autumn, as the three of us walked and stumbled in our dresses and heels, fully content in each other's company, into the night.

Acknowledgments

There are so many people who deserve thanks for their support along this journey that it feels impossible to fit them all in a single acknowledgements section, but I'm going to try to name a few.

To my wonderful agent, Alex Slater: I'm forever grateful for the way you immediately saw and understood my vision for this story. Thank you for your belief in it.

To my amazing editor, Sally Morgridge: you are such a joy to work with, and I've been so grateful for your thoughtful, apt, insightful edits through every step of the revision process.

An immense thank-you to everyone at Sanford J. Greenburger, and to the whole team at Holiday House, including Laura Kincaid, Chelsea Hunter, Kerry Martin, Rebecca Godan, Raina Putter, Miriam Miller, Michelle Montague, Terry Borzumato-Greenberg, Sara DiSalvo, Kayla Phillips, Elyse Vincenty, Alison Tarnofsky, Melissa See, Mary Joyce Perry, Morgan Hillman, Tova Seltzer, Kade Dishmon, and Hannah Finne.

To Beatriz Ramo: thank you for bringing Ros to life in your absolutely gorgeous cover art.

A huge thank-you to all of the English and creative writing teachers I had the pleasure of learning from, and all of the classmates whose work inspired me, during my childhood and teenage years:

in the Chappaqua school system, at the Iowa Young Writers' Studio, and at the UVA Young Writers Workshop. You cultivated my love for writing and helped it blossom into a lifelong passion. This book wouldn't exist without you.

To the Harvard English department and especially to the remarkable writers who led my workshops: your advice has stuck with me and shaped me into the writer I am today.

To the 2019 Tin House YA Novel Workshop: you all taught me everything I didn't know that I didn't know about writing and publishing. Thanks especially to my wonderful workshop leader, Lilliam Rivera, for providing guidance and inspiration, and to my workshop classmates—Becky, Gloria, Hugh, Kyrstin, and Ofelia—for your camaraderie, sparkling writing, and invaluable feedback.

Of course, I owe so much gratitude to the University of Wyoming Creative Writing MFA Program, for providing me with the time, encouragement, inspiration, and instruction that I needed to grow as a writer during this phase of my life. Thank you to Alyson Hagy for your mentorship, support, and enthusiasm for my projects. To Jenny Tinghui Zhang, for your sharp advice on the publishing industry and for helping me revise my query letter. To Harvey Hix, Ginger Ko, Caleb Johnson, and Steven Dunn, for everything you taught me about writing, revision, genre, form, and inspiration. A huge thank-you as well to all of my MFA classmates, and especially to my cohort: Caio, Hannah, Parth, Rae, and Rucy. I learned so much from your feedback, and even more from reading all of your sharp, strange, hilarious, and beautiful work.

To Aislinn, Alyn, Michael, Patric, and Tara: this book would never have become what it is without your support and advice (on this and other projects). I so deeply admire and appreciate all of you as writers and as friends.

To Adam: thank you for being a wonderful human and the best sailor I know (and for helping me revise the sailing portions of this book).

To Carrington: thank you for helping me revise an early draft, and for your artistic camaraderie.

To Sarah: thank you for being an amazing friend and for putting up with my chaos since high school.

Thank you to Arianna, Brandon, Edgar, Evie, Peter, Sal, Tate, Thomas, Travis, Will, and so many others (you know who you are), for your friendship, your enthusiastic support, and all of our shared adventures. Y'all mean the world to me, and I can't express enough how grateful I am to know you.

And, most importantly, thank you to my family. To my Anneanne, Dede, Farmor, and Farfar, for all of your love, encouragement, and perpetual belief in me and my work. To Derin, for keeping me up to date on high school happenings. To Emily, for your advice and optimism. To my brother Kenan, for inspiring me with your creativity and kindness, and for being the best ski buddy. And to my mom and dad, for helping me believe that I could do anything I set my mind to, and for giving me the tools I needed to make those dreams come true.